THE
BOATMAN'S
WIFE

BOOKS BY NOELLE HARRISON

The Island Girls

The Gravity of Love
The Adulteress
The Secret Loves of Julia Caesar
I Remember
A Small Part of Me
Beatrice

Noelle Harrison

THE BOATMAN'S WIFE

Bookouture

Published by Bookouture in 2021

An imprint of Storyfire Ltd.
Carmelite House
50 Victoria Embankment
London EC4Y 0DZ

www.bookouture.com

Written by Noelle Harrison

ISBN: 978-1-80019-198-3
eBook ISBN: 978-1-80019-197-6

For Corey & Helena
Always held in my heart

Chapter One

Lily had always been lucky. Her daddy said it to her from when she was a little girl.

'Darling, you were born under a lucky star.'

He described the night of her birth as if it were a fairy tale. Early December in Rockland, Downeast Maine, with the whole town coated in thick snow, the full moon iridescent and otherworldly. The lucky northern star beckoning as he held his newborn baby girl in his arms. Cradling her up to the winter night sky as if casting her in moonlit magic. Her parents had waited so long for her arrival. It had seemed a miracle. That was why her father had always said she was extra special, brimming with all the good fortune due her parents after years of disappointment.

Though Lily's mom told her daddy off for filling their daughter's head with nonsense, deep down, Lily had believed him. Her whole childhood, everything she had wanted had come true. Right from her first days in school, she had won all the competitions. Best at art, spellings, and sports. Lily had always been the first picked randomly out of the hat. Everyone wanted her on their team because that was the one which won. Her luck had lasted all these years.

She and her daddy had won the Lobster Races three years in a row. Of course, he'd named every one of his boats after her – *Lily May* – for luck. All those summers she'd spent working on his boat, early mornings banding lobster, shivering with cold from the streaming Atlantic chill, she'd felt lucky. Nothing was better than the look her daddy gave her when they brought back a big haul of lobster.

'You're a born fisher,' he would say to her with pride.

Lily knew she was everything to her daddy: son and daughter. It was she who made each lobstering season better than the one before, as if she were a lucky charm bringing them good fortune as soon as they set out.

Her first memory was of being on the boat, despite her mom's grumbling that she was too little. Lily had slipped out of her grasp and clambered onto her daddy's boat. Let him swing her in the air, laughing all the while.

'She belongs on the ocean, Sarah!' he'd declared, letting Lily sit on his lap as he began to steer their boat out of the harbour. Out into the wide blue open, while her mother stood on the wharf and watched, arms crossed and frowning.

It was true. The ocean was home. Lily loved every part of it. The days of stillness when she'd catch her reflection in sheer pools of silken water, and the rough days when it felt like they were riding a wild horse. Bucking all the way back to port. She loved the smell of the ocean. It sank into the pores of her skin, and her hair was always tangled and wild from the western winds.

Of course, Lily had stood out a little at school. None of the other girls wanted to fish, and Lily had no interest in fashion or movie stars. That all seemed so fake to her. Lily's idea of a great time was hiking. Scrambling up boulders, and dangling legs over ledges with fishing rods. She was too much of a tomboy for dates; had once punched a boy for trying to kiss her on one of those hiking expeditions. After that, none of the others dared ask her out. Lily hadn't cared back then. At sixteen, she'd rated herself lucky to be single when she could count the number of hurried weddings among her school friends on both hands. Girls just out of her high school with babies, already worried their husbands might not come back from sea one day.

That was it. Where to have luck was a matter of life and death. Working as a lobster fisher would never stop being risky, no matter what. Because the Atlantic Ocean could never be tamed. But Lily's star had shone bright. Always. So many times they'd been caught in storms, daunted by towering waves, but she'd never thought, not once, that she and her daddy wouldn't make it back.

As the years passed, though, Lily changed. Four years ago, on the morning of her twenty-first birthday, she'd woken up feeling lonely. Realised every single girl she had known at school was married, or at least had a fiancé. For the first time, she'd felt sneaking envy. What did it feel like to be loved the way her father loved her mother? Would she ever find a boy for herself? Thinking of all her fishing mates, not one of them made her think so. She'd seen them covered in fish guts, stinking and swearing. They were her friends, and she couldn't imagine touching any of them intimately.

On the December morning of her twenty-first birthday, on a rare day off lobstering, Lily had risen at daybreak and slipped outside. Icy air bit into her as she tucked her gloved hands under her armpits and made her way down the hill to the freezing wharf. It was cold, so cold, but there was no wind. Lily took the rowboat out, and as she rowed slow and steady through the thick, glacial water, she stared back to shore at the weave of white wooden houses along the craggy Maine coastline, the little one-rock islands and sparse pine woods. She lifted her face to the sky and asked silently for a soulmate. Felt the frigid air film her cheeks. She asked again, out loud.

'I want someone,' she said, unable to say the word 'husband' because it made her feel pathetic. In her heart, she wanted it more than her own luck. The husband and the babies. As she rowed back to shore, she felt a bit disappointed in herself. After all, she *was* like the other girls.

Here she was now. Four years later. Her twenty-first birthday wish hazy and near-forgotten. Yet it had come true. The very next summer, she'd met Connor. Had she ever thanked the ocean for him?

Lily turned over in bed and placed her hand on the empty space where Connor slept. So many hours had passed since he'd got up, the sheet had gone cold. She pressed her hand on the pillow where his head had rested. She reached out and pulled her cell phone off the nightstand. Connor had left her a message. She smiled to herself as she listened to his lilting accent. The love she could feel in the spaces between his words. Lily closed her eyes and rewound the past four years, remembering the first time she'd seen him: the tall, skinny young Irishman working in Moll's Bar down by the port. She had noticed him as soon as she had walked in with Ryan and some of the other fishermen. Felt an almost physical jolt as her eyes were drawn to his thick dark hair, and when he looked up, his big brown eyes. The gaze in them so slow and steady, as if nothing in the world could rush him. So unlike any man she'd met before in Maine.

As she'd perched up onto a stool, she'd felt herself blushing when he'd asked her what she wanted to drink.

She was the only woman in the bar. It was three in the afternoon. The time for the fishers to unwind before they went home to bed.

Lily had felt the new barman's eyes on her as she sat in the group of men, conscious of the old check shirt of her dad's she was wearing. She had no make-up on and her hair was pushed beneath a baseball cap. She took it off and pulled out her hair tie. Let it fall loose.

'Wow, Lily,' her cousin, Ryan, commented. 'Your hair has got real long. I remember when you used to cut it short. Folk always thought you were a boy. And you never told them otherwise.'

'It was easier that way,' Lily said, taking a sip of her beer.

'Lily, is it?' the barman asked, leaning across his counter, bar cloth in hand. He wasn't from America. She could hear he had an accent. 'Do you dye it, or is it naturally that shade of black?'

Ryan let out a laugh. 'Course she doesn't dye it,' he said. 'Our Lily is one hundred per cent natural.'

Lily wished Ryan would keep his mouth shut.

'It's like crow's feathers,' the barman said holding her eyes. 'Or ink.'

She took another sip of her beer. 'Say, where you from?'

His eyelids fluttered, and she noticed the curl in his lashes.

'My name's Connor Fitzgerald,' he said, putting the cloth down and reaching out his hand, all formal. 'From Ireland, west coast.'

'Better shake the man's hand, Lily,' Ryan joked.

She felt everyone's eyes on her as she took Connor's hand and gave it a shake. His skin was warm and soft. Embarrassed by her own rough hands, Lily found herself wishing she'd put lotion on them at night like her mom had told her to. She snatched her hand away.

'Nice to meet you, Lily,' Connor said, locking eyes with her. Again, she could feel colour creeping onto her cheeks. Why was she so damn awkward with men? She could captain a boat on the roughest seas, haul up lobster traps as fast as any man, and work like a dog for hours without stop, but when it came to relationships, no matter how casual, she was stuck.

'What're you doing here?' Ryan butted in.

'Travelling,' Connor said, answering Ryan but still looking at Lily. 'Got this job for the summer. They took me on to cook.'

'So are you Irish any good at cooking lobster the Maine way?' Ryan asked Connor.

'I'm curious,' Connor addressed Lily, ignoring Ryan's last comment. 'Are you a fisherman too?'

'I prefer the word fisher.'

'She's the only girl fisher in this town,' Ryan continued to interrupt, clapping Lily on the back. 'But she's one of the best.'

Connor looked at her with interest. 'Do you like it?' he asked. 'It looks like heavy work.'

'It's what I've always done,' Lily said. 'Sure it's hard work, but nothing beats being out on the ocean.'

'I know what you mean.' Connor smiled. 'I grew up by the Atlantic back in Ireland. Can't imagine living anywhere but by the sea.'

One of the other guys called Connor over for another beer. Lily watched him move behind the bar. He had long legs and looked strong.

She glanced at her phone. It was time to hit the road, and get some sleep. She finished her beer and stood up.

'You're only in for one?' Connor had returned. He appeared very interested in her, but then she was the only girl in the bar.

'Yeah, I have to be up before daybreak,' she said.

'Now, that is tough.' Connor's smile opened up even more. Ryan had moved off to talk with some of the others, and it was just her and Connor. She wanted to stay drinking on the stool, talking to him all afternoon, but at the same time, a part of her wanted to run away. It was a strange feeling.

'Do you surf?' Connor asked her.

She nodded, pushing her hair back into her baseball cap.

'Want to show me the best places, when you have time off?'

'You want to go surfing?' she asked, a little unsure. 'With me?'

'Yes, Lily.'

When he said her name, it sent a thrill through her. She looked at him and they just clicked. Lily knew straight out, from the first afternoon she met Connor, he was for her. By the end of the year they were married.

By the sounds outside and by the light, it was late. She picked up her phone off the bedside table to see it was nine fifteen. To think she was stretching in their warm bed, and Connor been gone since four in the morning, joining her daddy and Ryan to go lobster fishing in her place.

She had wanted to drive him down to the port, but he'd insisted she stay put.

'May as well make the most of your day off.' He'd kissed her on the lips. 'What time is your appointment again?'

'Twelve,' she'd said, feeling a pinch of anxiety in her stomach.

'Wish I could come with you,' he'd said, looking rueful.

'I know.' Lily had pulled him back down for another embrace. 'But one of us has to go out with Daddy. He only has Ryan.'

In the first year of their marriage, Lily and her daddy had taken Connor out with them to lobster trap. She had been proud of how Connor had thrown himself into the work. Following her instructions, he'd helped her pull up the lobster traps, emptying the old bait bags and tying in the new ones. But he could never go fast enough for her daddy's liking, and he often suffered from seasickness. Lily had known what her father was thinking: Connor wasn't a born fisher like the rest of them.

Eighteen months ago, Connor had got a job as a chef in town, and just a few weeks ago, he'd found the perfect lease for his own seafood restaurant. He'd handed in his notice the same day.

'Your dad will have to find someone else to fill in once I open the restaurant,' Connor had said that morning. 'And you might be otherwise occupied.' He'd given her a serious look. 'You sure about this, Lily?'

'I want to try,' she'd whispered.

She'd heard his pickup drive off, before drifting back off to sleep.

Lily swung her legs out of bed now and pulled on a sweater. Her body still felt wrapped in the sensuality of sleep. It was strange to be at home at this hour, rather than out fishing with her father.

Putting on some woollen socks, she pattered across the wooden floor to open the drapes. She could look at this view for the rest of her life, she reckoned. Their little wooden house was situated on a rocky ledge above a few other houses, including her parents'. It faced out to the small wharf, which was empty of boats right now; the yard, stacked with lobster traps which needed fixing; trucks belonging to her dad, Connor and Ryan; and the boathouse. Beyond was the bay, and an archipelago of tiny rocky islands, their contours fringed with granite and pine. From this window, she loved to watch all the seasons unfurl before her eyes. The snows fall and thaw, the spring blossoms erupt, and the dreamy calm of summer seas. Right now, in October, it was fall, and the whole world was burnished. Golden leaves reflected in the seas, burnt sienna sunsets, and big harvest moons. Today, though, the weather had turned from the day before, and dark clouds were beginning to stack in the sky, the ocean ruffling as the wind picked up. Lily had been out in choppy conditions plenty of times before. Yet as the sky darkened and it began to rain and then snow, she felt uneasy, a small spike of fear taking root in her belly.

It was a new feeling. As Lily hugged her sides, scrutinizing the cloud formations in the sky, she realised it was the first time she had not been with her father on rough seas. Not in all her years as a fisher. Not only that: Connor was out there, without her.

A gust of wind pushed through the chestnut tree outside the window, showering the ground with gold, green and brown leaves. The branches kept waving at her and she looked past them at the ocean. Trying to remain calm, as if the softness of her gaze could soothe the ocean's swells.

Dear God, make the storm go away.

She counted the boats returning to port, but none of them was the *Lily May*. She kept trying to push her anxiety away, but the fact was they should have been back by now if the weather was turning bad. Connor hadn't been out in the boat for weeks. Would he be able to cope with the conditions?

Lily remembered one of the pure days of rest they'd had, last winter out of season. She and Connor had risen in darkness and headed down to the wharf. Gone out in the boat with no agenda for the day. Just her and Connor, sailing to the island of Vinalhaven on a still January day.

There had been a bite in the air. The darkness filling them like cold soup, and then the joy of watching the sunrise together. Pink and orange seeping skyward above the blue horizon. Standing in the wheelhouse in silence, the putter of the engine as the boat churned frothy, icy water. The scent of gas wafting. Her hat pulled down to keep her ears warm. Connor had produced two pastries he'd made for them – almonds and marzipan – and a thermos of strong black coffee. He'd poured out two cups. The steam had twisted in the air as Lily had lifted it to her lips and sipped. Her first taste of morning brew: a little too sweet, but just how Connor liked it.

Lily pressed her forehead onto the cool glass of her bedroom window and closed her eyes. Listened to the wind stir the branches of the chestnut tree outside. Twigs tapping on the pane. She counted slowly to ten, willing Connor to come back to her across the ocean. But when she opened her eyes again to look at the boats bobbing in the harbour, the *Lily May* was still missing.

Chapter Two

Birds sang all around her. Dawn was a cacophony of sound and movement. Swallows swooping right in front of Niamh's bicycle, so she had to keep applying the squeaky brakes, afraid she'd knock into one. She tried to identify the bird songs, but she was bad at it. Her mam had tried to teach her when she was a little girl. Countrywoman that she was, she knew them as if they were family. Niamh recognised the blackbird, its consistent treble, and the wood pigeon, of course. Who didn't know their distinctive coo? But there was another bird, so loud this morning. A persistent rattle. She recognised its song, but couldn't quite remember the name. Her mam would know.

Niamh braked, balancing each foot on her tiptoes on the road. She scanned the thick green foliage. She could hear the singing so loudly, and then she saw the little creature. Of course: the tiny wren, with such a big voice.

'Good morning, Jenny Wren,' she greeted the bird, before pushing off again. She felt happy to have seen the little bird; it reminded her of the times she and her mam had spent listening to birds when she was little. Her daddy there, too. How many years had he been gone? She had been twelve. So, ten years. Hard to believe. She kept on pedalling, feeling weary now.

So many hours had passed since Niamh had gone to work the day before, and yet the short summer night had felt so fleeting. One moment, Niamh had agreed to stay on for the lock-in, and the next they were all stumbling out the door of the pub at day-break. It had felt like she'd drunk herself sober. She'd clambered onto her bicycle and pedalled off, waving her hand behind her as the others took off by foot.

Early morning was so pure. For the first time, she understood a little why her mam claimed her job was the best in the world. Up at the crack of dawn every day, in all weathers, driving around in her An Post van, delivering letters and parcels to all the local townlands. Up and down the twisty, bumpy boreens. Careful of all the little creatures of the hedgerows, which kept the same time as her mam. Right now, in the middle of summer, there were wild rabbits running hither and thither all over the road. Her mam was in a constant state she'd knock one down, taking hours over the post round, going at snail's pace, just to make sure.

Niamh kept on cycling uphill, the final push making it worth the effort as she caught sight of the Atlantic Ocean winking blue in the distance across the marshy fields and tumbled drystone walls. Every day, the Atlantic Ocean looked different, the play of light upon the water constantly shifting and transforming.

With the sea wind behind her, she slung her bicycle down the other side of the hill, her feet lifting off the pedals. Imagined herself as if from above, a lone speck spinning her way home in a tiny corner of north-western Ireland.

There was freedom to be had, away from the city. The rules which applied to city dwellers didn't stick to them. No one minded getting the post a little late because Rosemary Kelly didn't want to run over a rabbit.

Still, there were many days when Niamh longed for the anonymity of city life. There had been talk in her last year at school of going up to Dublin, and sharing a flat with her best friends, Aileen and Teresa. But in the end, Niamh hadn't bothered applying for college, and her mam had forgotten the closing date.

'You're so clever, Niamh,' her mam had complained when she'd found out. 'Why didn't you remind me?'

Niamh had shrugged her shoulders. 'It doesn't matter,' she'd said. 'I've the job in Murphy's.'

Her mam had snorted. 'You can't spend your days working behind a bar. Don't waste yourself!'

Niamh had known even then, three years ago, she couldn't leave Sligo. Her mam was part of why, but she couldn't tell her that. There was so much Niamh couldn't tell her mam.

She thought of the great days, when her mam was full of the joys. Baking soda bread as soon as she got back from her round, and feeding crumbs to the robin redbreast on the kitchen windowsill. Catching hold of Niamh and making her dance with her in the kitchen. But then some days, her mam didn't even make it out of her bed. The black clouds would descend and she'd burrow under the covers. Niamh would try to get her to shift, but her mam squeezed her eyes shut, begging her daughter to leave her be. On those mornings, Niamh had to deliver the post for her.

The truth was, her mam wasn't the only reason Niamh couldn't leave home. It was why she craved getting lost in a big city and disappearing forever. Becoming forgotten, in a way her father, and everything he stood for, could never be.

'He'll not be forgotten,' her father's cousin, Tadhg, had said to her at the funeral. Gripping her hand and squeezing it tight. Staring into her eyes with a look of fury which had matched her own. She'd been so angry.

Niamh pedalled hard up the last hill home. Could she ever move on? Aileen had got a green card in the lottery and was already set up in New York, and Teresa was in London. Her friends were in transition, but where was she going? She wasn't even at a standstill. Her life was going backwards, always. Back to the day she'd lost her father.

Niamh paused on the top of the hill. Behind her was the vast sweep of the Atlantic Ocean, and before her, fields and bogs. In the distance, she could see the blue hills of Donegal. They lived just a few miles from the border with the North of Ireland. Crossing back and forth had been part of her life since she was little. Back then, the troubles hadn't seemed to happen in the damp fields between counties Sligo, Leitrim and Fermanagh. They'd belonged in Belfast, with the car bombs and tit-for-tat shootings. Sure, Niamh had never considered how dangerous her home could be until that terrible day.

Niamh sucked in her breath. Why was she stirring it all up now? When her head was heavy from the drink and lack of sleep? She began to pedal down the last hill home, picking up speed, lifting her legs and letting the pedals spin. The rush felt good, as if she could take flight with all those sweeping birds. She let herself go faster and faster. There was nothing on the road; most people were tucked up in bed at this hour. The bike swept around the corner, and to Niamh's horror, she saw a flicker of movement as a man stepped out from the bushes, his back to her.

'Watch out!' she shouted, pulling on the brakes, but they were old and rubbish. The man heard her just in time, and jumped to the right, but she couldn't stop the bike now. She'd lost all control – it went spinning into the bushes as she fell off into the ditch.

'Hey, are you okay?'

Niamh groaned. She was tangled up in brambles, but nothing hurt.

'Give me your hand,' the guy said.

She looked up, noticing the accent now. American. He was tall, with dark hair and brown eyes. Without waiting for her to reply, the guy took hold of her arm and hoisted her out of the bushes. She took a wobbly step out onto the road.

'You were going real fast,' he said to her.

'Well, I wasn't expecting anyone on the road so early,' she said, flustered, aware of the state of her, and her boozy breath. Up close, he was even better looking. Really tall, and fit as a sportsman, with white, even teeth. He was wearing jeans and a red check shirt, a small rucksack on his back. She brushed down her jeans, noticing they were torn, and she could see a smear of blood on her knee.

'You're bleeding,' he said.

'It's nothing, just a graze,' she said, going for her bike and trying to pull it out of the bushes.

'Here, let me,' he said, helping her. He brushed against her arm as he pulled her bicycle out of the undergrowth, and the sensation set off a flutter in her stomach. She felt quite giddy. Well, of course: she'd been drinking all night, and had just fallen off her bike at breakneck speed.

'Looks like it's okay,' the guy said, wheeling the bike up and down the road. 'But your brakes need fixing,' he added, testing them.

'Right,' she said gruffly, still trying not to breathe over him. He looked like he'd had a good night's sleep, all freshly shaven, in his clean shirt. Whereas she must stink of cigarettes and a whole night spent in the pub.

'So, my name's Jesse,' he said to her, clearly wanting to engage her in conversation.

'Niamh,' she said, mounting the bike again. 'Are you on holidays?'

'No,' he replied.

'Oh,' she said, a bit surprised.

'I'm off to work, sort of,' he said. 'I'm in training with Joseph O'Reilly.'

'At the boatyard?'

'Yeah, I'm learning how to make traditional Irish wooden boats,' he said, smiling at her. Was he flirting? Niamh couldn't be sure. It was so early, and she was a bit dazed from her bike fall.

'I don't think Joseph will be at the yard yet,' she said.

Joseph O'Reilly was one of their regulars. Sure, he'd been in Murphy's until well after midnight last night. Most evenings he'd be in the bar at nine o'clock, after his dinner, to sink a couple of pints of Guinness. Niamh liked Joseph because he was always respectful and, unlike most, minded his own business. He was also held with respect in the community as a skilled boatbuilder. She'd been told he'd been offered jobs all over the world, but had chosen to stay put in his little boatyard in Mullaghmore. It was clear Joseph was a little too fond of the drink, but it was a vice which never seemed to change his quiet manner, unlike some of the others.

'I know,' Jesse said to her. 'Joseph gave me keys, so I can get started without him.'

'That so, Jesse?' She liked saying his name. Made her think of outlaws and the Wild West.

'We're fixing up an old yacht, see,' he said.

'Well, that's pretty cool,' she said. 'Are you going to sail it home to America?'

He raised his eyebrows, looked amused. 'I hadn't thought of that,' he said, giving her a cheeky grin.

They stood in slightly awkward silence for a moment.

'Sure your knee's okay?' Jesse asked her.

'Yeah, I'm nearly home,' she said. 'Well, see you around.' She pushed off again, and began to cycle, feeling self-conscious.

'Have a nice day!' Jesse called after her.

She still felt jittery as she leant her bicycle against the side of their house. Jesse had stepped out of nowhere. Had she imagined him altogether? He was so wholesome, which made her suspicious. Were Americans truly that friendly, or was it all an act?

'There you are, darling,' her mam said, pouring Niamh a mug of tea from the pot as she picked up the keys to the postal van. 'What happened to your leg?'

'Sure it's nothing, Mam. I fell off the bike.'

Her mam shook her head. 'Too many late nights!' She left the back door slightly open as she slipped out into the yard, the thick scent of the summer hedgerows wafting into the cottage.

Niamh stood at the kitchen window, watching her mam get into the green An Post van and drive off down the road. She was clearly in good form today. In fact, the whole month, her mam had been cheerful. But Niamh knew it was all a matter of time before she went down again. If her father were still alive, would her mam be better? Of course she would. Her lows had only begun after he was gone.

Niamh took some cotton wool out of the kitchen drawer, dampened it at the tap and applied it to her cut knee. It stung a little, but really it was only a graze and she didn't need a plaster. She applied a little Sudocrem to it, before pouring another mug of tea from the pot and wandering into the sitting room. They lived in a small two-storey cottage, with an outbuilding, Daddy's old workshop, across the backyard. Downstairs there was a big kitchen and a small sitting room. They spent most of their time in the kitchen. The TV was in there, as was the wood stove and a big old sofa to sprawl upon. But Niamh loved the sitting room best. Small and dark due to all the bookcases lining the walls. Her mam's desk was in the window, overlooking Bunduff Lough. The house was situated off a narrow lane which cut between two halves of the lough: they lived between water. Niamh sometimes worried about flooding when water levels rose, but her mam had absolute faith it would never rise too high. They were near the sea, too. You could hear the distant waves as they crashed upon Bunduff beach, but the only water they could see was the lake before them. Glimmers of still blue peeked out through the leaves of the trees which lined the road outside.

Niamh sat down at her mam's desk. Rosemary Kelly hand-wrote everything, sometimes typing it up herself on an old typewriter, but more often sending off her scribbles for her editor to unravel. Her mam had a publisher, but she hardly made any money from her slim volumes of poetry. The last royalty cheque had made a grand total of twenty-five pounds. They'd gone for fish chowder and pints of Guinness in Sligo to celebrate.

Niamh sipped her tea. She should go to bed. She was exhausted and sore from the fall, but her eyes dropped to a poem her mam was working on. She could see the ink was still a little wet on the blotter. Her mam even wrote with a quill pen. She often told Niamh that she woke up with the words of poems in her head and wrote before she was even properly awake. A notebook and pen were always by her bedside table. Niamh wondered if she had dreamt this one.

> *I see a child.*
> *His eyes are full of light and open dreams.*
> *I see his past, an agile mite, dashing through high, sharp grass.*
> *Sleeping with cows, upon their napes, sighting dreams of pure cloud shapes.*

Who was the child? A boy, so not her. Was it about her father? Nearly all her mam's poems were about Niamh's father. There was something about the poem which made Niamh want to read it again, and again. She could see an image in her head of a little boy running towards her: dimpled cheeks and outstretched arms.

The phone rang on the desk, making Niamh almost drop her mug of tea on her mam's poem. It rang so rarely. She put the tea down and picked up the receiver, already knowing in her heart who it was.

'How's it going, Niamh?'

'I'm just in from work, Brendan,' Niamh said, trying to quell the nerves in her stomach.

'Can you meet me later?' Brendan asked her, then gave her the details of when and where without pausing to hear her answer.

By the time they'd ended their brief chat, Niamh was wide awake. How could she sleep now? Whenever Brendan called her up, no matter how many years he'd been doing it, she was all in a heap.

Niamh had always known Brendan. He was her father's cousin Tadhg's son. Five years older than her. He had been her first love, the summer she'd turned fifteen, and seven years later, he was still calling the shots.

Chapter Three

Rockland, Maine, 18th October 2017

The storm had come so fast. Lily watched from the window in the kitchen, cradling her coffee cup in her hands, but not drinking. Willing the wind to drop. But it only got worse: the waves rolling larger, the rain turning to snow and then rain again, lashing against the window.

She picked up her phone.

'You seen this storm building?' she asked her mom.

'I know, honey,' her mom said. 'But your dad will have turned back the moment he saw it coming.'

'You sure?' Lily asked. 'I've been watching from the window, and all the other boats have returned. How come they're not home?'

'Your dad's boat is forty foot; he can manage more than the others. He was dropping a line of traps in a new gravel bar in deeper waters,' her mom said, not sounding as worried as Lily thought she should be. 'Your dad knows what he's doing,' she added, before pausing. 'Shouldn't you have left for your appointment with the specialist?'

'Mom, look outside the window! They called and cancelled, of course. Because of the storm.' Exasperated, she took a breath, tried to stay calm. 'It's going to be bad, Mom.'

'Honey, come on over,' her mom said. 'We'll wait it out together.'

*

Lily took her rain jacket off the hook in the back porch. Her whole body felt charged with nervous energy. Her hands shook as she zipped up her jacket. When the clinic in Portland had called to tell her the appointment with the fertility specialist had been moved to the following week, her anxiety had intensified.

'I'm sorry,' the receptionist had said. 'But there's a bad nor'easter coming down from Canada. There's weather warnings out and we're shutting for the day.'

Her words had confirmed what Lily knew already. This storm was serious.

But there was still no sign of Connor, her father and Ryan in the *Lily May*. Why the hell weren't they back yet?

As soon as she opened the back door, it felt as if the wind was slapping her back into the house. She put her head down and pushed into the icy bites of sleet, which stung her bare cheeks and plastered her fringe to her forehead. Lily was used to the wind. There was a part of her which liked the adrenalin rush of battling against the winds out on the ocean. If you knew what you were doing – as she did, as her father did – it was possible to ride huge waves in a relatively small boat, as long as they didn't smack you side-on. Even then, the wave had to break at an exact moment to overturn the boat. Lily liked the challenge of nature. Felt like a warrior when she was out on high waves.

She remembered a big storm, one night when she was around ten years old. She'd got out of bed and run to the window to look at the forked lightning on the horizon, the violent swells and surges of the ocean, glinting silvery in the dark. Excitement had coursed through her. Lily had opened her bedroom window, and been immediately knocked back by the force of the wind. The thunder had boomed, and it had felt as if she was being raised upwards. She had stood on her cold feet in the middle of her bedroom, spread her arms wide, and let the wind bounce off

her, the white drapes streaming like angel's wings, her nightie
billowing, her black hair flying all over the place. She'd imagined
herself taking flight, like a great big cormorant. Her books had
clattered off her shelves onto the floor and the window panes
had banged backwards and forwards, but Lily had been lost in
her own world. Not until her parents had come tearing into the
room had she come to with a jolt.

'Close the damn window!' her mom had shouted at her father,
who'd been laughing at the audacity of his child. But her mom
had been real angry. One of the rare times she'd used a curse word.

'Our child's pure wild, Jack,' her mom had said as she'd
grabbed Lily's hands and shaken her. Lily had never forgotten
the look of fear in her mom's eyes.

But her dad had shrugged. 'Good thing she's not scared of a
big storm,' he'd said, sounding proud. 'That's my girl!'

When she was older, Lily had liked to run with the wind. If
it were a blustery day, she would run from their house down the
road, past the pier and along by the beach. Thrilled by the roar
of the ocean, wanting to run into the waves. Yet knowing that if
she did so, within seconds she could be consumed and washed
away to a watery grave.

What was at the bottom of their ocean? The practical part
of Lily knew it was teeming with life. Most importantly for her
and her family, with lobsters. These giant crustaceous creatures
made their sand pits on the bed of the cold Atlantic, burrowing
to find a safe place to dispatch their eggs.

But as a little girl, Lily had daydreamed about kingdoms under
the sea. She had been a tomboy, never wanting to seem silly or
girlish with her cousin Ryan and his friends, yet out on a row
boat, her eyes had been hypnotised by all the light reflections
on the water. She'd gazed into the depths, wanting to slip off the

boat and dive right down to the bottom. Find a secret kingdom of mermaids and mermen.

The wind battered Lily seemingly from every direction as she fought through it, walking down the hill towards her parents' house. She cut across the front yard, through chestnut trees completely stripped bare. The last of their leaves swirled around her in a spiral of burnt umber. Rain, ice and snow flung against her, as if a great big sea giant was hurling them right at her. She found it hard to breathe, as if the wind were stealing her air. As she opened the gate into her parents' backyard, an old porch chair was picked up and hurled towards her. She leaped out of the way and it slammed against the fence. She dragged it into her father's garage.

Despite her rain jacket, Lily was completely drenched. Her clothing stuck to her skin; she had to peel her rain jacket off in the back porch. It must be like hell out at sea: at least sixteen-foot waves, which was way over the limit of her father's forty-foot vessel. Connor had never been out in such conditions before. Lily's stomach felt tight with dread. How would her husband cope? The one time they'd been out in rough seas – and it had been nowhere near the scale of this storm – Connor had been crippled by seasickness.

'Hi, Mom, I'm just grabbing a towel,' she called out as she ran upstairs to the bathroom.

She wrapped her hair in a turban, coming back down to her mom in the living room, who had the weather channel on. Lily didn't like what she saw on the screen. The nor'easter was bigger than predicted, and the weather warnings were clear. Stay inside. Ferries had been cancelled, but Lily's husband, her father and her cousin were out all on the Atlantic. Exposed and highly vulnerable. She didn't understand why her father wasn't back yet. Something must have happened to them.

Lily clenched her hands. No. She couldn't let herself think about it.

'Have you heard from the Coast Guard?' she asked her mom.

'No, honey,' her mom said, patting the seat beside her. She was looking pale now, and was no longer saying it would be okay.

'Did you call Cherie?' Lily asked, thinking of Ryan's mom, her aunt. Already she'd lost her husband – Lily's uncle and her father's brother – to cancer, when Lily had been twelve. She had to be in a terrible state at the idea her only son was in danger.

'Yeah, she was going to come over, but it's too bad to leave her house.'

'Where did the storm come from?' Lily asked, sitting down beside her mom. 'Like, it's got so bad real fast.'

It was a question which didn't need an answer. They both knew well enough how the weather could change in a heartbeat. There were times when Lily loved the fury of the sea, thrived on the challenge of riding the bucking waves in their fishing boat. Together with her dad in the helm, they had witnessed the power of the vast ocean. The rush of staying on course, and the high once you got home safe with a big lobster haul. But she didn't like being the one at home, watching and waiting for loved ones.

'I can't just sit here, Mom,' Lily said, standing up in agitation. Why had her appointment had to be today? Of all days, why had she let Connor go out fishing in her place? He wasn't experienced enough, even in the best of conditions. 'Let's go down to the point,' she suggested. 'See if we can sight them returning.'

'We shouldn't leave the house,' her mom said. 'There's weather warnings…'

'Well, you can stay here,' Lily said. 'But I'm going, and I'll pick up Cherie on the way back. She can't be alone.' She charged into the back porch to put her rain jacket back on.

'Okay, I'm coming,' her mom said, following her.

'I'll drive if you want, okay?'

Her mom nodded mutely as Lily took the keys off the hook.

'You got your cell phone with you in case the Coast Guard calls, right?' she said to her mom as they got in her station wagon.

The vehicle stank a little of sardines from all the bait trips her mom made. Before Lily had been allowed to go out fishing with her dad, this had been her job as well. Driving out to Booths Canning Company. She hadn't liked this minor role at all. Right back from as far as she could remember, Lily had wanted to be a fisher like her daddy.

At the age of five, she'd sat on the big sill in the front window, crying, waiting for her daddy to come home with the smell of the ocean on him, and a shine in his eyes from a big haul. Her mom would try to console her by getting her to bake cookies, but Lily wasn't interested in playing house. Every day, she'd asked if she could go fishing. At first her mom had told her she was too young, and then she'd told her that lobster fishing wasn't for girls.

Then when she was thirteen, her dad had started taking her cousin Ryan out with him. Lily had gone into a fury.

'Ryan told me he hates fishing,' Lily had complained. 'But I want to fish. It's not fair. Who says girls can't fish?'

'It's heavy work, Lily,' her mom had told her. 'You're not strong enough.'

'But I'm stronger than Ryan!' she'd complained. 'I beat him all the time at arm wrestling.'

'Let her go with me,' her dad had said to her mom, much to Lily's excitement.

'I guess once you see what it's really like, you won't want to do it again,' her mom had said, giving in.

But as soon as Lily had set foot on her daddy's boat, it had felt like a kind of home. Not a safe place, no: but somewhere she belonged. Way more than Ryan did. Sure, he was a good second mate now, but it had taken years for him to get it right.

Even her dad had been astonished at how quickly Lily had picked it up.

'Well, it's not rocket science,' Lily had said, making poor Ryan feel even more stupid. She'd always been fast at things. Lobstering suited her.

When they were both fourteen, Lily and Ryan had worked their first summer lobster fishing with her dad. Lily had felt sorry for Ryan. He clearly hated it, but lobstering was what Smyth men did. His father, Uncle Joe, had been a lobster fisher before the family had lost him to lung cancer. It was Ryan's destiny to follow in his father's footsteps. Ryan's lack of natural inclination for lobstering was one reason why Lily's father took her out with them. It was as if Lily was Ryan's shadow, helping her cousin.

That summer, Ryan had confided in her that he was having nightmares about giant lobsters chasing him across the ocean. Sea monsters with enormous pincers, crazy eyes on top of their hard shell heads, and long, spidery antennae.

'You need to lay off the pot,' Lily had laughed at him.

Lobster were living product to Lily. They were the means to her family's survival. There were rules and regulations, and of all industries, theirs was one which had always been focused on conservation. Their livelihoods depended on the survival of lobsters.

The next summer, her father switched Lily and Ryan's roles, and Lily became sternman. Her job was to pull each trap in as it was hauled up by the winch, then open it and take out the lobsters. Chuck the shorties, those too small to be legal to fish, back into the Atlantic, and throw the rest in a container ready to measure and band. She'd push the empty trap down to Ryan and he would take out the old bait bag, throw it in another box, then fix the new bait bag, before closing the lid of the trap and putting it on the shelf down the centre of the boat, ready to drop in a line with the others. Lily moved so fast, sometimes Ryan would be hollering at her to hold up. As soon as they'd emptied all the traps, she and Ryan would turn to the boxes of squirming greenish-brown lobsters and band their pincers. Of course, Lily flew through them, careful to measure any she was uncertain of, while Ryan laboured over the task. Now and again, a big mama egg-bearing lobster would land in their catch, and Lily got the job of snipping a V in her tail so other fishers would put her back in the sea. She never chucked the big ladies so hard – after all, they were carrying precious cargo – but dropped them gently into the ocean.

When Lily and her dad had taken Connor out with them the week after they'd got married, Lily had been astonished to see he was even slower than Ryan had been. All fingers and thumbs. But Connor, of course, was examining each lobster and thinking about which would be the best one to cook. His mind was always on food, or the creation of food. As fishing had been her passion, cooking was his. Over the past three years, his fishing skills had improved, but it had never been a consideration that he would become a fisherman like her father and Ryan. In Maine, fishing was an inherited occupation, and that was the way it was. Fishing licences passed down through the generations. You had to trust your fellow shipmates with your life. That kind of trust only came from family, even if you didn't get on.

Rain and sleet lashed into them and the wind buffeted the station wagon as Lily drove down the road, aware of the giant waves crashing onto the beach. Her mom's silence was enough to tell her she was deeply worried, too. They drove to the point, but it was too dangerous to get out of the vehicle and they couldn't see anything. It made Lily feel even worse. The thought of her family out in their small fishing vessel, trying to ride back into port over at least sixteen-foot waves was enough to make her want to vomit. It was one thing considering how her father and Ryan would manage, but what about Connor?

It was all her fault. If she hadn't have been so obsessed with wanting a baby, she wouldn't have made the appointment at the clinic, and Connor would be sitting in the station wagon with her mom right now. While she would be out on the ocean with her dad.

'Oh, Lily.' Her mom's voice cracked as she gripped her daughter's hand.

'It'll be okay, Mom,' Lily heard herself saying, although she was far from believing it. 'Come on, let's go to Cherie.'

Ryan's mom only lived another five minutes' drive away, but Lily crawled along the deserted coast road. Debris blew in front of the vehicle, causing her to repeatedly slam on the brakes.

At last, they pulled up outside Cherie's white board house. Lily grabbed her mom's hand as they ran across the front yard, the gale tearing into them.

'Have you heard any more?' Lily's mom asked Cherie as soon as they'd taken off their wet things.

'Nope,' said Cherie, her eyes wide with dread. 'Sarah, I can't lose Ryan, I just can't.' Tears started in her eyes.

'It'll be okay. Dad'll get them back safe, Aunty Cherie,' Lily said, though in her heart she, too, was fearing the worst. This weather was beyond any fisherman's skill.

'Shall I make some coffee, Cherie?' her mom said.

'Sure, Sarah.' Cherie wrung her hands and walked over to the window, staring out in desperation.

They were praying for their men to return. But as the storm accelerated and the light began to fade, the room turned dark with despair.

Lily's mom busied herself making sandwiches, which were left untouched to curl on the plate. Cherie smoked constantly, one cigarette after the other. Even Lily's mother ended up having a cigarette.

'I'm going to call the Coast Guard,' Lily said. As she did so, her mom's cell phone rang. She pulled it out of her pocket as Lily and Cherie waited, the two of them still and tense as they tried to hear what the man on the end of the line was saying.

'Okay, thank you, Ray, please let us know as soon as they've been picked up,' her mom said.

Lily turned on her mom. 'They found them?'

'Your dad radioed emergency to the Coast Guard an hour ago,' she said. 'You know the boat is narrow, even with the three of them, and taking on too much water. He feared it was going to capsize.'

'Did he mention Ryan?' Cherie said, putting her hands to her chest.

'Connor?' Lily asked. 'Are the boys okay?'

'Yeah, they're okay, I think,' her mom said. 'They've sent out a chopper. If the boys have to get into the life raft, they'll deploy a rescue swimmer.'

'Those guys are heroes,' Cherie said in a shaky voice. 'Wilfully being dropped down into the ocean to haul our men to safety.'

'Where are they?' Lily asked her mom.

'About thirty miles out,' her mom said. 'Remember, your dad will have a satellite signal. They'll find them quick.'

Lily glanced out of Cherie's front window at the raging ocean. The winds must be at least forty knots, she thought, the waves reaching tremendous heights as they slammed against the shore.

Trees bent over, big ones, so far it looked as if they might snap. Lily rubbed her wedding band, spinning it around her finger. As if by touching it, she could summon Connor, Ryan and her father to the door.

Her mom's phone rang again. She couldn't hear what was being said on the other end of the line, but she watched every movement of her mom's face for clues. It looked like she had aged ten years in a day. The lines furrowed deep in her brow as she spoke.

'They've sighted the boat,' her mom said as she got off the phone. 'It's capsized.'

'Oh God,' Cherie moaned. Lily couldn't speak as if all the air was being squeezed out of her.

'It's okay, the life raft's been seen, it's okay, they'll be on it.' Her mom just kept repeating 'it's okay', as if by saying it, all would be well.

But Lily knew all it would take was one freak wave. A big crest of ocean to wipe out a person's life.

Lily picked up her cell, tried ringing Connor's phone, which of course was pointless. He would have no coverage, and anyway right now he was probably just trying to stay alive. The phone went straight to voicemail and she heard Connor's cheerful voice telling her to speak after the tone. She listened to his message from this morning, feeling even worse. Shaken up from hearing him. Wanting him so badly to be there, putting his hand on her back and telling her he was just fine.

'My boy, my boy,' Cherie kept repeating. Lily went over and put her arm around her aunt. She was so small. Lily could see the snow white roots of her dark hair.

'He'll be okay, Aunty,' Lily said to her, glancing at the large photograph of Ryan on the TV stand. His big cheesy grin. Her stomach lurched. It was too much to consider that they might lose all three of them.

'Come on, Cherie,' her mom said, taking another of her sister-in-law's cigarettes and lighting it with trembling hands. 'Jack will take care of Ryan; they're made of tough stuff.'

'But so was Joe, and then within a year he was gone,' Cherie wailed. 'What if Smyth men are cursed?'

'No, Dad's lucky, Aunty Cherie,' Lily said. 'Ryan, too.'

But even as she said it, she was thinking that she was her father's lucky charm. And where was she? Back on land, not on the boat with him and Ryan, keeping them safe. Even worse, her husband was in terrible danger, all because she had wanted the appointment with the fertility specialist as soon as possible. Couldn't wait for end of the lobstering season, when she would have had all the time in the world to go to Portland for the tests.

Her father always said Lily belonged on the ocean. He'd known it from the first day she'd gone out with him, when she was sat up on his captain's chair at the wheel and had gripped on to it with both hands. So tiny she could barely see over it, let alone the way forward. But she'd been so happy on the ocean, and so excited when all they could see was water all around them. Not one tiny bit of land. She hadn't been frightened, not for one instant. But this was her world, not Connor's. If only someone else could have gone out today in her place – but every other fisherman had his own boat and crew. There had been no one else available. Connor had been the only option.

'Your dad and Ryan will look after Connor,' her mom said in a steady voice, her face rigid. 'The chopper is on the way out. They've got this.'

'I should have been there instead,' Lily whispered.

'Oh, honey,' her mom said, her eyes big. 'Can't tell you how glad I am you're not.'

Amidst the sound of the wind and the thrashing ocean, Lily heard knocking at the door. It was Cherie's sister, Lou, and her daughter, Angie. Not long after, another knock. Cherie's neighbours on both sides arrived in. This was what happened when a boat went down. The fishing community came together. Held hands, some prayed, and all of them waited for news. Lily made herself busy in Cherie's kitchen, making tea and coffee and more sandwiches, which none of them ate.

Everyone huddled on seats around the TV, keeping watch on the weather while looking out at the wind whipping the ocean, its spray spattering the windows. Lily stared at the grey bleak violence of the stormy Atlantic. If the boat had capsized, had they had time to get into the emergency suits her dad kept in the tiny hold? Or had they gone straight into the water, which was likely to be less than fifty degrees? How long could they survive before getting hypothermia?

Lily looked over at her mom, the wife of a fisherman and used to occasional dramas. Lily's dad had been caught in storms before. Lily remembered at least three from her childhood. Her mom pacing in the lounge, surrounded by friends and neighbours, glaring out the window as if to banish the bad weather. She had been through this all before. Yet Lily could see the fear in her mother's eyes now as she tried to stay calm for Cherie.

'Have you ever seen it so bad, Sarah?' Cherie kept asking her mom, who repeated again and again as if she was trying to convince herself:

'They'll be rescued. Our Coast Guard is the best.'

At last, her mom's phone rang and she snatched it up. Got off the couch and walked into the kitchen, as the rest of them waited in anticipation for her return.

'Okay, that was Petty Officer Grimes. They've picked them up and landed in Brunswick Airport,' her mom said. 'They've brought them to Mid Coast Hospital.'

Already, the wind was beginning to drop a little as Lily and her mom jumped into the station wagon. This time her mom drove, as fast as she could, while negotiating all the debris from fallen branches on the roads. Behind them followed Cherie, Lou and Angie in Lou's pickup.

The trees had been stripped bare of their golden bounty of leaves, and the roads were plastered with wet brown mulch. Lily's whole body was rigid with dread. She couldn't speak. Besides, her mom was concentrating so hard on driving she didn't want to distract her. It was over an hour to Brunswick. As they headed inland, they had to be so careful of the conditions. Lily knew all about the dangers of the ocean. Lived it every day. And yet she was shocked, because she had never thought something like this would happen to her.

The evening had never felt so dark to Lily as they raced along the treacherous roads to Brunswick. All the moonlight and stars obscured by dark clouds in the dusky sky. The hospital was on the way into the city centre, but they managed to drive right past the entrance. It was only after they passed the fire station and noticed Lou was no longer driving behind them, that her mom realised her mistake and turned the car. It was a good few minutes before they took a right onto Medical Center Drive and flew down the tree-lined road into the semi-circular car park, pulling up beside Lou's vehicle.

As they ran into the ER entrance, Lily's mom almost collided with Ray George, one of the coastguards her parents knew.

'They okay, Ray?' Her mom grabbed Ray's arm, and Lily saw Ray almost wince from her grip.

'It was one hell of a storm, Sarah, but Jack's okay,' he said. 'The boat capsized, but we picked him up in the life raft.'

Her mom's body sagged with relief. 'Thank God. What about the boys?'

Lily saw Ray's hesitation, the beginning of what he was saying. 'One of them—'

Lily couldn't wait to hear any more. She took off down the hospital corridor, her heart pounding with terror, rushing past surprised-looking medics in white coats and weary nurses in their blue scrubs.

'Connor!' she called, all the while praying inside her head. *Dear Jesus, make Connor be okay. Please.* Although if Connor was okay, did that mean Ryan was gone? 'Connor!'

She ran past an open door. Saw her daddy sitting up in one of the beds, the look on his face when he saw her. His expression told her what she didn't want to believe, but she couldn't stop. Kept calling out for Connor, until she came to the next open door. There, she saw him. Ryan.

Cherie, Lou and Angie were already in the room with him. Ryan was unconscious and all connected up to tubes and monitors. Cherie was wailing her son's name, Lou with her arm around her. But Lily's cousin, Angie, looked up at her with sorrowful eyes.

'Lily,' she whispered, walking towards her, reaching out her hands. 'Oh, Lily.'

'No,' Lily hissed, feeling as if she would fall down, never to get up again. She felt a hand on her shoulder and turned to look at her mother. Hunted her eyes for hope.

'I'm so sorry, honey,' her mother said, her eyes full of tears, her face gaunt.

'No!' she said, barging past her mom.

'Lily, come back!' Her mom followed her, pulling on her arm.

Lily spun around. 'They can't stop looking! He could still be out there, Mom. Clinging on.'

Her mom shook her head. 'He's gone,' she said. 'They're certain of it. I'm sorry.'

The pain inside Lily's chest was so intense, she thought she might stop breathing. This wasn't happening to her. Connor was only twenty-four. She was almost twenty-five. They were going to have lots of babies. They were going to share their whole lives together. This couldn't be the end.

Lily pulled away from her mom. Part of her knew she should go see her father, but she couldn't bear to be in the hospital one more minute. She ran back down the corridor, her mom calling after her, and outside into the wild darkness. The wind pushed and pulled her across the parking lot, and she kept running. Not thinking where she was going. Just following a narrow residential road as it wove through the tight pine trees. No one was about. Of course not: most sensible people were inside, snug and safe, watching the wildness outside. She ran on until she saw signs for Thomas Point Beach, and then just followed them all the way to the ocean.

The waves unfurled and crashed upon the shore, and the rain beat into her face, mixing with her tears. She fell to her knees on the wet sand and rough shingle, not caring as it cut through her jeans, and she howled. How could she live her life without Connor?

Chapter Four

So many times, she and Brendan had met in secret over the years. They used to go to the graveyard, where her daddy had been buried. Niamh had never liked meeting there. She felt the ghosts of all the dead souls, particularly her father, watching her. Besides, it made more sense to meet away from town, out on the bogs they both knew so well, or in the enclaves of nearby woodland. The bog was a territory which could be dangerous to a stranger who didn't know how to negotiate the lurking sink holes. Which could suck you into their black depths, as if they were quicksand.

Niamh pulled her bicycle off the road and hid it in the hedgerow, pushing it in as deep as she could without cutting her hands to shreds. It had begun to rain lightly as she crossed the fields, lacing her eyelashes with tiny drops, misting up her vision. But she could have her eyes closed and she'd know the way. Through the opening into the tight-knit spruce wood, then she kept on walking up and down root-exposed hollows until she saw the still silhouette of her cousin squatting at the base of a big lime tree, and smelt the scent of his lit cigarette wafting towards her.

'I can't stay long,' she said, as they hugged each other. 'I've to be in work in less than an hour.'

'Sure, old Murphy isn't going to sack you if you're a few minutes late opening up.' Brendan gave her a mocking look.

He never took her job seriously. She was not so important. He always made that clear, no matter what she did.

'Daddy says hello,' Brendan said to her, then stood up and began to walk fast through the woods. She followed him, almost breaking into a run to keep up. This was how it always went. Niamh following Brendan, blindly, without question.

The bond between them was deep. He was family, but not so close it was wrong. Their fathers were first cousins. Brendan had always been there for her. She would trust him with her life. At times, he almost felt like an extension of herself.

Although Brendan had never gone to college, barely finished school, he had been the greatest teacher of her life. Showing her and naming all the edible and poisonous plants of the woodlands, teaching her how to survive outside in the wilderness while they camped during the summer months of her teenage years. Most of all, Brendan had taught her about belief. Not the Catholic kind, which had always rung fake and hollow for Niamh. How she had hated being brought on Saturday afternoons to sit in the tiny confessional box on the other side from Father O'Donovan. Forced to share her deepest secrets with the old man, who had sounded like he didn't care one bit about what she was thinking or feeling, let alone about advising her on it. How relieved she'd been when one Saturday afternoon, just a few months after her father had died, her mam had marched into the church with her shopping basket hooked on her arm, and yanked Niamh out of the pew. All Niamh's school peers had looked at her mother in awe as she swore inside the church.

'By Jaysus, Niamh, I'll not have you in that box with the old pervert,' she'd said, dragging Niamh out of the church.

When Niamh had asked her mam to explain herself, she'd only shaken her head, and said she'd been told something about Father O'Donovan, and that it wasn't for a young girl's ears but there was no way she or Niamh would ever set foot in their parish church again.

Of course, Niamh had heard all the gossip at school about what Father O'Donovan had been up to. She'd been delighted at first that she no longer had to go to church every week, but thought it very strange no one else in Mullaghmore ostracised Father O'Donovan, and that the bishop did nothing about removing him. When she asked her classmates, they just shrugged, said their parents still wanted them to go to church, and they were all for an easy life. Their families had always gone to church every week, for decades, and then there were weddings, funerals and First Communions. These were important events. They couldn't just ban Father O'Donovan. But that was exactly what Niamh and her mam did. It set them apart from everyone in Mullaghmore, as if it wasn't already bad enough because her mam was a widow.

Despite her new freedom from Mass-going, if Niamh was honest with herself, there was a small part of her which had missed the sense of community she'd got from going to church every week. Because she had had a tiny bit of faith before her mam had exploded into the church that Saturday afternoon and had woken her up to the hypocrisy of the Catholic religion. Her whisperings to baby Jesus had kept her going in the dark months after the loss of her father. She had needed so much to believe in something, because it was the only way to keep going.

That was where Brendan had come in. On those summer nights, wild camping in the woods, he would fill her head with stories of Ireland. Not only the ancient mystic Ireland, but the suffering Ireland of the Famine, the new hope with the War of Independence, the sorrows of the Civil War. He filled her in on the history of the Troubles, made sure she understood it was the Loyalists and the Brits who had started all the violence.

Of course, she'd had a massive crush on Brendan. It had never occurred to Niamh it was inappropriate for a fifteen-year-old to be making out with a twenty-year-old, and her second cousin to boot. Brendan had made her feel adult in a way no one else had ever done.

She had lost her virginity to him. So long ago, the memory of the experience had faded. All she could recall was it had been quick, and clumsy. She hadn't even had time to take her skirt off as she felt the little stab of pain as Brendan pushed up into her. Afterwards, they'd shared a joint, and Brendan had talked about his beliefs again, as if it had never happened. After that, they'd had sex most times when they met up. Looking back, Niamh couldn't help thinking it was a miracle they'd never got caught out. He'd claimed he was doing the withdrawal method, and she wouldn't get pregnant, but she'd been so daft and flattered someone like Brendan would want to sleep with her, she'd never been too careful. Often, he stayed in until the end.

It had stopped when Brendan got a girlfriend. A blond girl with green eyes called Deirdre from Derry, who sometimes came with Brendan when he visited her. They'd been dating a long time now. Almost four years.

'How's Deirdre?' Niamh asked Brendan now, as she followed his tall figure stomping through the woods.

'Shush,' Brendan said, stopping so suddenly she almost slammed into his back. He turned and looked into her eyes. They stared at each other, and not for the first time, Niamh was struck how like her daddy's eyes Brendan's were. Such a brilliant, clear blue. His skin so pale in contrast, and the red hair like a flame upon his head. For a moment, as his gaze softened, Niamh thought he was going to bend down and kiss her – but of course, that wasn't why.

'We're so proud of you, Niamh,' Brendan said.

She wasn't sure if Brendan meant him and Deirdre, or him and his father Tadhg. But she didn't feel brave. She was doing what she always did for Brendan. It was easier to say yes than no.

*

The soft misty drizzle laced her hair with tiny droplets and covered her cheeks in a damp film. She inhaled deeply as she lugged the heavy bag across their overgrown garden. The scent of all the lush wildness distracted her from her task. The aroma of huge sprays of floral lilac and sweet unpruned summer roses filled her lungs as she stopped, put down the bag and pulled one pink waxen petal off a rose. Held it up to her nose. Inhaled its sultry perfume. She closed her fingers over the rose petal, felt it sticking to her palm. The scent was so deeply romantic, it made her yearn for something she'd never experienced in her life.

Niamh shook herself, dropping the petal onto the wet grass. What was she doing, mooning around in the back garden with Brendan's bag? What if her mam came home and asked her what was in it?

She pushed open the door of the outhouse. Inside it was exactly as if her daddy had just been in it. It was the reason why she always put Brendan's bags in here. She knew for sure it was the one place her mam would never enter. All of her father's tools were still in the same place on his workbench, covered now in a thick layer of dust. Niamh should have cleaned them and put them away in the toolbox on the shelf long ago. But every time she approached the work bench and looked at the big hammer, the saw, the screws and spanners, they all felt like messages from her father. The spray of sawdust where he'd been working. The half-made table still in the corner of the shed. Always, it reminded her of the injustice of what had happened to her family.

Niamh dragged Brendan's bag over to the other side of the shed by the one smeared window. The view was of the overgrown bushes outside, as if the outhouse had sprung out of a dense jungle of Irish weeds. Niamh knelt down and lifted up the loose floorboards, then slowly and carefully lowered the bag into the space beneath. She had no idea what was in it. She preferred never to look. She slid the floorboards back in place. No one had seen her as she'd pedalled home with the bag strapped to the back of her bike. Broad daylight, and so blatant. But Brendan driving over, day or night, would attract more attention.

The shed was growing dimmer as the rain intensified outside, hammering on the tin roof above.

Niamh pulled the string on the lamp and sat on the old mattress which was shoved against the wall. She took the joint Brendan had given her out of her pocket and lit it up. The scent of the rose petal she'd plucked in the garden was still on her fingertips. It was so tender and delicate, it made her feel such deep longing for a different kind of life. How had she got into such a mess? She couldn't tell her mam. She couldn't tell anyone. Brendan was lucky. He had Deirdre. But she'd no one.

Niamh lay down on her back, watching the smoke from the joint spiralling above her head. Could she run away? Would her mam be all right if she took off? It was so clear to her now. She didn't belong in Brendan's dangerous world any more. The anger was gone, and she just wanted out.

But Brendan had warned her, the night she'd been sworn in. 'Remember, Niamh, you can never go back,' he'd said. 'Once you join up, it's for life.'

She'd insisted she was sure. Raised her left hand and said the words:

'I, Niamh Kelly, promise that I will promote the objects of the Irish Republican Army to the best of my knowledge and ability, and that I will obey all orders and regulations issued to me by the army authority and by my superior officer.'

But she'd only been sixteen. Her cousin should have stopped her. He'd done nothing of the sort. Pulled her in deeper, and now she was stuck.

Niamh closed her eyes, let herself drift. She was going to be late for work, but she didn't care now. She let herself dream of leaving Ireland, dozing until she woke an hour later, stiff and cold.

Her mam had fallen asleep on the couch in the kitchen. She was still wearing her An Post pale blue shirt, with the little An Post insignia on the breast pocket. Her head was tilted back with Pixie, their collie, curled up on the cushions next to her.

'Get down, Pixie,' Niamh admonished the dog, who slunk reluctantly off the couch, giving her a guilty look.

Niamh leant over and gave her mam a gentle shake. 'Mammy, you need to go to bed,' she whispered.

Her mam woke up instantly, giving Niamh a wild-eyed look. 'Are you okay?'

'Strange dreams,' her mam said, stirring on the couch. 'What time is it?'

'Seven,' Niamh said, picking up her jacket. 'I'd best go.'

'Take the van,' her mam said. 'It's lashing. You'll get soaked on the bike.'

Time ticked slowly in Murphy's Bar on a wet Monday night. Niamh put the telly on with the sound off. The movement and light of the screen gave an impression of warmth and company. The bar felt chilly and damp, smelt of all the years of cigarette smoking and beer swilling. There were three regulars up at the bar – Paddy O'Mahony, Tommy Fox and Pat Feeney. She lined up their pints of Guinness on the counter and they waited for them to settle.

'Hey, turn up the volume, Niamh,' Pat asked her.

The news was on. More deaths up north. Three IRA members found dead in different parts of South Armagh. Suspected informers to the police in the north, the Royal Ulster Constabulary, or RUC. It was believed they'd been shot dead by the IRA.

'At least they weren't disappeared into the bogs like some of the poor bastards,' Paddy commented.

The news story made Niamh feel sick in her belly. Here they were, just a few miles from the border, almost too quiet, and yet across in the north, life was worth less. She thought about the bag Brendan had given her.

The door of the pub opened and in walked Joseph O'Reilly, but not on his own tonight. With him was the American boy, Jesse. Niamh could feel her cheeks blooming, much to her annoyance.

'Good evening, Niamh my dear,' said Joseph, tugging on his white beard. 'Have you met my young apprentice, Jesse?'

'Hi,' she said, drying a pint glass with a towel as she watched Jesse stride across the sticky floor of the bar.

'We've already met,' Jesse said, smiling at her. She didn't return it. His familiarity annoyed her.

'You have?' Joseph asked, raising his eyebrows.

'This morning, on my way to the boatyard, Joseph,' Jesse said. 'Though it seems so long ago now. How's the knee?'

'Fine,' Niamh said, stiffly. 'It was only a scratch.'

'Jesse has come all the way from his home in America, to study how to make boats just like me,' Joseph said proudly.

'My dad was Irish,' Jesse explained. 'Loved boats, and he told me about the tradition of wooden boatbuilding in the west of Ireland. It's always been my dream to learn the craft.'

'Well now, isn't that something?' Joseph said to the company in general, slapping Jesse on the back. 'Get the boy a pint of Guinness, Niamh.'

While Joseph settled at a table with the other three old fellows, Jesse stayed standing at the bar in front of Niamh, even after she'd served him his Guinness.

'Would you mind if I sit up here with you?' he asked her, hopping onto a high stool.

She shrugged, but couldn't help feeling a little flattered.

'You're the first person I've met my own age since I arrived,' Jesse told her.

'Have you not been into any other pubs in town?' she asked.

He shook his head.

'You should go to Flanagan's or the Harbour Bar; this place is dead,' she told him.

He gave her another smile. 'I'm happy enough for now,' he said, his eyes on her as she polished the last clean glass. She felt a little self-conscious.

'So, did you grow up here?' Jesse asked her, taking a sip of his pint.

She nodded.

'Oh boy, this is good,' he commented, admiring the black liquid in his pint glass.

'This place might be a dump, but we serve the best pint of Guinness in Mullaghmore.'

Jesse laughed. 'It's not such a dump,' he said.

She raised her eyebrows. 'Have you looked at the floor!' He was easy to talk with. Different from Irish boys, who said nothing until they were drunk, then never shut up.

'I've always loved boats,' Jesse told her. 'My father had a small sailboat and he used to take me out when I was a boy.'

'Was he a boatbuilder too?'

'Oh no, he was an accountant,' Jesse said, looking a little sad. 'He always dreamed of coming back home to Ireland. Learning how to build traditional clinker boats.'

'And did he?'

Jesse shook his head. 'He died last year. Heart attack.'

'Sorry,' Niamh said, her interest pulled to the young American. When he spoke of his father, his eyes gleamed with pride. He was doing what his father had wanted him to do.

Niamh picked up the cloth and wiped the bar down again. It was already clean, but she needed to shift the air between her and Jesse. It felt thick, potent, and it made her uneasy.

'So that's why I'm here,' Jesse continued. 'Learning from the best. Then I'm going to set up the boatyard my dad dreamed of when I get back home to America.'

Niamh raised her eyes to meet Jesse's enthused expression. She felt a twinge of envy. She had no such dreams. Tried never to think beyond the day she was in.

'Where are you from?' she asked Jesse.

'You heard of Cape Cod?'

As Jesse described the coastal town where he lived on the other side of the Atlantic Ocean, and the building his dad had bought for the boatyard before he'd died, Niamh looked at him as if he were an apparition. This American boy had it all worked out. But that wasn't real life, was it? Or maybe it was, and she was in the unreal world?

Niamh found her mind wandering to Brendan's heavy bag under the floor of the outhouse. How long would the bag sit below the floorboards? Until it was covered in cobwebs and mouse shit? Would Brendan come back soon? Or would a stranger turn up like the time before, with a thick West Belfast accent and a hard handshake? She'd been lucky her mam had been out at work that time, but what if it happened when she was home? What would her mam say if she knew Niamh was mixed up in the very conflict which had caused her husband's death?

'Hey,' Jesse said, pulling out a packet of cigarettes and offering her one. 'You okay?'

'Yeah, thanks,' she said taking the cigarette, and letting him light it for her.

She couldn't help noticing Jesse's hands. Strong from boat-building, but not too big or the skin rough like Brendan's.

'So enough about me,' Jesse said, taking a drag on his cigarette. 'Look, you want to go out on Saturday night? I don't know anyone round here apart from Joseph.'

Niamh was so astonished, she just stared at him. She'd never been asked out before, and so directly.

'Say, would you like to?' Jesse asked her again.

'I can't, I'm working here,' she said.

'What about Sunday then?' he pushed.

'No,' she replied quickly.

Jesse's eyes flickered. She could tell he wasn't used to being told no, but still, he wasn't so easily put off.

'Go on,' he said. 'I need someone to show me around. It's boring on my own.' He gave her a begging look. 'Besides, Joseph suggested I ask you.'

Niamh tilted her head on one side.

'Oh I see, so you don't *really* want to go out with me?' she teased. 'Merely doing what your new boss tells you to do.'

'You said no; I had to try to guilt you.'

She felt something. It disturbed her, and all her instincts were screaming at her to stay away from the American boy, but her body had a different notion. She found herself giving him a slow smile.

'Tell me where you live, and I'll come pick you up.' Jesse beamed at her, confident of her answer. She found it impossible to resist.

*

It was still raining when Niamh got back into her mam's postal van to drive home. The road was dark and she drove extra slow, watching out for frogs hopping across the wet black tarmac. She rounded the last hill, but kept going past the entrance to their house, on down the lane to the cemetery. She pulled in by the old gate, not turning off the engine, just watching the wipers going. The rain kept on falling out of the sky, illuminated like tracks of silver by her headlamps. Ten years had passed since the day she'd watched her father's coffin lowered into the ground, her mam clinging to her in hysterics. Though she'd only been twelve years old, she had felt so grown up. Brendan with his hand on her shoulder, always behind her. She still felt the weight of his hand on her now. Understood its full meaning. He had always had her back, sure, but he had also been marking her.

She had never let her daddy go. She'd turned his loss into fury, like a chained beast curled deep within. For years after her father's death, Niamh had come to the churchyard at night. Stood snarling at her father's headstone, twisted with rage. It was here that Brendan had found her on the three-year anniversary of her father's death. He had helped her take the impotency of her anger and turn it into revenge. But now, as she looked out at the bleak graveyard, she wished so hard he had never found her or helped her that night.

The American boy, Jesse, had spoken with pride about fulfilling his dead father's legacy with his boatyard, but what was her father's legacy? She knew in her bones, he would be so disappointed in her. More than that. Disgusted. As would her mam. Niamh recalled another memory from the day of her father's funeral. Brendan's father, Tadhg, holding up her mam as they walked back down the hill from the graveyard, but her mam shaking him off.

'This is all your fault,' she'd heard her hiss.

Her mam could never know her secret. Niamh stared out at the dark churchyard. She wasn't going in. Not tonight.

Chapter Five

At some point, Lily had to get up off her knees and stand up. She stumbled back to the hospital in the dark, soaked through to the skin. As soon as she walked through the doors, her mom ran up to her.

'Thank God,' she said, her face streaked with tears. 'Where'd you go?'

Lily shook her head, not answering.

'Where's Ray George?' she asked her mom. 'They've got to keep looking for Connor. He could still be out there.'

Her mom didn't contradict her, but she gave her a sorrowful look. 'He's in with your dad,' she said. 'Asking him what happened.'

'Is he okay?'

'Yes,' her mom said. 'All his vitals are good, but they're keeping him in for a precautionary measure.'

'And Ryan?'

'He's okay,' her mom said. 'The girls are with him. He has slight hypothermia, but okay otherwise.'

Lily marched down the corridor with her mom at her heels. She needed to see her dad. Of course she was glad he was alive, and Ryan, but she was devastated, too.

It was a shock to see her father in the hospital bed looking so washed out and weak. He was big and strong in ordinary life.

But now he looked old. His eyes bloodshot from the elements, his pallor sickly. Ray George was sitting on a chair by the bed, taking notes. As she came in, both men looked up at her. She saw the sympathy in Ray's eyes first as he stood up.

'I'm real sorry, Lily,' he said.

Lily didn't answer him, but looked straight at her dad.

'What happened, Daddy?' she asked him, unable to suppress the tremble in her voice.

'Oh Lily, darling,' her dad said, reaching out. But Lily stayed back, biting her lip. Her outburst on the beach had left her feeling strangely detached from her parents.

'What happened?' Her voice came out harsh and cold.

She could see the shock on her mom's face. But her dad looked down at his hands, cupped on his lap in the bed. In that one small movement, the dropping of his gaze, Lily detected guilt. She knew her father well. He blamed himself for what had happened to Connor.

'The storm came on so fast,' he said in a shaky voice.

'But all the other boats returned hours before it got bad.' Lily couldn't help the accusatory note in her voice. 'Why didn't you come back? Did you not get the weather warnings?'

Her daddy closed his eyes. 'It didn't seem to me like it was that bad,' he said, opening his eyes again, giving her a pleading look. 'We've been through worse, you and I. That's what I thought.'

'Jack, did you ignore the weather warnings?' Ray asked her father in a low voice.

Her dad shook his head, but didn't reply.

'Stop this now,' her mom intervened, approaching the bed, and standing protectively by it. 'He's not ready to answer any questions.' She turned to Ray. 'Can you not wait until the morning? Let Jack recover.'

'Okay,' Ray said, putting his notebook in his back pocket.

'Are you still looking for Connor?' Lily turned to the coast-guard.

'No, I'm sorry, Lily. He's gone.'

'But how do you know for sure? He could be clinging to a pipe, or hanging on to a piece of wreckage.' Her voice cracked at the thought of it. 'He could be out there on his own in the dark.'

'No, Lily,' her dad said in a quiet voice. 'I saw him go in.' He paused. 'It was getting real rough, and we were taking on water. I called up the Coast Guard to come and get us.'

'Why wasn't he picked up with you and Ryan?' Lily asked.

'Connor got caught up in the lobster trap line. It pulled him into the sea.' Her daddy paused. 'He just vanished.'

'Oh, Jack.' She heard her mother's despairing voice.

'No, no,' Lily said, her voice outside of her, while her whole body shook.

'Next thing I knew, we were going down...' Her daddy's voice petered out weakly.

'But didn't he have his suit on?' Lily screeched at her father. 'He might have made it to the life raft.'

Her dad kept staring at his hands. 'He was too far away. Gone too fast. I'm sorry, Lily.'

She closed her eyes and clenched her fists. Could see it all in her head. Connor flung into the sea, desperately trying to stay afloat, while a huge wave broke over him, swallowed him up. Her father and Ryan hanging on to each other as they got into the life raft, and watched their boat, the *Lily May*, go down.

Lily wanted to ask her father more questions. Every detail of each last moment before Connor had gone over, but a doctor came in and said they should let him sleep.

'Go home, get some rest,' she and her mom were told.

They lingered out in the hospital corridor.

'Shall we go see Ryan, see how he's doing?' her mom asked her gently.

'Sure,' Lily said, though all she wanted was to lie on the clean hospital floor and scream like a small child with a tantrum: *I want my husband back!*

Cherie, Lou and Angie were grouped around Ryan's bed. Her cousin was sleeping, and still attached to all the machines. All three of the women got up as soon as they walked in, and huddled around Lily. She felt herself falling into the circle of women, shaking with her grief and shock. Their tears were falling, words between them few, as the five Smyth women clung on to each other. Aunt Cherie took her hands, squeezing them tight.

'I'm here for you, Lily,' she said. 'We all are.'

But her words didn't make Lily feel any better.

All the long drive home in the car, she kept asking her mom what she thought had happened. But her mom couldn't answer her.

'You heard your daddy,' she told Lily. 'He got caught up in the lobster trap line.'

'But why wasn't it put away in the barrel?' Lily said. 'What were the traps doing set up to go out, when they should have been on their way home?'

'I don't know, Lily,' her mom said, her voice tense and tired.

'But I want him back!' she began to wail.

Her mom looked a little frightened. She'd never seen Lily like this before. Even as a little girl, she'd been stoic.

'It should have been me,' Lily said. Though they both knew, Lily would have never got caught up in the lobster trap rope.

*

As her mom pulled into their drive, flakes of snow fluttered in the light from the headlamps. The wind had dropped again, and after the violence of the storm, everything seemed so quiet and hushed. Lily looked across the front garden to the unlit windows of her and Connor's house, and her stomach felt tight with dread. How could she ever walk back through its front door?

'Why don't you stay in your old bedroom, with me?' her mom suggested.

'Okay,' Lily said. Her head was all over the place 'But I need to get my wash things.'

'They can wait, honey,' her mom said, taking her daughter's hand and leading her through their yard.

The house was as they'd left it when Lily had rushed off to Cherie's with her mom in tow. The TV and coffee maker had both been left switched on, the residue of coffee a hard brown stain in the bottom of the pot.

Lily stood swaying in front of the fireplace, staring at a picture of herself and Connor with her parents, taken the summer before at the Lobster Boat Races. Big smiles plastered on their faces. Oblivious of the tragedy that lay in wait for them just a few months down the line.

'You want anything to eat?' her mom asked, looking at her with concern. Lily could see how desperately her mom wanted to take her loss for her. But there was nothing she could do, so she'd switched to her default. Cooking, just like Connor always did. *Connor.* His name felt like a rock in the pit of her belly.

Lily shook her head. She felt like she'd never want to eat again.

'No,' she said, her voice sounding out of herself. 'I just want to go to bed.'

She stumbled into her childhood bedroom and fell onto her old bed, still dressed in her damp clothes. She didn't care if she got a cold. Cared about nothing. The wall was hung with photographs of her dad, Ryan and herself on fishing trips when she and her cousin had been thirteen. One of her grandfather's old buoys, painted in stripes of the Smyth colours – blue, red, white and green – leaned up in the corner of the room. Seashells were lined up on the windowsill, and trophies of all the competitions she'd won stood on the shelves.

In darkness, tears streamed down her face, until exhaustion pushed her into unconsciousness.

Lily woke up with a jolt. Where was she? Not in her and Connor's bed. The room smelt different. As her eyes adjusted to the light, she recognised the outline of her childhood dressing table. She was at home, in her old bed. What was she doing here?

The truth slammed into her, made her gasp in her horror. No. It couldn't be true.

She got out of bed and ran across the hallway into her parents' bedroom. She could see the single hump of her mom in the bed.

'Mom!' she called out. 'Mom!'

Her mom sat up in the bed, leant over and turned on the beside lamp, pushing her hair out of her face.

'It's not true, is it? Mom, tell me it's not true.'

Her mother's face folded like a small child's.

'Oh, Lily,' she said.

'No, Mom, no!' Lily wailed, climbing onto the bed, and clinging on to her mom. It couldn't be true.

Her mom wrapped her arms around Lily and she clung on to her, but it didn't make her feel any better. She prayed to God, asked him to send her a miracle. Make time go backwards. Start today all over again. She would have held on to Connor's hand. Told him to stay in bed with her.

*

She must have fallen asleep again, because next thing she felt sunlight on her face, and her mom's phone ringing. Her mom leant across her to answer it.

Lily could hear the voice at the other end of the line. It was the hospital telling them they could go collect her father.

All she wanted was to hide in her parents' bed, pull the covers over her head and sleep forever. She had never felt so tired in her entire life. But she was tough. All the Smyth women were. She had to get up. Go to the hospital with her mom. She wanted to talk to Ryan and ask her dad more questions. She had to know exactly what had happened.

As if to mock her grief, it was a gentle fall day. As they drove to Brunswick, Lily could see gentle ruffles of blue sea matching the cloudless sky, as the sun beat down upon the road before them. Sticks and leaves were strewn in front of them, but already drying out, as a thin icing of snow was sprinkled upon the bare branches of the trees and the sides of the road. The Maine landscape looked so beautiful, it made Lily angry. As if God was taunting her. Without Connor, the sun should never shine again.

Her dad was still shaky and weak. Her mom helped him out of bed to sit in a chair while they waited for the doctor to discharge him. Lily stood back, watching her father. He couldn't meet her eye, and there was an awkwardness about him, which was more than shock and weakness from the accident. There was something he wasn't telling her.

'Hey, I'm going down to see how Ryan is,' Lily told her parents.

'Give him our love,' her mom said, as she smoothed her husband's hair down.

Her dad finally looked her in the face. 'How are you doing, Lily girl?' he asked in a faint voice.

'Not good, Dad,' she said, and he flinched. She was never one to lie. She wasn't going to start now, no matter how fragile her father looked. His behaviour was stoking the anger she already felt towards him.

Lily had learnt all about the ocean and its vagaries from her father. He had taught her to always be humble to the dominance of nature. To never attempt to push against it. And yet that was exactly what he had done when he'd not turned around like all the other fishermen had yesterday.

Why had her father kept going? What recklessness had possessed him to take the most precious thing in her life, her husband, and lose him at sea?

Ryan was sitting up in his bed, awake and alone. As soon as he saw her, his eyes began to brim with tears. It made her want to cry again, too. She'd never seen Ryan cry, and it made her feel frightened.

'Aw, Lily,' he kept repeating.

All the wires which Ryan had been hooked up to the night before had been removed. Lily sat on the end of the bed and leant over. She and her cousin embraced each other. All the years they'd spent together lobster fishing, culminating in this moment. The trust they had shared was deep-rooted. Of course she was so grateful he'd survived, but at the same time seeing Ryan here, alive in the hospital, made the loss of Connor even harder.

At last, she pulled back, took out a tissue and blew her nose. 'Want one?' she offered Ryan.

He nodded and she passed over the packet of tissues.

'Lily, I'm so sorry,' Ryan said, wiping his eyes.

'Thanks, Ryan.' Her voice came out small and tight. 'I'm glad you're okay.'

There was an awkward pause.

'Did you…' She took a breath. 'Did you see when he went in?' she whispered. 'Daddy said he got caught up in the lobster trap line.'

'It was all so quick, Lily,' Ryan said. 'It got rough real fast.'

'But how did he get tangled up? Surely you were on your way back by the time the storm hit?'

'We were trying to drop the last line of traps,' Ryan said, not looking her in the eyes.

'In the middle of the storm?' Lily asked, incredulous.

'It was only a bit choppy when we got to the gravel bar,' Ryan said. 'We'd gone a long way, and we were ahead of the storm.'

'But didn't you know it was coming?' Lily said, astonished at her father's stupidity. He was an experienced fisherman. He should have known better. She knew Ryan and Connor's instincts weren't so great. If only she'd been there, she would have told her dad to hell with the traps. They needed to get back home.

She gritted her teeth as fury began to build in the pit of her belly. Her father had been reckless. That was how it was looking to her now.

She turned to Ryan as he sat in the bed. 'Was it my dad's fault?'

'No! Lily,' Ryan said, but she could tell he was lying.

'We know what we do is dangerous,' Lily said to Ryan. 'I mean you, me, Daddy, but Connor wasn't a fisherman. He shouldn't have been there.'

She didn't have to say it aloud. They both knew getting tangled up in the lobster trap line, no matter how bad the weather, was a rookie mistake.

'Has your daddy been interviewed for the Coast Guard report?' Ryan asked her. 'Ray George was in earlier, asking me questions.'

'Yeah,' Lily said, chewing her lip. 'He was interviewing Daddy last night.'

Ryan sighed, closed his eyes. He looked worn out.

'Look, I'll let you rest,' she said. 'Your mom coming in?'

'Yeah, and Lou and Angie,' Ryan said faintly. 'They just went home to change their clothes.'

When Lily returned to her father's hospital room, the doctor was there doing a last check-up.

'A bit bruised and battered, but you're good to go, Jack,' the doctor said, in a voice which was far too cheerful.

Her father walked shakily across the room, leaning on her mother's arm. 'Let's go, girls.'

'I'll drive,' Lily said. Her mom would sit in the middle seat between Lily and her dad.

She couldn't be close to him right now. Not the way she was feeling.

On the way home, her mom told Lily to stop at the store so she could get some groceries.

'Now? Do you have to?' Lily snapped, not wanting to be left in her pickup sitting next to her father.

'We've got no milk, and no food for dinner,' her mom said.

'How can you think about food right now?' Lily complained.

'We've got to eat, darling,' her mom said, gently.

After her mom got out of the car, the silence hung heavy and tense between Lily and her father. She broke it first.

'How are you feeling?' she asked him.

'A bit sore,' he said. 'Bruises. Okay.'

Again, silence. Her father coughed. She could hear the nervousness in his voice as he spoke. 'How are you, Lily?'

She felt a spike of anger in her belly. 'Well, how do you think I am, Daddy?' She turned on him.

He looked at her and flinched. She must look real mad, she thought, but she didn't care.

'Why the hell were you laying down traps when there was a big storm approaching?'

Her father shook his head. 'I've done it before,' he said. 'We were unlucky.'

Lily shook her head, the word 'unlucky' wounding her. She'd always believed in her good fortune, but it had been a lie all her life. All that luck had built up to this moment of catastrophe.

'That's just not good enough, Daddy,' she said. 'Connor wasn't experienced. Not like me. He wouldn't have known to tell you to go back, nor Ryan.'

'Ryan's been fishing as long as you—'

'You know what I mean, Daddy,' Lily interrupted, exasperated. 'Ryan wouldn't stand up to you.'

'It was an accident, Lily,' her father said.

Lily's hands gripped the steering wheel tight, and she felt as if the very breath was being squeezed out of her. She couldn't speak, the pain of her loss hurt so much.

Her mom came back with the shopping and they set off again, her mom fussing over her dad, asking him every two minutes if he was okay.

Lily pulled up outside her parents' house.

'I'm going back home for a bit,' she said to them.

Her mom looked alarmed. 'Are you sure, Lily? Don't you think you should stay with us for a while, until—'

'Until when, Mom?' Lily snapped, giving her dad a hard stare so that he looked away. She couldn't be near him right now. She felt so confused and angry.

'I'll call you, Mom,' she said, softening her voice.

*

She had left the door unlocked. Lily stepped across the threshold of her and Connor's home.

Everything was exactly how it had been left yesterday morning, as she'd rushed out the door. The whole place felt like a museum now. A stray sock of Connor's on the radiator, her mug of half-drunk coffee, and his good coat hanging by the back door, were all exhibits of their marriage. She could still smell her husband. His soft sandalwood lingering in each room. How could she ever sleep in their bed again? She lay down on its covers and closed her eyes. Inhaled deeply, to try to catch his scent off the pillows.

They'd bought this little wooden house with its views of the ocean the year they'd married. Used the money she'd saved from lobster fishing all her high school summers with her father as the deposit. Spent nearly a year doing it up. Painted the outside green, her favourite colour, and planted up the garden with hydrangeas and rose bushes. Lots of roses – that was their thing. Inside, the house was small, but had everything they needed. A cosy front room with a woodstove, and a kitchen with a high table and stools for breakfast. Upstairs, there were two bedrooms. In the bigger one, they'd put the old mahogany chest of drawers and closet that Lily had inherited from Pap when he died, and their new white ironwork bed. Mom had made them a quilt for the bed, patterned with red roses and blue forget-me-nots, with yellow trim.

The best thing about their bedroom was that from their bed, Lily could look out of the window and see the ocean. If she got out of bed and stood at the window, she could also see her parents' house, which was down the road a way, also facing out to the ocean. Every time she stood at her bedroom window and looked at the ocean, at her parents' house, and at the whole of their neighbourhood in Rockland, she had felt such peace. She had never wanted to be anywhere else, or go anywhere else in the world.

The second bedroom, Lily had named 'the nursery' in her head. Even though it was currently Connor's den with his computer and gaming stuff, in her imagination, Lily had planned exactly how it would look one day. She'd seen the wallpaper already in a store in Portland. Yellow, with little green apples. She had her old baby blanket tucked away in a box, along with a mobile of fishes, starfish, and seahorses that she'd bought as a gift for her cousin Angie's baby, Sam, but had fallen in love with so much she'd ended up keeping it.

Everything was set up to start their family. Lily had thought it would be like plain sailing.

Perfect, like when she and Connor were out to sea on her boat, cutting through pristine blue water, and feeling the sun on their cheeks. Welling with gratitude for all they had.

It had been December almost two years ago, on her twenty-third birthday, when it had all come up first. She'd been a little drunk after the birthday meal at her parents'. Connor had his arm around her to stop her from slipping as they cut across the thick snow on their front lawn on the way home.

It had been a clear night sky filled with glistening stars, and the air had felt so pure and clean. It had made her think of her daddy's lucky star story. Had the night she was born been just like this?

'Let's make a baby,' she'd said, turning to Connor as he'd unlocked the front door. Full of good feelings, bursting with excitement at the idea, she stood, arms spread out, as if summoning all that starry magic from the sky. 'Let's do it, honey!'

But it was as if Connor hadn't heard her. 'You're letting the warmth out, Lily.'

She didn't want to walk in until he acknowledged her request. At that moment, it seemed the most important thing in the world.

'Hey, did you hear me?' she said. 'I want a baby!'

'Come on, missy, time for bed.' Connor pulled her inside and she tottered in. He helped her off with her boots, as if she were a child, and she felt a little wounded. But maybe she was being over the top? She had drunk way more than him, and he looked tired. So, she let it go.

But when she'd woken up the next morning, it was the first thing she'd thought about. In fact, she wanted them to have not just one baby, but lots. She'd been an only child and though she'd been happy, sometimes she had wished for a sibling. She lay on her back in bed and pictured their children. Could almost hear them running around, playing games downstairs. Their little house, filled with the sound of a happy family. She'd wanted it so much it made her tummy ache.

Lily had turned on her side and put her arms around Connor. Breathed him in. He was so gorgeous. What beautiful babies he'd make. That morning, as they'd made love, Lily had imagined Connor and herself making their first child. Of course, it had been a fantasy, she'd still been on the pill then, but she would never forget the sweetness of the first time she'd made love with the desire of creating new life – and without knowing what challenges were before them.

Right after, as they'd eaten breakfast together, Lily had said it again. She'd never been one to wait. Besides, she assumed Connor would want the same as her. Why else had they got married?

'Honey, I want to start a family,' she said to him, as she dug into her pancakes.

'Not yet,' Connor had said back. 'We're still so young.'

Lily had been so surprised, she'd dropped her fork on the plate. 'That's the point,' she said. 'I want to start now, so we'll have energy for our kids.'

She could have sworn Connor had winced when she said the word 'kids'.

'We're so perfect together, why spoil it?' Connor had said in a low voice, not meeting her eye.

'Don't you want to have a baby with me?' she asked him bluntly, her heart heavy with dread.

'Sure, I do, it's just… I'm not ready yet.'

He had that look on his face. The same one he got whenever she asked him about his grandmother in Ireland.

She had let the baby discussion go that morning, but not for long. All her friends were having babies. Even her cousin Angie had just had baby Sam. Lily wanted their kids to grow up playing together.

So, Lily didn't let up. She had learnt that was the way she got things from her daddy, and she did the same to Connor. Every day, badgering him about trying for a baby. But weeks went by and he wouldn't relent. It was only after baby Sam's christening party the following January when Connor found Lily sobbing in the bathroom, that he had finally agreed they could try. Jubilant, Lily had gone off the pill right away. She had thought that would be it. Like everything else in her life, pregnancy would happen easily for her. But month after month, she'd been disappointed when her period arrived.

'Be patient,' her mom advised her. 'Remember, it took me a long time to get pregnant too, Lily, and you've not even been a year trying.'

But Lily wasn't used to waiting. She got things to happen, through hard work, determination, and her good luck.

It wasn't just her inability to get pregnant which had floored her. It had been her reaction to it. She had always been so tough, and strong. It took a lot to get her upset, and yet often when she caught sight of another woman in the store with her baby she was consumed with jealousy.

Nearly two years had passed and still no pregnancy. To make it even harder to bear, Angie had just got pregnant for a second time. Lily found herself irritated by her cousin when she complained she hadn't planned another baby so soon. She snapped at her mom, too, when she suggested working on the lobstering boats might not help if Lily wanted to get pregnant.

'Don't see how that makes one bit of difference, Mom,' Lily had said.

The situation was made even more intense by Connor's lack of enthusiasm. She felt like she had to push him the whole time. When Lily asked Connor if he'd go to the doctor with her and get some tests, he'd got annoyed.

'If it's meant to happen, then it will,' he said. 'Let's just enjoy what we have right now. We've plenty of time.'

But Lily couldn't enjoy what they had any more. The nights they stayed in watching movies cuddled up together felt pointless now, because there was no baby upstairs asleep. She wanted so badly to carry Connor's child, because she loved him to the extent she wanted a part of him forever. It hurt her that he didn't feel the same way. Moreover, there seemed to be babies everywhere she looked, every time she went into town. The only peace she got was out on the ocean. Just her, the boat, and the other fishers.

It was her mom who gave her the idea of going to a fertility specialist.

'But Connor won't even go to the doctor, Mom,' Lily had said, almost on the verge of tears. 'He said it'll happen at the right time. But what if it never happens!'

'Oh, honey,' her mom had said, squeezing her hand.

'Besides, we don't have the money for a specialist.'

Her mom had tucked her hair behind her ear and gave her a wan smile. 'Yeah, you do.'

Her mom revealed she'd been saving for Lily's college fund ever since the day she'd been born. But of course, Lily had never gone to college. All she'd ever wanted was to be a lobster fisher like her dad, and his pap before him. She'd been lobstering ever since she was fourteen.

'But, Mom.' Lily had been stunned. 'Why didn't you tell me about the money before? Give it to us when we got married?'

'Because I could see you and Connor didn't need it right then, honey,' her mom had said. 'And this money is for you and your dreams.'

She'd hugged her mom tight.

'So, make yourself an appointment, darling, if having a baby is your dream,' she'd said to Lily.

'It is, Mom, it's what I want most in the world,' Lily had sighed. 'But what about Connor?'

'Why don't you go first?' her mom suggested. 'Go get some tests done on your own.'

Lily had taken her mom's advice and contacted a fertility clinic in Portland.

She had been nervous about how Connor would react to her news about the appointment, so she decided to go all out and cook his dinner. Soften him up with good food and a glass of wine. She was nowhere near as good a cook as he, but he always appreciated it when she did make food for him. She had spent hours in the kitchen that evening, making homemade pizza with butternut squash, ricotta cheese and cranberries.

'This is great,' Connor said, biting into a big slice. Lily took a sip of her glass of wine to give her courage.

'Honey, I need to tell you something,' she said. Taking another breath to steady her nerves, she ploughed on. 'I've an appointment with a fertility specialist in Portland. Tomorrow.'

He stopped eating and stared at her.

'My mom has been saving up money for me; she paid for it,' Lily added.

'Why'd you go behind my back, Lily?' Connor said, frowning at her.

'Because I just wanted to know if it was me,' she continued.

'Well, I'm not the problem,' he said, looking furious.

'How do you know that, unless you take the tests?' she flared up.

He didn't reply. Sat staring at her, his eyes dark, but his face almost expressionless. Lily had never seen him like this before.

'I mean, maybe it's just us,' he said, his voice flat. 'Now's not the right time for a baby.'

But that wasn't good enough for Lily. 'Don't you want to have a family together? Why else did we get married?'

'Because I love you, Lily!' Connor reached out and took a hold of her hand. The blank look was gone, and instead his eyes were loaded with hurt. 'Am I not enough for you?'

She dropped her gaze and pulled her hand away, despite hearing the hurt in his voice. Connor never got upset. So calm, keeping her level, putting her first always. Why was he being so stubborn? She was going to be the pregnant one. It was her life which was going to be turned upside down.

'It's not enough,' she said, because she couldn't lie. 'I want our baby, Connor. Our beautiful baby.'

She slowly looked up, pleaded with her eyes, but he shook his head.

'I'm sorry, Lily,' he said. 'Maybe you picked the wrong guy.'

'No, I want you to be the father of my children,' she said, confused by his words. It was the first time he'd ever said anything like this to her in during the four years of their marriage.

'Sorry, Lily,' Connor backed down. She had never seen him look so upset. 'It's just, all I need is you.'

He walked out of the kitchen leaving his pizza unfinished, and went upstairs to bed. He'd never walked away from her before. She was left reeling from his words. Connor had been pretty clear – he didn't want kids with her. She looked at the years stretching out, just the two of them, and she knew it wasn't enough for her, even though she loved him so much.

She closed her eyes, took a breath. A part of her felt so angry. He should have told her this before they got married. It wasn't fair she had to choose.

He was asleep, or pretending to be, by the time Lily got into bed. She shouldn't have drunk two extra glasses of wine, but she'd not been able to bring herself to go upstairs to bed. She still hadn't asked him to take her place on her dad's boat in the morning. She needed to wake him up and ask. But rarely for Lily, she felt anxious about doing so. Was this the end of their marriage?

It was no good. She had to wake him up. Even if it was to know to cancel the appointment. She gently shook his shoulder.

'Connor, are you awake?'

Her husband stirred in the bed, turned to her. 'What?'

'Did you mean what you said?'

She sensed him choosing his words carefully.

'I don't want to lose you,' he said, pausing. 'I'll go to the clinic if you really want me to.'

Her heart took a little jump of hope. 'You will?' She sniffed.

'Sure,' he said, beginning to stroke her body. 'I just need time, honey. You know, to get my head around it.'

She kissed him on the lips, and he pulled her even tighter.

'Will you go out with Daddy and Ryan tomorrow, so I can go to Portland for the first appointment?' she asked him.

Connor groaned.

'You know how I hate fishing with your dad,' he said. 'I always feel I'm never good enough for him.'

'But it's for a good cause,' she said, wrapping her legs around his waist.

'I guess,' he said.

Lily's heart felt like it was going crack open with pain. Two days ago they had made love in this bed. Connor so alive in her arms. How could he be gone?

She sat up, remembering the voicemail Connor had left her that morning. With shaking hands, she pulled her phone out of the back pocket of her jeans.

'Morning, darling, hope I didn't wake you. Wanted to call before we're out of coverage. Am just out on the ocean, thinking about you. That you gave me this. The ocean, and your family. Even lobsters for the restaurant.' She heard his soft laugh in the background. The sound of Ryan calling him, and the noise of their boat starting up. 'You gave me everything, Lily. I'm sorry about last night, baby. I want to give you everything… If you want a baby, so do I.'

Lily wiped the tears from her face with the back of her sleeve. She knew where she got her bull-headedness from. It was her father. He always wanted more, too. But for him it was lobsters. Always pushing them to keep going and drop the maximum quota they were allowed. Always searching for new underwater ledges, further away from port.

It just couldn't be true. She wouldn't accept that Connor was lost. Lily looked up the number of the Coast Guard on the phone and rang them.

'Hey, it's Lily Fitzgerald here.'

'Hey, Lily.' She heard Ray George's tired voice. 'I'm sorry, but Connor's not been found.'

'Please can you keep looking for him?' she pushed.

There was a pause. She knew what he would say, but she had to hear him say it outright.

'No one could have survived those waters, Lily, you know that,' Ray said. 'He's gone. I'm sorry.'

The next day was still and glorious. The foliage that remained on the trees shimmered in the soft fall light. Lily woke from a night of disturbed dreams to reality again. Connor was gone. She drew her knees up to her chest and buried her head in her hands. How could she get through another day without Connor?

There was a soft knock on the door. She didn't bother to answer, but she heard it open. Felt the weight of her mom sitting on the end of the bed.

'Honey, you need to try,' her mom said, putting her hand on her arm. 'You need to do something, occupy yourself. How about going fishing with one of the other lads? They'll pay you decent money.'

Lily shook her head. The idea of going out lobster fishing was horrific to her. For the first time, it hit her. They'd not only lost Connor, but the *Lily May* too.

'We'll be getting another boat on insurance,' her mom said, as if reading Lily's thoughts. 'Your dad will be back on his feet soon. He only has some bruising on his ribs.'

Lily looked up at her mom, and saw that her eyes were loaded with pity. A look she'd never given her ever before. It felt almost as if she were a stranger.

'We need to do something for Connor,' her mom suggested.

'Like a funeral?' Lily whispered in horror. 'But there's no body! I can't even say goodbye to him.'

'I know, honey, I know, but what about we have a memorial, make a tribute to Connor?'

Lily felt sick. 'I don't want to, Mom.'

'I think it would help us all,' her mom said. 'And Lily, you need to contact Connor's grandmother.'

Lily felt instantly guilty. 'Mom, I haven't even thought of his grandmother.'

'Do you have a number for her?'

'No,' Lily said. 'If there is one, it would be in Connor's phone.' She and her mom looked at each other. The sentence left hanging. The phone, which was with Connor at the bottom of the ocean.

'I know we've never met her,' her mom said. 'But you must contact her. Connor was her grandson.'

Her mom reached and squeezed Lily's hand in encouragement.

It had always been in the back of Lily's mind. The story behind Connor's family. But the odd time she'd brought it up, he just kept repeating himself: mother dead, no idea who his father was. It was his grandmother he loved. He told Lily her name was Rosemary and she was a postmistress who also wrote poetry. She had encouraged Connor to go study in America. Had no idea he'd dropped out to work in bars, and then train as a chef. So, when Connor had told Lily his grandmother couldn't come to their wedding, was too frail and ill, if she was honest, she'd been a little relieved. What if Connor's grandmother blamed Lily for leading her grandson astray, away from his studies? Thought a non-college-going lobster-fishing girl wasn't good enough for her boy? Decided Lily had turned her grandson into a barman, a cook, and now a dead fisherman?

Oh, God. Lily felt a piercing pain in her belly, and her skin felt hot and irritated all down her arms. How could she possibly tell Connor's grandmother what had happened?

'I don't know where she is,' she said, rubbing her itchy arm, looking at her mom with pleading eyes.

'Honey, you've got to try to find her,' she said. 'It's the right thing to do.'

'I don't know where to start,' Lily said.

'What about having a look in Connor's emails?' her mom suggested. 'Or there might something in his desk in the office.'

Her mom went back home, but only after making Lily promise she'd come over for her dinner. Neither of them mentioned her father. As if her mother sensed Lily's anger with him.

Lily dragged herself into Connor's office, or the nursery, as she had thought of it. Her desire to have a baby felt so vain and stupid now. All she wanted was Connor. There was Connor's blue sweater, lying on the chair. She picked it up, held it to her face, and breathed in. There it was, faint sandalwood. She put the sweater on over her own. Hugged her sides, before sitting down in the chair at the desk.

Her eyes scanned the neatly shelved graphic novels, the framed picture on the wall of Connor in a wetsuit, surfing on a big wave on Higgins Beach his first year, and the desk with Connor's laptop. She stared at the photograph, picked it up. How happy he looked, because he'd loved the ocean, just like her. The ocean which had turned on him and taken him away. Lily forced herself to put the photograph back down. She had to stay focused on finding his grandmother's contact details. Just keep her tasks simple right now. She opened Connor's laptop up and turned it on, then realised she didn't know his password. She typed in her name and birthdate, but it didn't work. She sat thinking for a few minutes. She knew some of the passwords Connor used. One was the name of the place where he'd grown up. She closed her eyes. What was it called again?

The word came to her. He'd talked about the ocean there often enough. Lily typed in 'Mullaghmore'. Immediately she got onto his desktop screen and clicked onto his emails, which were already logged on. She did a search under 'wedding', but all that came up were a few emailed invites to their wedding sent to friends of Connor's in Boston, who had all attended. Had he even invited his grandmother? Lily chewed her lip. Wasn't that a bit strange?

Lily sat at Connor's desk. All around her were small mementos of her husband. An abalone shell they'd got on honeymoon in Hawaii, a dish they'd bought in a store in Rockland on their first wedding anniversary, decorated with pink lobsters and filled with spare change, her notepad with a list Connor had started to write on it: *Butternut squash with caramelised apples, cinnamon, nutmeg, maple pecan muffins, Lily's birthday?*

Her birthday was six weeks away and yet he'd begun listing her favourite foods in preparation. How could she ever enjoy any food again, now he was gone?

Lily took a deep breath and steadied herself as she trailed through Connor's inbox. Nothing seemed to fit an email to his grandmother. Would she even have email? The way Connor had talked about her, it hadn't sounded like she was very technical. Lily opened up his spam box just in case. Scrolled down the screen through the sea of rubbish, until an email made her stop. The screen swam before her eyes, and her breath caught in her throat. The subject line of the email from redshamrock@hotmail.

com stood out: *DOES YOUR WIFE KNOW WHO YOU REALLY ARE?* She looked at the date. The message had only been sent a couple of weeks ago.

Lily's hand trembled as it hovered over the keyboard, her arms incredibly itchy again. She clicked on the email.

Chapter Six

Mullaghmore, 12th July 1992

On Sunday, the rain stopped. All week long, it had been pouring down, but now as the sun came out and warmed the damp air, it felt as if all the undergrowth had exploded. The garden had become a wild green jungle overnight, and all the hedgerows along the lanes were bursting and overflowing.

'It needs to be cut back,' Niamh commented to her mam. 'Must be dangerous, hard for you to see when driving round corners.'

'Sure, I slow down,' her mam said back. 'What about all the little creatures living in the hedges. That's their home!'

'Oh, Mam, you know it'll get cut back any day!' Niamh said, handing her mam a cup of tea.

Her mother looked at her, eyes widening, clearly noticing for the first time something was up. 'Are you going out today?'

Niamh was trying not to show her excitement, but it was rare she put on a dress. She'd bought this one on a trip to Galway last summer. It was purple, with little silver stars on it, and shoestring straps. She was wearing it with her black DM boots, and had her leather jacket, of course, in case the weather turned.

'Yeah, didn't I tell you?' Niamh said, knowing full well she hadn't.

'Well no, you did not,' her mam said.

'It's no big deal,' Niamh said, at the same time as they heard the roar of a motorbike engine in the yard outside. Niamh ran to the window. It was Jesse, pulling off his helmet and getting off his motorbike. He was dressed in biking leathers.

'Oh, shit.' Niamh looked down at her dress. 'He never said he had a bike.'

'He's very dashing,' her mam said, coming to stand next to her at the window. 'Who is he?'

'Dashing!' Niamh snorted at her mam. 'His name is Jesse, and he's Joseph O'Reilly's new boatbuilding apprentice.' She went to the door. 'Mammy, please don't embarrass me!'

'As if!' Her mam raised her arms in mock offence.

Niamh went out into the yard to head off her mam. Jesse had placed his helmet on the seat and was turning towards her.

'You've a motorbike?'

'Yeah, I bought it for while I'm here.' Jesse turned to her, giving her a big smile. 'Thought I told you.'

'No!' Niamh said, astonished. 'Wasn't it expensive?'

'I had some money,' Jesse said. 'Needed wheels when I was here to see the countryside. She's a Honda CB400 Four Classic. Beautiful, isn't she?'

Niamh had never been interested in motorcycles, but looking at Jesse's bike, she couldn't help but admire the streamlined curves and lines of the machine.

'Yes, she is,' Niamh said, running her hand along the maroon fuel tank before turning to Jesse. She saw him look at her dress.

'I don't think that dress will work on the bike,' he said. 'Though it's real pretty.'

'Give me a minute, and I'll change,' she said. 'You'd better come in. Meet my mam.'

Niamh left Jesse downstairs with her mam, who went into a frenzy of tea and sandwich-making, despite Jesse telling her he wasn't hungry. She prayed her mam wouldn't relate any embarrassing anecdotes about when she was little. She grabbed her jeans and pulled them on under her dress, yanked the dress off over her head, and then hunted around for a shirt. She really wanted to wear purple today. She had a deep violet shirt somewhere, but could she find it? Of course, hunting around in her mother's wardrobe, the violet shirt appeared on a hanger. There'd be words about that later. Niamh fiddled with her hair in front of the mirror. She'd better tie it up if they were going on a bike. She was a little nervous about going pillion; she'd never been on a motorbike before. Though she wasn't going to tell Jesse that.

Downstairs, Jesse was sitting at the kitchen table, politely nibbling one of her mam's salad sandwiches, while her mam was asking him questions about Cape Cod.

'It sounds so beautiful,' she said, turning to Niamh. 'Your dad and I nearly emigrated to Boston, you know.'

'You did!' Niamh exclaimed.

'Yeah, Cormac had some cousins over there, working in construction and house painting,' her mam said. 'But then you came along, and Cormac insisted we raise you in Ireland.'

'Come on,' Niamh said, a little brusquely to Jesse, not wanting her mam to talk to Jesse about her father. 'Let's go.'

Jesse stuffed the last of his sandwich into his mouth and gathered himself up. In his biking leathers, he looked even taller than she remembered him.

'Nice to meet you, Mrs Kelly,' he said to her mam.

'Call me Rosemary, please,' her mam said, giving Jesse a sweet smile. 'You two have a great time.'

Niamh instantly felt guilty for being cross with her mam. Most parents would be interrogating them, asking where Jesse was taking her. Worried about them going for a bike ride on the twisting Irish roads, where everyone drove too fast. Her mam just looked so forlorn, sitting on her own at the kitchen table.

She went over and gave her mam a big hug, kissing the top of her head.

'See you later, Mammy.' She didn't care if she looked daft.

Outside, Jesse lifted up the pillion saddle and took out a spare helmet, then pulled down pegs for her feet.

'So, unlike newer bikes, there's no handle at the back of the saddle to hold on to,' he said, giving her a flirtatious smile. 'So, you'll just have to hang on to me.'

The rush was immediate as soon as they took off down the narrow lane. She was shocked at just how different it felt to being in a car. At first, she felt very vulnerable each time he went around a corner, as if she might slide off the bike onto the road. They were going fast, and yet it felt like she was suspended in space. When Jesse stopped at the junction, she held her hands encircling his entire waist. It felt too intimate, yet it was the only way she also felt safe. As they sped along the roads, she realised she hadn't asked him where they were going. All she could tell was they were heading south and towards the coast.

Jesse took her down by the sea. The sun was behind them, and the blue Atlantic at peace for once. The sea looked silken as it slowly moved in and out against the rocky shoreline, as if in time to the breath inside her head. Just before Sligo, Jesse took the turn for Rosses Point. How did he know this was her favourite place to be? Where she and her parents had spent the best summer days of her childhood. The innocence of it a bubble of memory inside her head. Mammy in her red bathing suit, lying down on one of the beach towels. Growing smaller and smaller as Niamh's daddy took her by the hand and led her towards the sea. She remembered him lifting her onto his back as he waded into the water, and feeling the sun on her cheeks.

Jesse pulled up in the car park and switched off the bike. Niamh clambered off the back, a little clumsily, stretching her back and stiff arms.

They walked down the sandy path, through the dunes and the long rushes to the perfect crescent beach. It was still early, and despite it being a glorious summer's day the beach was relatively empty. Just the odd dog-walker in the distance.

'Do you like it here?' Jesse asked her.

'Yes,' she said, taking a breath and inhaling the scent of the sea. 'I love it.'

She closed her eyes for a second, listening to the sound of the waves sweeping onto the shore, the gulls calling above. Felt the wind whipping her hair around her face.

When she opened her eyes again, Jesse had walked on down the beach. She watched him as he trailed the water's edge, tall and dark in his biking leathers, looking out to sea.

She followed him, and he turned and waited for her, smiling, his eyes creased against the sunlight.

'It always makes me feel good, being by the ocean,' he said. 'Reminds me of good times with my dad.'

'Me, too,' Niamh said in a quiet voice. Jesse turned and looked at her.

'My dad's dead too, but a long time ago now,' she said.

'Yeah, your mom told me while you were upstairs,' Jesse said.

Niamh shook her head. 'Typical Mam,' she said. 'Sorry.'

'Don't be stupid,' Jesse said. 'Hey, come on, this is supposed to be a date, not a wake!'

He turned and ran towards the dunes, clumps of damp sand churned up by his boots.

'Come on!' he called out, trying to climb up the sandy hills and sliding back down every time. She followed him up, and he held out his hand to her, dragged her to the top of the shifting dunes.

They fell back on top of the sea grass, out of breath from climbing to the top. Niamh could feel Jesse looking at her. She must be a bit of a mess, wind-blown from the bike (was her eyeliner smeared, surely?) and her hair had fallen out of its plait. But still, she felt the heat of his gaze and turned.

As she looked at Jesse, Niamh felt a confliction of attraction but also fear. No one had looked into her eyes like this before. Not even Brendan, who knew her the best. It was too much, and she broke away first. Pulled her bag towards her, opening it up and hunting for her papers and tobacco.

'Want a joint?' she asked him, feeling a desperate need to calm her nerves.

'Sure,' he said, leaning back in the grass and looking out to sea. Niamh peeked at his profile. His stillness, as if captured in an old photograph, reminded her of all the young men in the past who had maybe sat in the same spot, staring at America, and their new beginnings across all the miles of ocean. Jesse had come in the other direction, though. He was looking back at his home.

As they smoked, they lay on their backs in the sea grass, watching the clouds shapeshifting above them. Niamh's body was softening, surrendering into the soft contours of the dunes as they passed the joint back and forth. Jesse circled her palm with his finger. The slightest of touches, and yet it felt as if it was magnified in her body, rippling outwards to her fingers and toes. It was such a long time since she'd been touched with such tenderness. Niamh sat up, passing the joint back one last time.

'Let's walk,' she said.

Jesse raised himself up on his elbows, and looked at her with mild surprise.

'Sure,' he said, standing up and putting out the joint with the heel of his boot. He held out his hand to help her get up. His grip was sure, and she felt the strength in his body as she stood up.

'You okay?' he asked, looking at her beneath heavy lids.

'Yeah,' she said, dusting sand off her jeans.

They walked the length of the beach and continued along the coast, clambering up rocks and down again until they came to a tiny cove.

'Hey, want to go for a swim?' Jesse asked her.

'I've no swimsuit,' she countered.

'That's not stopping me!' he laughed, pulling off his biking leathers until he was down to his boxers.

'It's going to be freezing!' she protested, but his enthusiasm was infectious. She hadn't been in the sea for so long, and now she craved it more than anything.

Niamh tore her jeans off, but kept on her shirt, embarrassed by her old faded bra. Jesse charged into the sea, and Niamh followed him, hypnotised by his smooth broad back spraying sea water in his wake.

'Oh my God, it's so cold,' she squealed, as she floundered in the shallows.

'Go under,' Jesse said. 'Do it quick!'

He dived into the surf, and disappeared for a second. She wasn't a good swimmer at all, but she was also high. The seawater was making her skin feel so alive, tickling with sensation. She pushed her head under the water, and then leapt up, screaming with exhilaration as sea water cascaded around her. Jesse appeared again, swimming towards her. Taking her hand, he began to tug her further out to sea.

'I'm not a great swimmer,' she admitted.

'It's okay,' he said. 'I got you.'

He held both her hands, dragging her weightless into the sea. For a moment, she felt a twinge of unease. How much did she know about this boy? She'd grown up suspicious of strangers. Yet all she had to do was look into Jesse's honey eyes, and she melted. She didn't care if she was being reckless. It was so long since she'd had any fun.

They swam together. He held her hand, and she was buoyed by the sea. The sun warmed the back of her head, though her limbs were cold beneath the water. But still, she didn't want to get out when Jesse began to tug them both back to the beach.

They staggered out of the sea. She pushed her toes into the damp sand, and squeezed her feet.

'That was so cool,' Jesse said, as they landed on the beach. She shook herself like a dog, spraying him with her wet hair.

'Hey, you!' he laughed, catching her by the arm and spinning her away from him.

'My top is totally soaked!' she declared.

'I can fix that,' he said. 'You can wear my shirt.'

'What are you going to wear?'

'My leather with nothing underneath.' He grinned at her as he sat on the beach, his wet chest gleaming with rivulets of seawater.

'Well, I could do that too,' she remarked, trying not to stare at his body, as she sat down next to him.

'True, and it would be a lot more sexy,' he said, and she felt herself blushing. 'But not very gentlemanly of me, so here you go.' He threw her his T-shirt.

She pulled it on over her head, catching his scent. Fresh and citrusy.

'Oh, the blue suits you,' he said. 'You should keep it.'

She shook her head, not knowing what to say back, but wanting more than anything to keep his T-shirt.

Jesse leant over and put his hand to her face, traced the side of her cheek, cupping it with his palm. The air felt tight between them, and a voice inside her head was screaming at her to pull away. But she did the opposite, let herself be drawn towards him.

The taste of Jesse's kisses was salty like the sea, and she felt the same as she had in the water. Lost in sensation, as he pulled her over to him and they embraced. His wet chest against the damp T-shirt. He slipped his fingers under the soft cloth, and unclasped her wet bra. Pulled it off and away from under the T-shirt. She was falling into him, and she wanted to so much, but then she remembered where she was, who she was, and she jerked away.

'Sorry,' Jesse said, concern on his face. 'Too far?'

'No, it's just, we're out in the open, anyone could come along,' she said.

'Course, sorry,' he said, looking apologetic, and releasing her. Immediately, she regretted her caution. All she wanted was to kiss him again. But Jesse was already slinging on his jacket.

'Come on,' he said, 'I'm starving.'

They drove further down the coast and into Sligo town, parking the bike down by the river. They paused for a moment to watch two swans gliding along the water, before Jesse took Niamh's hand in his. She felt a thrill pass through her. Brendan had never walked down a street with her, holding her hand. Not once in all the years she'd known him. In fact, no boy had ever held her hand. She felt her pale cheeks blooming again, but she didn't pull her hand away. She was aware of Jesse's T-shirt against her bare skin, of being braless and walking down the main street in Sligo with the American boy.

'Oh wow, I love this place,' Jesse said as they stepped into the dim interior of Hargadon Bros with its panelled walls of dark wood, and black and white photographic prints of Irish characters from bygone times.

'It's the best pub in Sligo,' Niamh said.

Inside Hargadon Bros, Niamh was at home, as if she were in the front room of her beloved Ireland. The woody tobacco scent of the bar, the cluster of tweed-capped men on high stools, and the glittering motes spinning in the shafts of afternoon light through the dusty windows, all sunk deep into her soul.

It was so different from Murphy's, where she worked. There, the cracked linoleum, crooked old chairs and tables, the brown wallpaper, and freezing outside toilet was in stark contrast to the soft-focus haze of Hargadon Bros.

Niamh took the lead and showed Jesse into the snug. They slid into a cosy booth and ordered fish chowder along with two pints of Guinness.

'Man, this Irish soda bread is awesome,' Jesse said, crumbling it into his chowder. His action brought a memory back, sharp and painful. Her daddy had used to do the same thing with his bread. Crumble it into his food. Drove her mammy nuts.

'Cormac, why would you ruin a perfectly good Irish stew with lumps of bread?'

'It's how I like it, Rosie!' her dad would laugh.

'You're a strange man, Kelly,' her mam would say, but smiling all the same.

'That I am.' Her dad had winked at Niamh, while her mam continued to give out.

Niamh swirled her chowder around with her spoon, her appetite gone.

'Hey, are you okay?' Jesse leaned over. 'Did I say something wrong?'

'No, sorry,' Niamh said, annoyed with herself for slipping into the past again. 'Tell me more about your family. Do you have brothers? Sisters?'

'Yeah,' Jesse said. 'I've three big sisters. There's ten years between me and my closest sister, Maisie.'

'So you were a bit of a mistake?' Niamh teased him. Trying her best not to be distracted by the thought of his naked chest beneath the zipped-up biking jacket.

'You could say that,' Jesse said. 'How about you?'

'No brothers, no sisters,' she said. 'But I've a cousin. Brendan. We're close.'

As soon as she told him, she regretted it.

'That's cool,' Jesse said, not noticing her sudden tension. 'I got lots of cousins too.'

But Niamh wasn't listening. She shouldn't be on this date with Jesse. Brendan wouldn't like it. He'd told her it was the price they had to pay. Never get involved with civilians. But was she supposed to be alone forever?

'Hey, are you even listening to me!' Jesse said, giving her a poke, but looking amused.

'Sorry, I'm a bit spaced out, the joint and the swimming,' she said, coming back to look into his rich brown eyes.

Jesse gave her a slow, lazy smile.

'Yeah, that was great,' he said, cocking his head on one side. 'So, your place or mine?'

He was so confident, a part of her wanted to push him away for his audacity. And yet it didn't put her off him. There was a rebel spirit inside her. Countering the voice in her head telling her to stop. Why couldn't she do what she wanted, just for once?

'Mine,' she replied, looking down at the table at Hargadon's, counting the grains of old wood in time to the steady beat of her heart.

Chapter Seven

Does your wife know who you really are, Connor Fitzgerald? I don't want you to ever forget not one day goes by when I don't want to get you back for what you did. You're not welcome in Mullaghmore ever again. So, don't ever think you can come home with your new wife. Because if you do, I swear I'll kill you.

Lily stared at the email. Read it yet again. She knew it by heart, and her instincts told her the content was too specific to be spam.

Lily had become obsessed. The last twelve days, she'd spent hours trying to work out who'd sent the email, but when she googled 'redshamrock@hotmail.com', nothing at all came up. It had to be what she'd heard called a 'guerrilla account'. Set up temporarily and never used again. Even so, she felt the mention of 'shamrock' pinpointed an Irish connection.

She'd also been trying to find Connor's grandmother, Rosemary. All she'd had to go on was Connor's surname, which was Fitzgerald, and the place name of Mullaghmore. She'd already searched the internet endlessly for Fitzgeralds, but there were none in either of the two Mullaghmores in Ireland, because most likely his maternal grandmother had a different second name.

She had searched for Mullaghmore on Google Maps. One Mullaghmore was a mountain in the north of Ireland, so it had to be the other one, a village in County Sligo. The first images which came up were of the ocean, huge waves, and sites about surfing. This had to be Connor's Mullaghmore, because he had loved surfing. She remembered he'd said he had learnt as a teenager in Ireland, which had always surprised her. It wasn't a country she associated with surfing, but Connor had told her the place where he grew up had some of the biggest waves in the whole of Europe.

'Swells up to thirty metres,' he'd said, eyes shining.

Lily had clicked on a website called *Wild Atlantic Way* and read about all the allures of Mullaghmore as a holiday destination: a small fishing village with stretches of beaches, views of sea cliffs and a castle. She was stunned by the images of this place. It looked so beautiful, and Connor had never told her this. Yes, he'd talked about the sea and surfing, but he had made it sound like he'd grown up in a boring country village.

There was no doubt in her mind that Mullaghmore was the place where Connor had been raised. She looked up Mullaghmore again on Google Maps, and went to satellite view. The village was on the edge of a peninsula, jutting right out into the blue ocean. She could see the slim gold curve of sandy beaches, and the white lines of surf. What struck her most was all the green, and so few houses. Just one road appeared to wend its way around the coast. She zoomed in to Mullaghmore itself. She could see an old walled harbour, and the main road running along the seafront. There seemed to be very few businesses: a sailing club, a B&B, and a hotel. As she pulled out again, she got a sight of just how beautiful the landscape might be. The green fields. And the white foaming edge to the land told her there were cliffs.

Lily took up another piece of paper and began scribbling again.

What does the email mean? Who wrote it? Why? Why?

She tore the piece of paper out of the pad, scrunched it up and threw it across the room. Why had Connor never shown her the nasty email? How could it possibly be meant for *her* Connor? Kind, loyal, funny, honest Connor.

Lily closed her eyes. Right in the early days of their relationship, when they'd gone for all those romantic strolls on the beach together, she remembered Connor talking about Mullaghmore and his grandmother.

One day, the summer after they were married, she and Connor had been walking in the sea. The water had been thick with bladderwrack and lush, honey-coloured fronds of kelp.

'The seaweed here is so rich,' Connor commented. 'We should harvest it.'

'Ourselves?' Lily asked. She loved eating seaweed. Often had a craving for the kelp bars that Maine Coast Sea Vegetables made with sesame seeds, or their apple-smoked seaweed, which tasted so much better than jerky.

'My gran used to hang dulse seaweed up on the line to dry it out, and then put it in her stews,' Connor told her. 'We could start a seaweed business one day.'

'Sure, but lobstering is better money,' Lily pointed out.

'Yeah, but I really like the idea of harvesting sea vegetables. Have you ever had a seaweed bath?' Connor asked her.

'Sure, I love the seaweed soaps Mom gets,' Lily said. 'Made from Maine seaweed, too.'

'Sometimes my gran would fill a bath full of really hot water, so the steam would be billowing out of it, and put loads of fresh seaweed in it,' Connor said. 'I'd sink into the bath and lie there for hours, until my fingers were pruned and the water had gone cold.'

'Aw, not too sure I'd like to lie down in all that sliminess,' Lily commented.

'It's very good for your skin,' he declared. 'Great for the hair, makes it thick and glossy.'

He scooped up some kelp, drops of seawater spraying her face, and made to put it on her head.

'Don't you dare!'

She'd run out of the sea, laughing, and he'd chased her down the beach. She'd let him catch her, because she knew he'd never put a pile of slimy seaweed on her hair really. Once he had her in his arms, he dropped the strands and kissed her. He tasted of the sea and made her feel so good in herself.

Lily's heart began to accelerate. How could Connor be dead? Her darling man from across the Atlantic ocean, who had kissed her all over, and told her she was the most beautiful girl in the whole world? Fury ripped through her. She'd always loved the ocean, but now she hated it. She was mad with Connor for leaving her, but most of all she was furious with her dad.

She pulled out another piece of paper, started writing again.

Why didn't you tell me who you were? Why didn't you bring me to Ireland to meet your grandmother? I promise I'm going to find her.

Lily heard her front door open, and her father's voice call out for her.

'Lily! Where are you?

Her whole body stiffened. She got up off the chair and stomped downstairs.

'I've been calling your phone,' her father said. 'We need to talk.'

Lily looked at her father, incredulous. How dare he walk into her and Connor's home unannounced and tell her she needed to talk to him?

'Well, Dad, I'm not sure I want to talk to you right now.' Lily shrugged, pushing strands of greasy hair out of her face. She couldn't remember the last time she'd taken a shower.

'Want a coffee?' her father said, ignoring her hostility and heading towards the kitchen. She could see by the slow way he walked that he was still sore.

'I'd prefer a big glass of vodka,' Lily said, following him into the kitchen.

Lily sat up at the counter and watched her father make a pot of coffee. It occurred to her that she couldn't remember an occasion when her father had ever made her a cup of coffee before. Her mom or Connor had always been the ones in the kitchen. Lily knew her dad was trying to make things right again between them. They had always been so close. That's why he had been suspicious of Connor when Lily had first met him. Not wanted him going out with them fishing lobster, as if he might sell her dad's secret locations of where the best hauls might be got. Even after she and Connor had got married, her dad had been wary of him. He was a Maine man and it had thrown him that his daughter would choose to spend the rest of her life with an outsider.

But over the past two years, Connor's charm had worked its way on her dad. It made it easier that Connor had no family nearby, because he had become absorbed in theirs.

Lily's dad placed a steaming mug of black coffee in front of her.

'Come on, get that down you; you look like hell.'

She felt irritated by his care. The burning pain returned to the rash on her arm, reminding her it had arrived right after Connor had died. She took a big gulp of coffee to try to steady herself. She had to hold it together somehow.

'Your mom and I got the memorial booked for Friday the ninth, Lily,' he said, as he sat up on a stool next to her. Lily put her mug down again.

'No.' She shook her head. 'It's too soon.'

'It's been nearly two weeks. You need some closure.'

'They haven't found a body,'

'You know they never will,' her dad said. 'You have to be able to lay his memory to rest, Lily, so you can have a life.'

'But I don't want one without Connor, that's just it.' She clenched her fists. 'You've no right coming in here and telling me what to do.'

'I can't say anything that's going to make it better, I know, but everyone here needs a memorial,' her father said in a gentle voice. 'We're all real upset. We need to say goodbye to Connor.'

'Thought he was an outsider, anyways.' Lily held her father's eyes.

'That's not true. It took a while, but he was part of our community. We want to honour him, Lily.'

'But I'm not ready,' she protested.

Her father sighed. She'd never seen him look so sad.

'I know you're mad with me,' he said. 'I get it.' He leant forward, his elbows on the counter. 'Believe me, I wish I could change what happened that day. Lily, I wish I could have taken Connor's place.'

'It doesn't make it better, you saying that,' Lily said hotly.

Her father sat back on his stool. 'A memorial will help you,' he said. 'I know it did for me with your Uncle Joe.'

'That's different,' Lily said.

'It's loss, Lily,' her father said, before pausing. 'Your mom told me you were going to try to find Connor's grandmother in Ireland. Did you have any luck?'

'No,' Lily said tightly. Should she tell her dad about the email? Her instinct was not to. She felt protective of Connor's memory.

'That's a real shame,' her dad said. 'You have to keep trying. But we'll make it special, Lily. Connor might have been from Ireland, but he became one of us, a Downeaster from Maine.'

Lily was cornered. She didn't want to have to say goodbye to Connor, but deep down she knew her parents were right. Her husband was never coming back and she had to face it. But who had her husband really been? The anonymous email seemed to indicate a man she didn't really know at all. She felt a flash of anger, and she wanted to hurt someone. It was the only way she could feel better.

'What happened, Daddy?' Lily said to him, standing up off her stool. 'Tell me the damn truth. Why were you out in the middle of nowhere when there was a raging storm?'

Her father's face shut down.

'I've told you everything, Lily,' he said. 'I've been interviewed by the coastguards several times. I don't want to talk about it right now.'

'You don't get to tell me that, Daddy!' Lily's voice rose. But her father got up off his stool, his face closed, and walked out of her house without another word.

The afternoon of the memorial, it began to snow. Big, sloppy wet flakes which thawed as soon as they hit the ground, crossing over into sleety rain and back to snow again during the drive to the church. Lily's mom had organised a service in Rockland Congregational Church with Pastor Anderson set to officiate. It was the same church they had got married in, although afterwards, Connor had told her he'd been raised a Catholic. A fact which seemed to amuse him immensely. Lily had never bothered to tell her parents about Connor's religious background, despite the Congregational Church being far from Catholic. But Lily did believe in God. Or she had believed in him, until Connor had been taken from her. Now she didn't know what to think.

All she knew was she felt as if her whole world had been blown up. She was in pieces. Tiny particles of blasted dust.

Lily walked into the church with her parents behind her. She was wearing a long-sleeved black dress to hide the angry rash all down her left arm, but it was itching like hell. Although it was bright outside from the snow-swirling sky, the wooden walls and rafters of the church interior glowed with soft lighting. She looked up at the ceiling, not for the first time thinking how it looked like the bow of a boat. The stained-glass windows were rich with colour, and the red carpet made the whole interior feel warm. The place was full; she was surprised to see so many from Rockland had turned up. Fishermen dressed up in suits, with their wild hair flattened down, and faces shaved for once. All looking awkward and out of place, like mermen not used to land. As Lily walked down the middle aisle to take her seat in the front pew, she was struck by the overpowering scent of lilies. Big vases of them were up by the altar, beside a framed photograph of Connor, beaming away at her. Her Mom had had to push her to find a photograph she didn't mind being blown up. She had taken one of him standing by the sea, a close-up of his face, the wind blowing his hair, but looking free. That was important.

The scent of lilies was really getting to her. It was a cruel irony her name was the same as her husband's funeral flower. Had no one else thought of it? They could have replaced the lilies with any other flower. She should have done it, she thought, squeezing her hands. She'd been so removed from the memorial and now she felt a crescendo of regret. What had she been thinking of? She'd let her husband down again. Let them pile the church with these stinking, tall white waxen flowers. She hated lilies. Hoped she never had to see or smell one ever again.

The congregation were singing 'The Lord is My Shepherd' to the accompaniment of Aunt Cherie on the piano. It sounded forlorn, not comforting. Their voices faded out as Pastor Anderson stood up before the altar to say meaningless nice things about Connor. They had to be meaningless, because he hadn't known him. Why hadn't Lily taken control like she usually did, and written the eulogy herself? She wanted desperately to get up and say something about Connor, but then she didn't know what to say. The moment passed and everyone knelt down in the pews and prayed. Lily pressed her palms together and closed her eyes. Tried to pray for Connor in the next life. But her prayers felt forced. Her parents sat beside her in the pew. She could hear the quiet sobbing of her mother, and sensed her father at her side. Lily remained dry-eyed. As if floating above everyone in the church. She turned in her pew to look at her father. His head was bent in prayer, remorseful. She felt seized with a desire to scream at him. It was all his fault. How could she ever forgive him?

The memorial reception afterwards was in her parents' house. Her mom and Aunt Cherie must have been days at the preparation. Platters of food were on every surface, and a myriad of aromas filled the small house. Lobster cakes and little pies, creamy lobster, leek and corn chowder, beer-steamed clams (Connor's favourite), fresh poppy seed bread, split top crab rolls, and blueberry buckles. Despite the fact they were lobster fishers, they didn't eat lobster that much because of its value – but the whole community had clearly gone all out. As more and more platters of food arrived, gifted by local wives, it felt like the whole of their little neighbourhood and the fishing community was stuffed into her parents' sitting room, placing plates and napkins on their laps, drinking her dad's supply of beer and whisky.

It was worst when someone came up and shook her hand. Told her what a great guy Connor had been. She nearly lost it so many times. *Stop it, stop it*, she was wailing inside. *Don't talk about him as if he's gone. Not yet.*

With her mom busy with the food, her cousin Ryan hung by her side most of the time, batting some of the more insensitive folk aside.

'Good guy, you'd think he was a real Downeaster,' she heard time and time again. *Solid. Honest. Hard-working. Straight-up guy, just like your dad.* That made Lily mad. Especially when she saw all of her dad's fishing mates crowded around him. Consoling *him*, as if he'd lost a son.

But did any of these people really know her husband? At the back of her head, she could see the words of the awful email swimming around. The one phrase that kept sticking:

I swear I'll kill you.

What had her husband done to deserve such an email? And who was it from? A man? Or another woman?

'I remember the time Connor just came right on over and cleared our yard of snow,' their elderly neighbour, Arthur Pickford, was saying to her. 'I invited him in for coffee and a little drop of bourbon after. He was such a decent fellow.'

Lily nodded, trying to smile at Arthur. Ryan had disappeared, and she just wanted to get away from the kindly old man. She'd no memory of Connor ever telling her he went over and swept Arthur's yard. She thought she knew everything about her husband, and she didn't even know this little thing. She felt hot all of a sudden. Her polo neck on her black wool dress was choking her, the rash on her arm felt like it was on fire, and her face was reddening. She needed air.

*

Outside on her parents' back porch, it was already dark. Another day without Connor had passed. The snow was still falling, no longer wet, but dry and light, tickling her face as it landed on her cheeks. She saw the glow of a lit cigarette as Ryan turned around. He was mostly in shadow, some of the light from the house falling across the side of his face.

'How are you holding up?' he asked her.

'Not great,' Lily said, pulling up her sleeve and scratching her arm. 'Say, give me one of those.'

Ryan offered her his packet of cigarettes, and she took one. He cupped his hand around it and lit it for her, and she inhaled deep into her lungs, letting smoke slowly plume out her nostrils.

She and Ryan watched the snow falling in silence as she took another drag on the cigarette. She was grateful he didn't try to say anything to make her feel better.

'I can't take any more inside,' Lily said. 'Everyone's so fake. Most of them treated Connor as if he was an outsider when he was alive.'

'Aw, that's not fair, Lily,' Ryan said. 'He sure was part of the community here. People liked him. Loved his cooking.'

'But I *loved* him,' Lily whispered.

'I know.' Ryan nodded, looking at her.

'Ryan, tell me again about what happened out there?' She saw Ryan tense up, and she knew it must be upsetting for him, but she had to know all the details. 'I mean, weren't there weather warnings? How did you get caught up in such a big storm without knowing?'

Ryan shifted his feet from side to side.

'I don't know what to say, Lily,' Ryan said. 'Surely your dad has told you everything? I mean, it was like any other day. We'd hauled all the traps up, emptied them out, and banded all the lobster.'

Lily imagined Ryan and Connor out on deck, hauling up the traps. Ryan as sternman would be pulling out lobster and measuring them, while Connor would be putting the fresh bait bags in and stacking the traps ready to drop. Her dad would be up in the wheelhouse, keeping an eye on the charts, listening to the weather reports.

'Did Daddy come down and help Connor because he's slow?' Lily asked Ryan. 'If I'd been with you, would he have been in the helm, heard the warnings from the Coast Guard about the storm coming in?'

'No, he didn't come down,' Ryan said. 'Me and Connor were doing good. I remember looking up into the sky, and I said to Connor, "It's gone so dark." It was the sky I saw first, and I knew by the clouds things were going to be rough.'

Lily said nothing. She wanted to hear the whole story. She needed to hear about the last hours of Connor's life.

'I called up to the wheelhouse, said to your daddy about the sky, and we could see the ocean getting real choppy. I told him we needed to head back quick like.' Ryan looked away from Lily. Out at the falling snow. 'He said we'd be okay. Drop the line of traps.'

'What?' Lily's voice came out hoarse.

'He said we'd be okay.'

'But you said he also told you to drop the line of traps?'

Ryan shook his head, as if he were waking up. 'It was getting real wild then. The wind lashing into us, and we're staggering all over the deck, and taking on water. I said we should go back, like to hell with the traps. But Connor said we could drop the line.' Ryan sighed. 'I think he wanted to prove to your daddy he was a good lobsterman, you know, and also he knew how much money they could make.'

Lily pulled on her cigarette. It was making her feel sick now. Why had Connor been such a fool? Because he wasn't brought up in Maine, working every weekend as a kid on the lobster boats. Ryan knew, as did Lily, when to let be. But what about her dad – he knew that too, surely?

'But it got so bad, what with the boat taking on water, your daddy changed his mind, said let the traps be, and we needed to head back sharpish.'

Lily stared at Ryan. Saw his face go still with the memory of what he'd endured.

'It takes just one big wave, Lily,' Ryan said to her, his face solemn. 'I saw the lightning forking on the horizon, and the ocean boiling and frothing. I saw that big wave coming. I shouted to Connor, "Hold on," but that's when he tripped, got caught up in the line.' Ryan's voice was hoarse with emotion. 'He'd left it out, see. And then the end of the line went over the side, and all the traps were pulled off the boat.' Ryan paused. 'Connor after them.'

Lily squeezed her eyes shut. She could see the whole scene in her head. The terror, the panic. Had Connor been swept away immediately, pulled down to the depths of the ocean in a moment? Or had he desperately tried to swim back towards the boat?

'I should have been there, Ryan.'

'I'm glad you weren't, Lily,' Ryan said.

Lily looked up at Ryan, his eyes glassy in the half-light. She crushed her cigarette beneath her shoe. She was shivering with the cold now in her black wool dress.

'Me and your dad both made it to the life raft, and we were hollering and hollering for Connor. But Lily, he was just gone.'

Her daddy was talking to Pastor Anderson. He had a glass of bourbon in his hands, filled with ice, and was taking small sips of it, as if it were medicine. Her father had never been much of a drinker. She couldn't help noticing he seemed to have shrunk. He looked broken, his back stooped as he held on to the drink.

It was the wrong time and place to ask him, and yet she needed to know right now what had happened on the *Lily May*. In all her father's decades fishing, he'd never let himself get caught out in such a bad storm. Had he really ignored the weather warnings?

She marched across the room, ignoring her mom, who was calling her over. The snow had melted on her woollen dress and she felt damp, halfway between cold from outside and hot from the warm room.

'Daddy, I need to talk to you, alone,' she told her father, not caring if the pastor thought she were rude. This was her husband's memorial and she could behave how she liked.

Her father looked over at her. She saw something in his expression. An apology? Shame? Dread began to seep into her heart.

'Now's not the time, Lily,' her daddy said, as the doorbell rang.

'There will never be a good time, Daddy,' Lily said, but her father wasn't looking at her anymore. His eyes had widened as he looked over her shoulder. For the first time in her life, Lily saw her daddy look frightened. She turned around to see two cops approaching them. She recognised one as their local sheriff, Bill Frederickson.

'Mr Jack Smyth?' Frederickson asked her father in a formal tone of voice, as the whole room fell silent. Lily sensed the eyes of all their family, friends and neighbours on her father as the sheriff and his fellow cop, Seth Bailey, walked into the centre of the room.

'What the hell, Bill!' her father exclaimed, his face turning a deep shade of red. 'What're you doing here?'

'I'm sorry, Jack,' Frederickson said.

Lily's father looked furious. 'God damn you, Bill, you can't come barging in on my son-in-law's memorial! Have you no respect?'

'I got my orders, Jack,' Sheriff Frederickson said as Seth Bailey produced a pair of handcuffs. Lily heard her mother gasp behind her, and the ripple and hush of shock that ran through the whole gathering.

'I'll come by the station later if you want to talk to me,' her dad said to the sheriff. 'But you can't do this, not right here, not now – in front of Lily!'

Frederickson kept his head down, unable to even look in Lily's direction as she stood in stunned silence.

'I'm sorry, Jack, but on the authority of the US Attorney's Office I am placing you under arrest on the charge of seaman's manslaughter.'

Lily took a step back, gripping her shaking hands. Seaman's manslaughter? It was so rare for anyone to be accused of such a crime. The last time she'd heard of it was eight years ago. Another captain over in Portland had been sent to prison for ten years for being responsible for the deaths of two of his crew. They'd all gone out drunk and stoned, and got swept overboard. But because he was captain of the vessel, he was responsible for their welfare.

Lily watched in horror as Seth Bailey approached her dad with the handcuffs.

'Hey!' her dad challenged him. 'What do you think you're doing?'

'Don't resist, Jack. Don't make it worse for yourself,' Frederickson said, as her father put his hand out in defence.

'Leave him alone!' her mom screeched.

'I've got to cuff you, Mr Smyth,' Seth Bailey said, looking apologetic. 'I don't want to have to use force.'

'I don't believe this is happening,' her mom said tearfully.

'It's okay, Sarah,' her daddy said, looking at her mom, and then at the whole silent group of witnesses – although he turned his gaze away when it came to Lily. 'I sure am sorry for the drama, folks.' He turned to the sheriff. 'I'll come, but you don't need to cuff me, okay?'

Frederickson continued to read her father his rights, but Lily couldn't watch it any longer. She backed away, shoving through the crowd, feeling their pity as she turned and ran up the stairs to her old bedroom. She slammed the door behind her and pushed a chair up against it. The room was full of flashing blue light from the cop car outside. She flung herself on her bed and buried her head under the pillow. Her nightmare had just got ten times worse.

Was her husband dead because of her father?

Chapter Eight

Mullaghmore, Ireland, 12th July 1992

Niamh snuck Jesse past the cottage and across the back yard to the shed. She could hear her mam's folk music on. The diddly-aye fiddles she adored.

'Are we not going into the house?' Jesse asked as she fumbled with the door of the shed.

'Course not,' Niamh said, turning to him. 'My mam's home.'

'Seriously?' Jesse said, laughing. 'I mean, how old are you?'

'Don't be so smart,' she said, opening the door and pulling him inside the musty shed.

'Very cosy,' Jesse teased, flicking his Zippo open to look around.

'You'll see,' Niamh said, lighting a candle and popping it inside a lantern. She carried the lantern over to the window side of the shed, with the view of the back undergrowth, and popped it on a stool. 'Want another joint?' she asked, feeling nervous.

'Sure,' Jesse said, walking towards her. She watched him as he stepped over the loose floorboards. For a minute she imagined his weight crashing through, his foot landing on Brendan's heavy bag.

As they shared the joint, Jesse told her more about his family. How he'd grown up more or less an only child because of the age gap with his sisters.

'When Dad died, my mom went to live with Maisie in Boston,' Jesse said. 'So it was just me in the house and the boatyard. A bit lonely.'

'Is that why you came to Ireland?'

'I thought, why not? I mean, this was where my dad was from. My heritage, right?'

'Is your dad's family from Sligo?'

'No, Galway, but when I found out about Joseph O'Reilly's boatbuilding yard, I had to come here.'

Niamh tucked her feet up on the mattress, hugging her knees.

'What about you?' Jesse asked. 'What's your story?'

Niamh shook her head. 'Enough stories,' she said.

They stared at each other, and for a moment, she thought she'd got it wrong. Maybe nothing was going to happen. But then he leant forward and tucked a tendril of her hair behind her ear, before kissing her on the lips.

They sank back onto the old mattress as she tugged her jeans and then her pants off. She didn't care if she was being too easy.

Niamh felt the weight of Jesse upon her and banished thoughts of any memories of her times with Brendan. She closed her eyes, put her hands on his hard hips and pressed herself to him. She sought to reconnect with the moment they'd shared on the beach, damp with seawater and full of longing. Jesse's hand slipped between her thighs and he began to stroke her. She sighed from deep within her belly, felt herself opening outward, as if to the light. She pulled him to her, pulled him in.

Afterwards, she rolled them both cigarettes with her Golden Virginia tobacco and papers, lighting his before handing it to him. He put his arm around her shoulders and she nestled her head against his chest. It was a clear night, and moonlight found its way into the shed even through the dense foliage outside the window. Along with the lantern, it illuminated the side of the shed where her father's tools still lay upon his workbench, and the half-made table leaned up against the wall.

'Are those your father's things?' Jesse asked her softly, seeing her looking.

'Yes, this used to be his workshop,' Niamh told him. 'He was a carpenter.' She sighed. 'He's been dead ten years, but I still haven't managed to put his stuff away.'

'Maybe you don't have to.'

'Look.' She pointed at the table. 'It's not even finished. I should break it up into firewood.'

'No, Niamh,' Jesse said, stroking her hair. 'Don't do that.'

They lay in silence for a while, finishing their smokes. Niamh had never been held like this before. With Brendan, they'd always been half-dressed and hurried, but here, after just one date, she was lying totally naked against Jesse's bare skin.

Jesse stirred, but still held her as he shifted his position. 'What happened to your father?' he asked, in a low voice.

She had known the question was coming. Joseph O'Reilly was bound to have said something to his young apprentice.

Niamh had imagined the scene so many times in her mind. Gone over every little detail, time and again over the past ten years. Now, as she described what had happened to her father, she could see it before her, as if she'd stepped back in time.

'It was close to this time of year, the twenty-first of August,' she told Jesse. 'When all our laneways are choked with tractors and harvesters. I remember that.'

It had been late on the warm golden afternoon when Daddy had set off to go fishing on Lough Melvin. He was meeting his cousin, Tadhg, at the lake. A pastime her daddy and Tadhg had enjoyed since they were boys. Even though the border between the north and south had always separated them – Tadhg living just across the border in County Fermanagh – they'd never missed their annual summer jaunts to the lough. It wasn't even about catching fish. Niamh never remembered her daddy bringing back any to eat. The year before, she'd asked him why he kept going if he'd never caught any fish. He'd told her it wasn't about that for him and Tadhg.

'Sure, I might catch a fish,' her father had told her. 'But we always put them back in.'

'What's the point, then?' Niamh had asked.

'That is precisely the point,' her father had laughed at her. 'It's about the journey, not the destination.'

'What are you on about?' Niamh had demanded.

'I mean, my darling, the reason Tadhg and I go fishing is not to tot up how many fish we've caught. It's about sitting together in silence, enjoying the lake. It's about a bit of peace.'

'That sounds totally boring,' twelve-year-old Niamh had said at the time.

'We've always done it, since we were boys.'

Niamh had rolled her eyes. 'Boring!'

But inside, she'd been a little jealous. She'd wished she and her cousin Brendan could have gone fishing with them too, but her daddy was always insistent: adults only. It was the way things always were. Her daddy would go off fishing with Tadhg two or three times during the summer, and the same evenings her mam would make jam from summer fruits they'd gathered. Niamh's job was to help her mam collect raspberries – consuming and collecting in equal quantities, until their lips were stained so pink her daddy always said they looked like a couple of harlots when he got back.

So many times, Niamh had tried to drag every last moment of memory from that day before her father died. But the truth was, there were so many gaps. She couldn't remember breakfast, or going out with her mam to collect raspberries in the morning. Her dad had been in the shed, working on the table, she remembered that. She'd brought him a cup of tea in his big BEST DAD mug she'd given him for Father's Day that year. She'd sat on a stool and watched him work for a while. Fascinated by how he shaved the wood, as if he were peeling vegetables. She remembered the scent of wood resin, and the sawdust spinning in the air like tiny particles of gold glitter as sunlight shafted through the dusty window. Every time she looked at that half-finished table now, she saw her daddy wearing his blue work shirt, the same colour as his eyes. Bent over, so focused she'd wondered if he even knew she was still there, watching him.

She couldn't remember what they'd eaten for tea that day, but it was not long after that her dad had gathered up his fishing rod and tackle and laid them on the back seat of his car.

'Will you be making jam with your mammy, my little ray of light?' he'd said to Niamh, tickling her under the chin.

'Don't call me that any more, Daddy, it's silly.' Niamh had wriggled away. She'd felt she was too old for her dad to tickle her.

'But that's what your name means, Niamh – radiant – and that's what you'll always be to your daddy.'

Her father had kissed her on the forehead, and she'd stepped back.

'Too grown up for Daddy to give you a hug, too?' he'd asked. She had never forgotten the hurt look in his eyes.

'Course not, Daddy.'

Niamh had fallen into her father's embrace. For years, after he was gone, she'd dream he was still hugging her.

'Can I come with you?'

'Ah, darling, I told you – men only, and anyways, you'll be bored silly,'

'I won't, I promise.'

Her daddy had cradled her face with his hands. 'I tell you what, how about next year, right?' he'd said. 'You and Brendan can come along. Okay?'

'Okay,' she'd said, disappointed.

Her daddy had got into the car, and her mam had come running out the house, a Tupperware box in her hands, packed with cheese and salad sandwiches for the two men.

'You forgot your sandwiches! Got your thermos of tea? The hip flask of whisky?'

'Thanks, darling.'

Niamh remembered her mam bending down, and her daddy kissing her through the open car window. Her mam stepping back, and the car setting off down the bumpy lane. A jaunty wave of his hand was the last she saw of her daddy as he turned out of their front gate.

Niamh had gone over in her mind so many times what she'd heard had happened next.

Her daddy would have been whistling as he drove along the country lanes, bumping up and down as he traversed old bog land. Perhaps slowing down to let Paddy O'Mahony's bullocks amble past the car, escaped yet again from their field. Looking out at Aghavogil Bog as he sped by its marshy contours, the earth rising black and fecund, gatherings of reeds sharp and high. Pools of still water reflecting the slow, gentle descent of the summer sun. He would have been driving towards the summer moon, looming ahead in the pale blue. Looking forward to sharing his night of peace with his cousin, away from his work shed, and his women. Solitude, the still lake, and perfect companionship in silence.

Usually, it was Tadhg who drove over the border, from the north to the south, and they met on the southwestern shores of Lough Melvin. But they'd changed their minds this time. Tadhg had explained to Niamh and her mam at the funeral: he'd been out earlier in the fishing season and had left the boat tied up on the northern edge of the lough. Where they lived, it wasn't dangerous to cross over the border. It was only irritating, because the British Army had blown up most of the roads, so you had to either pick your way over craters, or drive on a long detour, as her daddy had that night, to pass through a checkpoint and backtrack all the way to the lake.

'He was only going fishing,' she told Jesse now, turning to look at him. Her breasts were pressed against his bare chest, her eyes fixed on his. He looked back at her. She could already see the pity creeping in.

It had been about seven in the evening when Tadhg and her daddy had eventually met up, got into the small row boat and pushed out onto the mirror-clear waters of the lough. They sat at either end of the boat, casting their lines. A few words exchanged, and then the purity of quiet.

Meanwhile, Niamh and her mam had been making a sticky, sugary berry mess in their kitchen. Ladling sugar into the simmering pots of raspberries. The scent divine, the flavour intense, with an edge of tartness, when Niamh dipped in a teaspoon for a taste. She had stared into the pot, stirring the bubbling mixture, fascinated by the intense crimson of the raspberry pulp.

The sun was falling low in the sky, staining the air red as if with berry juice, and dark was seeping up from the land. Trees whispered out by the home lough. There came the lone hoot of an owl, and the sounds of all the night creatures coming out.

At this point in the story, Niamh stopped. She had been so lost in her memories, but now, Jesse's face was right in front of her, his expression intent.

'It's okay. You don't have to go on,' he said.

She touched her cheeks and realised they were damp with tears. Nearly ten years, her dad had been dead, and she still wasn't over it.

'I want to tell you all about it,' she whispered. 'Because if I don't, someone else will, and they might get it wrong.'

'Okay, then,' Jesse said, kissing her gently on the forehead. Niamh swallowed down the lump in her throat.

'He never came home,' she said. 'My mam woke me in the night, and she was worried.'

'"Did your daddy tell you what time he'd be back?" she asked me. And I said, "No, is he not home?" My mam must have had some kind of feeling, because she looked really shaken up and I said, "Mammy, don't worry, he probably went out for pints with Tadhg and is staying over."

'"But he never rang," Mam said, looking at me, all pale. And then she said, "I dreamt about him, Niamh, like he came to me." And I know it sounds dramatic, but we both knew something bad had happened.

'When the Gardai car turned up, we weren't surprised. Mam had been on the phone to Tadhg's house and his wife, Mary, had answered. Woken up Tadhg, who'd told Mammy that he'd said his goodbye to Daddy long before. Like, hours and hours ago. Daddy should have been back by dark.'

Jesse took Niamh's hand, gripped it between his. She knew it was breaking all the dating rules to come out with such heavy stuff on their first night. He might bolt for it as soon as he could, but she was beyond worrying. Now that she was talking about the night her father had died, she couldn't stop. She hadn't spoken to anyone about it, apart from Brendan. Who had always had a different take.

'When the Gardai knocked on our door, we knew something had happened to Daddy, but we still didn't expect what it was.

'Those Gardai, they lied to us. Said there'd been an accident. Said they were sorry. Daddy was gone. I remember Mam fell down onto a chair, and she was just staring into space. Couldn't say a word. So, I asked them. I said, "What accident? What happened?" The younger Garda couldn't look me in the face.

They weren't local. I don't know where they were from. But then the older one told me that Daddy had been shot by accident up north, and they were talking to the RUC about it.'

'What's the RUC?' Jesse asked her.

'Royal Ulster Constabulary,' Niamh told Jesse. 'The police up north.' She felt the fury return, like an old wound throbbing. 'Mam came to her senses and she said to the guards she wanted to talk to the RUC man on the phone, right now. I can't even remember that Ulsterman's name, but it was him who told us the truth.'

Niamh took a breath. Looked into Jesse's brown eyes and said it straight out, just as her mother had been told, so brutally:

'Daddy had been shot at a fake checkpoint – most likely by a member of the UDF.'

Jesse frowned, and Niamh could see he didn't understand.

'Have you heard of the UDF?'

Jesse shook his head.

'Well, it stands for Ulster Defence Force. They're a terrorist Loyalist group fighting the republicans, or the IRA.'

'I know about the IRA,' Jesse said. 'The Irish Republican Army, right? They want a united Ireland?'

'Most of the troubles are in Belfast,' Niamh continued to explain. 'There've been the bombings in Enniskillen, about an hour away across the border in County Fermanagh, but not much trouble near us. Only the odd random incident.'

'So was your father in the IRA?' Jesse asked.

'No,' she snapped, defensive. 'He was totally against violence. But some of his relatives were in the IRA.' As Niamh said this, a memory returned to her of her daddy. Right here in this very shed, her father kneeling down, with his hammer in his hand, tapping her head gently. Making her promise never to get caught up in the Troubles. She'd broken that promise.

'So why was your father killed?' Jesse whispered, and she realised the expression on his face was one of awe. For a second, she was tempted to tell him her secret. But of course, there was no way she could do that.

'He was unlucky. A Catholic in the wrong place at the wrong time,' Niamh said. 'He came across a fake checkpoint. Two UDF men, dressed up as British soldiers. When he stopped the car, they shot him point blank. Then fled across the fields.'

'What?' Jesse looked aghast. 'But why?'

'No reason why – just because our car had a southern Irish registration plate,' Niamh said, though the truth was she'd always known deep inside her it had something to do with Daddy's family. She just couldn't tell Jesse that.

'Did they catch the men who did it?'

'No,' Niamh said bitterly. 'The RUC never catch the UDF guys.'

'But they had British soldiers' uniforms on?' Jesse looked so confused. 'They were posing as soldiers. Randomly shooting civilians. Why didn't they go after them?'

'Exactly.' Niamh heard her own voice, hard and cold.

'The authorities up north covered it all up,' Niamh said. 'We never got justice. Because the RUC, the British army and the UDF are all colluding.'

'That's totally insane,' Jesse said, pulling her close. 'I'm real sorry, Niamh.'

'It's okay,' she said. 'It happened a long time ago. I've let it go.' She was lying. Of course she had never forgiven what had happened. How could she? Instead, she had directed all her grief into hatred. Become part of the situation her father had tried so hard to protect his family from.

But protecting them hadn't worked, had it? They had got him in the end.

'Come here,' Jesse said, his eyes deep with compassion.

Niamh wrapped her legs around his waist and guided him inside her as they began to move together. Rocking gently back and forth, as if they were on western seas, not on the old mattress in her musty shed. She closed her eyes. Imagined herself and Jesse on a little rowing boat, drifting. Each time he pushed inside her, she wanted to bring him up deeper within her, as if they were diving into the deepest blue. She wanted their love-making to take her far, far away from her tragic corner of Ireland and her hidden past.

Afterwards, they clung on to each other, breathless. It felt as if they'd swum the longest distance together. Through riptides and swirling whirlpools, to reach their own little island. As Niamh drifted off to sleep, she let the feeling of such liberation wash over her.

Niamh woke with a start. A bright light was directed right into her face. She put her arms over her eyes to try to stop it, snuggling into the warmth of Jesse's sleeping body, but felt a hand shaking her shoulder, and a familiar voice hissing in her ear.

'What the fuck, Niamh?'

'Go away,' she murmured, and then suddenly jolted away in alarm. Brendan was here. In the shed, and so was Jesse. Fast asleep on the mattress next to her. He couldn't wake up.

She reached around to the end of the bed for Jesse's T-shirt and her jeans, very aware of Brendan's dark figure standing over her.

'Come on,' Brendan hissed as she struggled to get dressed, half-covering her naked body with the sheet while also trying not to disturb Jesse. 'Move it, will you, Niamh? I've seen it all before.'

Niamh tried to ignore his comment, but it hurt all the same. 'I didn't know you were coming,' she whispered.

'Clearly.' Brendan's voice was still sarcastic. 'I called as usual. Let it ring three times. Nine o'clock.'

'Fuck, I forgot,' she said. 'I was out.'

She detected the disapproval in Brendan's silence. 'Come on,' he said, eventually. 'I've got to go.'

'What if he wakes up?' Niamh asked, panic fluttering in her chest.

'You'd better hope he doesn't, cousin,' Brendan said, his voice flat and emotionless.

She glanced back at Jesse, but his face was in the shadows. She could hear the steady rhythm of his sleeping breath, at least. Brendan directed the light from his torch at the floorboards, and Niamh dropped down onto her knees, feeling around to find the loose ones. She yanked them back, and then moved away to let Brendan pull out the bag. He handed her the torch, and she led the way out of the shed and into the garden. The grass was damp and cold on her bare feet. The full moon illuminated the garden, the roses silvery and lustrous. She could hear Pixie scratching at the back door.

'I'll just let Pixie out, else she'll wake up Mam barking,' Niamh said, hopping across the wet grass.

Pixie came barrelling out the door, charging towards Brendan. Once she sniffed and recognised him, she calmed down and trotted off to pee in the bushes.

'So who's the fellow, Niamh?' Brendan asked her, putting the bag on his shoulder.

'Just a boy,' Niamh said.

'What's his name?'

'Jesse. He's American,' Niamh said, reluctant to reveal any more.

'Be careful, Niamh,' Brendan warned her, shifting the weight of the bag to his other shoulder.

'It's nothing, a fling,' she said.

'I didn't think you were that sort.' Brendan eyed her.

'How's Deirdre?' she asked, unable to keep a bitchy note out of her voice.

'Grand,' Brendan said evenly. 'Waiting for me in the car down the lane.'

'Well, you'd best be going, then,' Niamh said, tightly.

He began to lope across the garden, but she found herself running after him, tugging on his jacket.

'What's in the bag, Brendan?'

He turned and gave her a good look.

'I'll be in contact,' he said, not answering her question.

'Brendan, I don't want to do this anymore,' Niamh heard herself saying. But Brendan kept on walking. Had he even heard her? More likely, he was ignoring her yet again. He would only tell her there was no way out, after all.

Niamh felt a flare of anger. This was her life, and she wanted it back. She followed him across the yard, although the stone was brutal on the bare soles of her feet.

'Brendan,' she hissed.

He swung round.

'What is it, Niamh?'

'I want out. I'm serious,' she said.

They stared at each other. She'd known him all her life, but she still had no idea what he was thinking.

'I'll ask Daddy,' he said, after an awkward pause. 'Okay?'

'Okay,' she said, surprised by his answer, beginning to feel a tiny seed of hope.

He disappeared out through the gate, and she imagined him running down the lane to Deirdre, waiting for him in the driving seat of the car. Deirdre, with her curves clad in a little bomber jacket and mini skirt. Deirdre with her scarlet lips, cat-kohled green eyes, and long blond hair. Brendan opening up the boot. Hiding the guns – she was certain they were guns – under the spare tyre, while Deirdre turned the key in the ignition, her fingernails flashing red. She always drove, to distract the soldiers.

Niamh remembered when Brendan had first mentioned Deirdre. Four years ago now. Told Niamh that Deirdre was the most beautiful girl he'd ever seen.

'And a believer, too!'

It had made Niamh jealous. Motivated her to ask for more. To do more for the cause. She had wanted Brendan's attention back.

Niamh stumbled across the yard, shivering, with Pixie at her feet. She let the dog back into the house and then crossed the garden to the shed, praying Jesse hadn't woken. As she opened the door, she stepped on something sharp and gave a little squeal, lifting up her foot and squinting. A big thorn from the rose bush was sticking out of the pad of her heel. She pulled it out, then hopped into the shed.

To her relief, Jesse was still asleep. She slid back in next to him, still shivering, and nestled up to his warm body. Her foot was throbbing. She put her arms around Jesse and held him even tighter. But she couldn't find sleep again. Brendan's rude awakening had brought her back to reality. A nagging dread, as constant as the pain in her foot.

Chapter Nine

Lily lay on her childhood bed, pressing her palms over her eyes to blot everything out, but all she could see was the look on her daddy's face when Sheriff Frederickson had arrested him. What a spectacle the whole thing had been. Not that the gossip wouldn't be all over town anyway, even if the memorial reception hadn't been going on. But still, it felt as if her whole family had been stripped naked. She was so confused. What had just happened?

She lay there, listening to everyone leave. Next, she heard her mom's footsteps outside on the landing. The door handle turned – but of course, she couldn't open it as it was wedged shut with the chair.

'Lily, will you come on out?' her mom begged. 'Come with me to the county jail to bail your father out.'

'No, Mom, go away,' Lily said.

'I've got to go now,' her mom said. This time Lily didn't answer. 'Okay, well, I'm off then.'

Again, Lily responded with silence.

A few minutes later, the house was quiet. Lily looked out of the window and all the cars, including her mom's station wagon, had gone.

She pulled the chair away from the door handle, and opened it. Walked back downstairs into the deserted rooms of her husband's memorial service. The half-eaten plates of food and dirty glasses. The flowers filling every vase. Someone had brought the hateful lilies back from the church, and their awful, cloying scent was filling the whole of her parents' house.

Lily flung open the back door, ran across the garden to her own home, and slammed her door shut. She locked it. She didn't want see or talk to anyone.

No one was who they seemed. Her father had been her icon. The whole of her childhood, she'd looked up to him. She had thought he was the best man in the world, until she had met Connor, of course. How lucky she had thought she was, to have two such wonderful men in her life. Her and Connor's only issue had been about the babies, but they'd sorted that out. Just the night before he was taken from her.

Lily sat down at Connor's desk. Stared at the computer screen, before accessing Connor's emails again. She clicked on the email and read it once more.

She felt everything smashed inside of her. All she believed in, and who she was. Her father was a liar, and a coward. It was his fault Connor was gone. At the same time, Connor had lied to her, too. Who had sent him the email, and why? It was gnawing away at her. Her grief was now tinged with hurt. Why could her husband not have confided in her? What secret did he possess, to have invited such a vicious missive from a person who was a complete stranger to Lily?

Lily shivered, a chill passing through her as if she was cold from the inside out. Her skin was hot, arms on fire, the rash spreading up to her elbows – but inside she was so cold.

Lily went into her bedroom and lay down on the bed, closing her eyes. She wanted to sink into the mattress, through the base of it, and through the floor. She wanted to fall away to nothing.

She was woken by the sound of her phone ringing, but by the time she'd found it she'd missed the call from her mom. She walked over to look out of the window and saw the light on downstairs in her parents' house. Her mom's station wagon was parked outside the front. She listened to the voicemail. Her mom had successfully bailed her father out, after a wait of about three hours. Lily couldn't help but feel a sense of relief. She was mad with her dad, yet she didn't want to see him in jail.

She went downstairs, put her coat on over her woollen dress and slipped on a pair of boots.

Her parents' back door wasn't locked. She pulled her snowy boots off and hung her coat on a hook. Her mom had now cleared up everything from the memorial reception. Plates of food were covered with plastic wrap and every surface had been wiped down. Only the light under the stove was on. Lily walked down the hall and into the main living room. Her dad was sitting in his chair. Lily could see a bottle of bourbon and a half-full Old Fashioned glass on the table beside him. He started when he saw her. She could tell by the look in his eyes that he was drunk, which felt strange because her daddy never drank too much.

'Lily, your mom was trying to talk to you,' he said, his words slurring slightly. 'She rang your phone, but you didn't pick up.'

Lily sat down on the couch. 'I fell asleep,' she said.

Her dad nodded.

The tension between them was thick. Lily had never felt like this with her father before. She couldn't bear it. They had to talk about what had happened. Get it all out.

'What happened, Daddy? Why did Frederickson take you off to Knox County Jail?'

Her father sighed. 'Man, they actually booked me.' He shook his head and took another gulp of whisky. 'I'm being charged with seaman's manslaughter for Connor's death.'

'I know,' Lily snapped. 'I heard Frederickson when he arrested you. But what I want to know is why, Daddy? On what evidence?'

'Honey, you came over.' Lily heard her mother's voice behind her, and felt her hand on her shoulder. 'Jack, you need to go to bed. You've had too much to drink.'

But her father stayed put, looking down at his glass of bourbon before draining it.

'It's going to be okay,' her mom said, coming down to sit next to Lily, although she didn't sound like she thought so. Her voice was trembling. 'We managed to post bail.'

'And how much was that?'

'Twenty thousand dollars,' her mom answered, in a flat voice.

'But how did you get the money?'

Her mother turned to her, a colour high in her cheeks. 'I had to use the money I'd saved up, that I was giving you for your fertility treatment,' she said. 'You'll get it back.'

'Well, I don't need the money now, anyway,' Lily said bitterly.

'They have to drop the charges. It's crazy they're charging Jack with seaman's manslaughter. He didn't do anything negligent. Just got caught out in a storm, but because he's the captain, he gets the blame...' Her mom's voice petered out.

Lily looked across at her father. 'Is that what really happened, Dad?' she challenged him, feeling her anger raw in her throat like heartburn.

He stared back at her, his eyes unfocused, before turning to pour more Jack Daniels into his glass. She felt her mom watching him, sensed her concern, but her mom didn't say anything. Instead she turned to Lily, picking up her hand and looking into her eyes.

'Your dad can't lobster fish until this gets sorted, and we lost the boat,' she said. 'At least it's the end of the season, so we've some money saved, but honey... Do you think you're ready to go back to work? Could you go out with one of the other crews? We're going to need the money.'

'But if it does go to trial, when will that be?' Lily asked.

'It won't,' her mom said firmly. 'It wasn't Jack's fault.'

'How do you know, Mom?' Lily burst out. 'You weren't there.'

Her mom looked genuinely shocked. 'How could you say such a thing, Lily?' she said, but her eyes were flitting, and she was clearly trying to divert Lily's attention to more practical matters. 'The insurance won't cover us if Jack is found negligent,' she said in a quiet voice. 'But I don't believe they'll bring it to trial—'

'Three years,' her dad interrupted. 'If they decide to prosecute, that's what my attorney said.'

'They wouldn't even consider prosecuting unless they had good reason for doing so.' Lily walked over to her dad. 'So come on, Dad, spit it out. Tell me the truth.' She could hear the harsh anger in her voice, yet at the same time she was scared. What would happen to her father if he was sent away to prison for three years?

'Lily! We all need to pull together,' her mom said, twisting her hands in her lap, her face pale with nerves.

'Pull together because my husband has died, or because my own father caused his death?' Lily said, pointing at her dad, looking at her mom. She looked so frightened, but Lily didn't feel sorry for her, because she had taken her dad's side.

'How could you say such a thing, Lily? We adored Connor like our own,' her mom said, her voice trembling with emotion. 'Of course it's not your father's fault. It's Ray George, he's twisted around some of the things your father told him the night they got rescued.'

'I knew the storm was coming, but I just kept on going,' her father interrupted, his voice slurred and shaking.

To Lily's horror, her father was crying.

'Did you ignore the weather warnings, Daddy?' Lily asked him, her heart tight in her chest.

'I thought we'd be fine,' her father said, tears streaming down his cheeks. 'I've been out in storms like that before.'

'Come on, Dad, not as big as that storm! You risked Connor's life, and Ryan's too.'

'I asked them if they wanted to turn back, and they said no, it was fine,' her dad said defensively.

'That doesn't make it okay! You should have known!' she wailed.

'But I'm telling you, what happened to Connor was pure accident, with the lobster trap line…'

'What was it doing out, Daddy?'

Her father buried his face in his hands. 'You're right, Lily. I was the captain and Connor was my responsibility. It's my fault he's dead.'

Her father's confession didn't make Lily feel any better. In fact, she felt cold with fury. 'I will never forgive you.' She turned on her mom. 'You can forget about me going out to make money to help Dad. I never want to get on a boat, ever again. I'm done fishing.'

She stormed out of the living room, leaving her mom aghast and her dad sobbing into his hands.

While Lily was pulling on her boots and coat, her mom appeared in the kitchen.

'Lily, honey, please. Your father's devastated,' her mom said, reaching out for her. 'He's so sorry, but we all need to stick together. He needs you, Lily.'

'No!' Lily hissed at her mom, pulling back. 'No, you don't get to tell me to think of my dad's feelings right now. Because it's *my* husband who drowned all alone out there, and I can't even say goodbye to him by burying his body. *My* husband, not yours, Mom, not Daddy!'

Lily took off across the snow and back up the hill towards home. There was a tiny crescent moon, which lit up a narrow silvery pathway for her. At the top of the hill, she turned and looked down upon Rockland, her Downeast town by the ocean. The water was still and rippling beneath a shaft of moonlight, the wharf icy and all the harbour buildings covered in thick snow. She inhaled deeply, remembering the last time it had snowed. She and Connor had had a snowball fight out back. He'd told her it never snowed back in the west of Ireland the way it did in Maine.

'It never sticks like this,' he'd said, lying on his back in the snow and sweeping his legs and arms to make a snow angel.

Lily imagined Connor by her side now. Warmth upon her chilled cheeks as if he was blowing softly on them.

'Okay,' she whispered. 'I hear you. I'll take you back. Promise.'

She already had some of the savings from her mom in her own bank account – her mom had transferred enough to pay for that first appointment. Fertility treatment was pointless now, and she wasn't going to give the money back to her mom for her father's court case. But she had another use for it. She had to go to Mullaghmore and find Connor's grandmother, Rosemary. If not for him, then for herself, because she felt like an outsider in her own hometown. The way things were right now, she never wanted to see her parents again.

The last line of the email from the mystery sender in Mullaghmore rose in her mind. *I swear I'll kill you!* Whoever had sent the message had known about Lily and her life with Connor in Rockland, but she had no idea who they were. What was the secret in her husband's past that had motivated someone to threaten him so dramatically? Lily knew she had to go to Ireland. She'd never rest until she got to the truth.

Chapter Ten

Mullaghmore, 9th August 1992

Even her mam had noticed Niamh was different. She glanced up from scribbling on the back of a shopping receipt to comment on how well Niamh looked as she was going out the door.

'It's great to see a smile on your face, Niamh,' her mam said, before going back to writing whatever verse she was conjuring up.

Niamh had seen Jesse nearly every day since their first date. Doing exactly what Brendan had warned her not to do. But she just couldn't stop herself.

Every evening, Jesse would come into Murphy's after work and have a pint of Guinness up at the bar, taking the whole evening over it. Waiting until her shift was over. Then he'd walk her home if the night was fine, which involved a great deal of kissing, often with a detour to his little attic room – although Niamh was mindful not to be seen by Joseph O'Reilly.

If it were a rainy night, which it often was, then Jesse would pick her up on the bike, with waterproofs for her to put on, and speed her home. Sometimes, he'd stay overnight in the shed with her.

Jesse awakened all of her senses. The whole of nature became their lovemaking. The fluttering of butterflies in the long grass by the lough, and the bright blue damselflies hovering over the still lake. The feeling of the water on their bodies as they waded in, the sun kissing her forehead as they lay down together, and the scent of the woods as they walked into the cool shade, quiet as they could be in case they saw a red fox.

Was being with Jesse so intoxicating because she knew it couldn't last forever?

The beginning of the change between Niamh and Jesse started the Sunday morning that Brendan rang to remind her of the border road rally and festival.

'What time will I pick you up?' Brendan asked.

'I'm not sure I can come now,' Niamh said. It was going to be a hot afternoon, a rare one, and she and Jesse had planned to go swimming in the sea out at Rosses Point again.

'You can't miss it, Niamh,' Brendan said. 'We need all the hands we can get hold of, and there's going to be bands playing. You promised.'

Niamh's body tensed. She knew how important promises were to Brendan. 'Okay,' she said. 'I'll be there, but you don't need to pick me up. I'm bringing someone.'

'Fuck, Niamh, not the American boy?'

'His name is Jesse,' Niamh said tartly. 'And yes, I want to bring him. His father was Irish.'

'I warned you not to get involved with anyone else,' Brendan said.

'You're not in charge of my life, Brendan,' she said, her heart thumping.

There was a pause.

'True,' he said, careful always, in case someone else was listening in.

To her surprise, Jesse was a bit nervous about going to the festival.

'But aren't there armed soldiers at the checkpoints?' he asked her, frowning. 'I mean, do you really want to go after what happened to your father?'

'It wasn't British soldiers who shot my father, Jesse,' Niamh reminded him. 'It was Loyalists dressed up as soldiers, remember?'

'But still, I'm not keen,' he said. 'Can't we hang out at the beach? Just the two of us.'

She wanted so much to say yes, but she knew Brendan would be raging if she let him down. Besides, she wanted to see if he'd asked Tadhg about her situation. It was a chance to try to do something about it. Especially if they all met Jesse. Saw how good they were together. Surely her father's cousin would want her to be happy?

'We have to cross the border all the time,' Niamh reassured Jesse. 'It will be good for you to see what it's like for people who live in the border counties.'

Jesse didn't look like he agreed, frowning and looking at her intensely as he chewed his lip. 'I'd rather go to Rosses Point,' he repeated.

'But I promised my cousin Brendan I'd help build the road again,' Niamh said, looking at Jesse with big eyes. 'We're doing something for the people in his community.'

'What's the point, if the British army just blow it up once you're done?' Jesse said, still resistant.

'That's exactly the point,' Niamh said, feeling a little irritated. 'It pisses them off. Come on, your ancestry is Irish, right? This is something small you can do to make a statement.'

'Not sure I understand the political intricacies enough to make a statement,' Jesse said, his eyes dark and pensive.

'It's not that complicated, Jesse,' Niamh said, crossing her arms, and for the first time feeling real friction between them.

'I'm sorry,' Jesse said, clearly seeing her annoyance and backing down. 'Must bring stuff back about your dad.'

'That's why I want to go,' she pushed. 'It's my duty, and besides, it'll be fun. There's live bands playing and there's always a great session in the pub afterwards.'

*

Before they got on the bike, Niamh gave Jesse instructions on which route to take and the approved checkpoint they were going to pass through. They were heading just south of the border, all the way to Monaghan, to join in rebuilding the Munilly Bridge road just outside Clones.

There were two soldiers at the checkpoint. Niamh and Jesse had to take off their helmets and tell them where they were going. One of the soldiers looked very edgy, his gun almost cocked at them, but the second one was more relaxed, especially when he heard Jesse's American accent.

'Where you from?' he asked Jesse.

'Cape Cod,' Jesse said, looking a little nervous.

'What are you doing in this backwater?' the soldier asked.

'Just curious,' Jesse said. 'I've never been to the north.'

'Nothing to see, mate,' the soldier said, turning to Niamh. 'Where're you going?'

'We've visiting friends,' Niamh said stiffly. 'In Rosslea.'

The soldier narrowed his eyes at her, and she waited for more questions. She hated the soldier and everything he stood for. This was her land, and he didn't belong here. Then to her surprise, the British soldier waved them on through.

There was already a large gathering at the crater site at Munilly Bridge. They parked the bike in an open field and followed the crowd. There were way more people than Niamh had expected. A makeshift stage was set up for bands in the field next to the cratered road, and there was a van selling burgers and chips. The early heat of the morning had waned; it was slightly cloudy. Niamh spotted Brendan with his distinctive red hair up ahead with a group of friends, most of them local – though a couple she recognised as mates of his from Belfast. There was no sight of Deirdre, which pleased Niamh. No matter how she tried to get on with her, the girl left her cold.

'There's Brendan!' she said to Jesse, and dragged him through the crowd to her cousin. Better to get the introductions over with right away.

She waved like a maniac at Brendan and he gave her a big grin, waiting for her and Jesse to catch up to him.

'There's a great turnout,' Brendan said to her. 'The lads have some big telegraph poles. And we've a digger coming, too. I reckon it won't take many hours to get the road up again.'

'Brendan, this is Jesse.' Niamh's voice was jagged with nerves as she introduced them. She felt Jesse's eyes on her in surprise at her awkwardness.

'How's it going?' Brendan said, deadpan. No hint he'd already seen the American butt naked in Niamh's shed. But she could already sense the hostility coming off her cousin in waves. What had she been thinking of? She should never have persuaded Jesse to come with her.

'So, does this happen a lot?' Jesse asked Brendan, evidently trying to be polite for Niamh's sake.

'What do you mean? The Brits blowing up the roads, or us building them back?' Brendan said, in an arsey tone of voice. Niamh wanted to give him a slap. For the past four years, she'd had to be nice to Deirdre, although she hadn't liked her from the minute she'd laid eyes on her. But she had done it, for Brendan's sake. Could her cousin not do the same for her?

'Well, both,' Jesse answered, clearly a little unsure of how to take Brendan.

'Well yeah, the road building has been going on since the seventies.' Brendan looped his arm around Niamh's back, the intimacy of his action in front of Jesse making her blush. 'All these blown-up border roads are our Berlin Wall.'

'It's not really the same,' Jesse said, his eyes on Brendan like a hawk. Her cousin gave her a possessive squeeze before turning to her, as if Jesse wasn't even standing in front of him.

'You told me his dad was Irish, Niamh?'

'I'm American,' Jesse said, staring at Brendan's hand on Niamh's waist.

'Yeah, I got that,' Brendan said, his tone sarcastic as he released his grip on Niamh.

She didn't even need to look at Brendan to know what he was thinking. In her cousin's eyes, Jesse was an ignorant American who knew nothing of their real lives.

No one said anything for a minute, but the tension was thick between the two young men. Luckily, one of the bands started up. It was a Wolfe Tones cover band and went straight into a very loud version of 'Come Out, Ye Black and Tans'.

'Come on, let's listen to the band before we help with the road,' Niamh said, dragging Jesse away from Brendan, who now had his hands in his pockets and his head on one side, looking at her critically as if to say: *What are you doing with the American eejit?*

Why did she always feel she had to impress Brendan?

After the band finished, they shared a bag of chips from the chip van, before joining the others at the roadside. Their job was to clear some of the debris with the digger so Brendan and some other men could drag the telegraph poles over the cratered road and build it up from there.

Despite his evident dislike of Brendan, Jesse worked hard. They flung their jackets down on the grassy banks of the River Finn, and got stuck in. One of Brendan's friends, Liam, passed her a joint, and she took a big drag before passing it on to Jesse.

A folk singer from Cavan, Dolores Sheehy, played her guitar and sang some old Gaelic ballads. Some in Irish, and some in English.

'Ah, I adore this song,' Niamh said, stopping in her work and tugging on Jesse to listen as Dolores began to sing 'Wild Mountain Thyme'.

For a brief while, it felt good. They were all as one, working together for a common cause. Niamh had always liked the border road rallies. Made her feel like she was doing one small thing to honour her daddy's memory. By being together, they were all safe.

It was late afternoon by the time the road was completed. One of the local men drove a red Ford Fiesta slowly across its wobbly surface to the sound of cheers all round. It wasn't going to be too safe a road, although the locals were determined to use it, but that wasn't the point. It was the symbolism of what they were doing which was important.

'Want to join us for a pint in town?' Brendan asked Niamh as she and Jesse gathered up their jackets.

'Let's just go for one,' Niamh said to Jesse.

Now they were all a bit stoned, and Brendan had seen how hard Jesse worked on the road, surely having a pint together would break the tension between them? Besides, it was rare that Deirdre wasn't around. An opportunity for Niamh to talk to her cousin without the blond girl listening in.

'Okay,' Jesse said as they gathered up their helmets and jackets, although the expression on his face told her he didn't want to.

As soon as they were out of earshot of Brendan and his friends, Jesse turned to her.

'Let's go, Niamh,' he said. 'We might make it back in time for a swim in the sea.'

'But we agreed to meet them,' she said.

'So? I doubt he'll care if we take off,' Jesse said, kicking his bike off its stand.

'No, he'll be really mad with me,' Niamh said, aware she was sounding petulant.

Jesse raised his eyebrows at her in surprise. 'Do you care that much what he thinks?'

'Of course I do, he's family,' she said. 'Come on, just one pint. Please.'

'Okay,' Jesse said, shaking his head.

They drove back into Clones. For a moment, she thought Jesse might keep going, but then he pulled in outside the Creighton Hotel bar, where they'd agreed to meet Brendan, Liam and a few of the others.

'You sure you want to go in?' Jesse asked her again, once they'd taken off their helmets.

'Just a quick one.' She kissed him on the lips to placate him.

'Okay, if you insist,' Jesse said, pulling her towards him and giving her a long kiss back. 'But I want to get you home soon, right?'

Niamh regretted her decision as soon as they walked in the bar, and saw Brendan and his group had taken over an entire corner. Their loud banter filled the whole pub – but Brendan had summoned her. She couldn't just go home.

There were already pints on the table for them, Niamh saw, as she and Jesse sat down. Jesse didn't take part in the chat, stiff by Niamh's side. Brendan and his friends were talking about football. Surely all boys liked football? But Jesse said nothing. Did he think he was better than them? Niamh shook the thought out of her head. He was just outside of his comfort zone. Didn't know about football, obviously, because he was American. She gave him an encouraging smile, but he returned with an unsmiling look. Despite the drink, Niamh was rigid with tension.

Jesse went up to the bar and bought Brendan a pint, but not one for himself, which somehow seemed insulting to Niamh. On his way back to the table, he leant down and whispered to her. 'We'd better get back.'

'Have another pint?' Niamh said. 'We've just got here.'

'I can't,' he said tightly, glancing over at Brendan, who was laughing loudly at one of Liam's jokes, though his gaze was on Jesse, cold and hostile. 'I'm on the bike.'

'We can stay over at Brendan's. You're off tomorrow, aren't you?'

Jesse looked at her, as if he was trying to tell her something with his eyes. 'No, Niamh, I want to go,' he persisted. 'You coming with me?

She should have known better than to bring Jesse with her. Of course he wouldn't mix with these people. She downed her pint and stood up, turning to Brendan.

'We're off,' Niamh told her cousin.

'Ah no, it's early still,' Brendan said. 'You'll miss the session. Stay for another. You can crash at the house.'

'Jesse has to be up early,' Niamh said. The first excuse she could think of, and she felt Jesse shift beside her at the lie.

'Well, that's okay,' Brendan said, staring right at her. 'He can go on. And I'll drive you back tomorrow morning. You can stay over.'

'Oh no, I should go,' Niamh began to say.

'Didn't you want to talk to Daddy?' Brendan cocked his head on one side.

Jesse stood waiting, holding his helmet in his hands. What should she do? She turned to look at him, begging with her eyes.

'Can you not stay?' she asked him.

'No, but you can if you want,' Jesse said gruffly. 'I know the way back, and it's still light.'

'Are you sure?' Niamh said, conflicted by her duty and her desire. A part of her hoping Jesse would insist he needed her to accompany him.

'Yeah, it's all cool,' he said, clearly trying to sound breezy, but Niamh could detect the hurt beneath his words. 'Nice to meet you guys.'

Brendan and his friends barely acknowledged Jesse's departure. He walked off looking tall and dignified in his biking leathers. Niamh wanted to run after him, but if she stayed the night, she had a chance to talk to Tadhg. It was an opportunity too important to let go.

As the session began and the fiddler struck up, Niamh looked down glumly at the contents of her pint glass. This was not how she'd imagined the day was going to end. Listening to diddly-aye music on the piss with Brendan yet again. She imagined Jesse riding away on his bike, dipping round the corners of the country lanes.

Niamh picked up her glass and slugged back the contents, before following it with a shot of whisky as everyone in the bar began to sing 'The Fields of Athenry'. This was where she belonged. She was a fool to believe anything else.

Niamh woke with a banging headache, curled up on the sofa in cousin Tadhg's house. Brendan hadn't even made it up to his bedroom and was sitting in the armchair, an empty bottle of whisky on the table, his mouth wide open in deep sleep.

She groaned as she stretched her stiff body. She'd been so drunk she couldn't remember getting back to the house, or ending up on the couch, but catching sight of an empty tumbler on the floor, she must have helped Brendan demolish the bottle of whisky. She sat up on the sofa, taking in the small living room. It hadn't changed in all the years she'd been visiting her cousins. Everything in tones of brown. Faded wallpaper, striped brown and beige, and the maroon-tiled ceramic fireplace. A picture of the Sacred Heart over the armchair where Brendan was sleeping, and the brown velvet footstool indented with the weight of cousin Tadhg's legs, which she'd used to sit upon as a little girl while she listened to him telling his stories.

She got up and perused the mantelpiece. All the same framed photographs. Brendan at the age of fourteen, with a mess of curly red hair, pimples, and the beginnings of a moustache, grinning like mad at the camera. A picture of his parents and her parents together at a lakeside picnic, before either she or Brendan had been born. Her dad and mam looked so young in the photograph, and so very carefree. Next to the photographs was a statue of Our Lady of Lourdes, which had been one of her Aunt Mary's most prized possessions, brought home from when she'd accompanied her sick mother to the holy grotto as a young woman. The room smelt musty, and in need of a good airing. It certainly wasn't as clean and tidy as Aunt Mary used to keep it.

Niamh dragged her feet across the living room and went into the kitchen. She leaned at the sink, filling up a glass of water and glugging it down in one go, before refilling it and repeating the process. She looked out the window. It had rained overnight, and her cousins' back yard and garden was lush with greenery, the mud glinting wet, puddles formed in tractor tyre tracks. She opened the back door and Patch the collie dog came trotting over, pushing her muzzle into Niamh's hand. This was her father's homeland. The place his father and his brother – Tadhg's father – had moved their families to from West Belfast in the fifties. Cormac Kelly had been born and bred down the road. It was Niamh's mother who'd grown up in Sligo, by the sea. Her daddy's home had been on this very farm, growing up by the bogs, woods and loughs of the border country.

Niamh wandered over to the hawthorn tree, which had been left untouched by her cousin Tadhg, despite the fact it was right in the middle of the garden. It was bad luck, her daddy had told her, to cut down the hawthorn. It was a fairy tree, and belonged to the Little People. He'd been dead serious when he'd told her this story. Her daddy, though a practical man, had believed in the fairies – as did most people where Niamh had grown up. She couldn't help wondering what Jesse from Cape Cod would make of the Little People. He was so different from her. She was stupid to think it might have worked out.

She closed her eyes and took a breath. The air felt thick and smelt earthy, heavy with summer weeds.

'There she is!'

She opened her eyes to see Tadhg walking towards her. He was using a walking stick, and she was shocked to see how much he'd aged since she'd last seen him.

'Well, how's the head?' Tadhg asked her, a smile cracked wide on his face.

'A bit sore.'

'Not surprised,' he said, eyes merry. 'The two of you made an awful clatter last night.'

'Sorry,' Niamh said, embarrassed she'd let herself get so drunk she couldn't remember their arrival in Tadhg's house. She hoped to God Brendan hadn't driven them, the state he was in.

'Not at all,' Tadhg said, lifting his stick and giving her a gentle poke in the ribs. 'It was great to hear a bit of a laugh in the house. It's been a morgue since Mary passed on.'

It had been a bad year for Tadhg. With no warning, Mary, his wife of thirty years, had died of a brain aneurysm the previous summer. She'd collapsed in the kitchen while making the dinner. Tadhg had rushed her to the hospital in Enniskillen, as Brendan was away at the time, but it had been too late. About a month later, he'd had the stroke.

He'd had it rough. But then Tadhg was one of the old vanguard. Despite losing his wife so suddenly, and his poor health, he was no victim.

'How's your lovely mother?' Tadhg asked now, linking his free arm through Niamh's. 'Still writing her poetry?'

Without fail, Tadhg always asked Niamh about her mother, as if they were the best of friends. But the truth was, her mam refused to talk to Tadhg. His enquiry was a pretence and they both knew it. She could hear a slight resentful edge in his voice.

'She's grand, yes, she's still writing,' Niamh said, thinking of all the scribbled notes on the back of shopping receipts littered around their house.

'She should come visit with you next time. Sure, I haven't seen her in years. She didn't even come to Mary's funeral.' He gave Niamh a doleful look.

'She's been very busy, with her job,' Niamh said, knowing it sounded lame. But Tadhg was well aware Niamh's mam would never come visit him. He was just playing with her, as he always did. Like a cat with a mouse. Waiting for her to speak the truth. Her mother blamed her husband's family for Cormac's death. Had never forgiven Tadhg in particular.

'It's hard to believe your daddy's been gone ten years,' Tadhg sighed.

Niamh couldn't tell if Tadhg was being sincere. When she was younger, Niamh had believed so fervently in his tears every time his brother's murder had been mentioned. She'd listened avidly to his rants on the injustice of what had happened. An innocent man, gunned down by Loyalist terrorists, and the Royal Ulster

Constabulary in collusion with them so the inquest had barely lasted one day. Tadhg had fuelled Niamh's fury. It was why her mam had stopped bringing Niamh up north to see her husband's relatives. But Brendan had kept up the contact in secret. Calling Niamh up, driving down and arranging to meet her in the woods when she was a teenager. Bringing her to visit his father. It had seemed perfectly normal to keep the secret from her mother at the time, because her mother's depression had been so bad. Niamh hadn't wanted to complicate her mother's life further. It was all her mam could do to get out of bed every day.

As Tadhg led her away from the house across the yard, Niamh wondered how much was for real. Did he really care about her?

'I'm glad Brendan brought you back last night,' Tadhg continued. 'I've been wanting to give you my old car for a while now.'

Niamh started, turning to look at him with astonishment. Tadhg gave her a wonky smile – one side of his face had shifted because of his stroke. 'You're such a good girl, Niamh. You deserve a car of your own.'

'No, really, thank you, but I can't,' she said. The last thing she wanted was to accept a gift from Tadhg.

'I can't be driving right now, and sure we have Brendan's car,' Tadhg insisted, leading Niamh around the front of the house, where his dirty white Toyota Corolla was parked up. 'You'll have to change the registration of course, to the south.'

'I can't accept it, Tadhg,' Niamh protested, wondering how she would explain the car to her mother.

'Think of it as a late twenty-first birthday present?' Tadhg chuckled, dangling the keys in front of Niamh. 'It's going to fall apart if someone doesn't drive it.'

She should say no. But then… Her own car! No more cycling in the rain, or trudging the lanes. She could nip into Sligo any time she wanted. Drive to Galway, all the way to Dublin. The car would give her such freedom. But she had to make sure it was what Tadhg said it was. A present, with no conditions attached.

'Cousin Tadhg, I need to ask you something.' Niamh licked her lips nervously. Her head was still aching and her mouth was dry to the back of her throat. The last thing she wanted to do was face Tadhg with her request. But this was her chance, and she had to say something.

Tadhg looked at her. The smile was still plastered on his face, but already she could see his eyes hardening. The warning.

'Did Brendan speak to you about me?'

'No, darling, what is it?' Tadhg said, still smiling as warmth leached from his eyes.

'I, well, you know, I might be leaving home soon,' she said, surprised by her own words.

'Is that so?' Tadhg said. 'Where're you going?'

'America.' She swallowed, not knowing why she'd said it.

'Well now, isn't that grand,' Tadhg said. 'We've lots of family in America. You'll be well looked after.'

Niamh's heart sank. Why couldn't she just tell him out straight? But inside her head were Brendan's words. *You can never get out.* Membership of the IRA was for life.

'I wanted to ask,' she said, stumbling over the words with nerves. 'Well, I'd like to stop.'

'Stop?' Tadhg asked her, his voice suddenly sharp, as Patch pushed up against them, sensing the sudden tension.

'Yes,' Niamh ploughed on. 'I don't want to be involved…'

'Darling, that's not up to me,' Tadhg said, his eyes wide with apology – but now Niamh could see his expression was fake. 'Sure, do you not know that?'

'Well, who is it up to?' she asked.

Tadhg shook his head. 'You'll have to ask Brendan,' he said, his face shutting down. The smile gone.

'But he told me to talk to you!'

Tadhg released her arm. 'Have we not looked after you all these years, Niamh?' he said, his tone sharp. 'We're family.'

'It's just dangerous,' she whispered.

'You knew that,' the old man said, shaking his head. 'Where's your conviction, girl?' He threw the keys at her, and they landed in the mud. 'Take the car,' he said. 'It's yours now.'

Part of her wanted to refuse, to go inside and shake Brendan awake. Make her cousin drive her home and then tell him she never wanted to hear from him or his father again. But she didn't. What made her bend down and pull the keys out of the muck? Shame, deep down, as she heard Tadhg's stick hard against the concrete on his way back into the house. What if Tadhg was right? Had she gone soft? Where was her faith gone?

She didn't turn around, and she didn't go back inside. What was the point? All she wanted was to leave.

Niamh wound down the window and let her hair blow in the breeze. She'd never owned her own car before. She should be elated, but this sense of freedom was an illusion. Her conversation with Tadhg had left her feeling even more frustrated. She wished she'd had the guts to throw the car keys back at Tadhg. Stomp away down their tiny country lane, and hitch a lift home. But she knew what the truth was. In all Tadhg's enquiries after her mother, he was letting Niamh know what she risked if she betrayed them. Her mam. Of course, she would never, ever inform. She just wanted out.

She banged the steering wheel with her hands. What had she done? Just made things worse. She put her foot down as the car gathered speed, racing to get away from Tadhg and Brendan. To put the brown house and those dark obligations behind her.

A she tore round a bend in the road, a checkpoint appeared out of nowhere. The soldiers on alert, guns raised because of her speed. She slammed on the brakes, her heart beating frantically. They lowered their guns as she screeched to a stop, the heat from her brakes stinking up the air. Her hands were shaking as she wound the window right down. She must never forget where she was, or who she was.

Chapter Eleven

Maine to Mullaghmore, 14th November 2017

Connor,

The ocean was always my safe place. All my first memories are by the sea. I could swim almost before I could walk. It was the same for you. I remember you saying it to me on our honeymoon. Why you loved surfing, because the ocean made you feel freer than you had ever felt your whole life. It was your passion and your love before you met me.

Of course, you surprised me with a trip to Hawaii for our honeymoon! You'd talked enough about going there and riding the waves, ever since the day we found out we both loved surfing. We could get swell in Maine, but not much in the summer, and fall was a bit cold. Sure, the waves were great for surfing in winter, but the payoff was extreme: icicles hanging off the end of your nose, and full head and body wetsuit. You told me you'd never surfed out of a wetsuit, that it was your dream to get on a board, in your surfer shorts, and slice through those big blue Pacific waves. I was excited too, but nervous to fly so far. White-knuckled the whole way, downing vodka after vodka. I don't like to travel. I told you that right from the start. If you wanted to be with me, then we'd stick where I grew up. I'm a homebody and all about family.

Once we had settled into life in Maine, you told me you liked to keep it simple, too.

'I get it, Lily,' you said to me, the first night we moved into our house, gazing at a shimmering sunset over the Atlantic Ocean. 'We don't need to go anywhere.'

I did wonder sometimes why you never went back to Ireland, or suggested we went together, but it was never mentioned. Since I hate flying, I wasn't going to bring it up. Did you resent me for it, Connor? Should I have pushed you to take me to where you grew up? I mean, you would have been there right beside me the whole way, holding my hand as the plane took off. You worked hard to get my parents to accept you as the man for me, and yet I never could do the same for you.

Back to our honeymoon, and after the terror of the long – oh, it felt so long – flight, we landed in paradise and it was all worth it. We were staying up on the northern shore of Oahu, in a resort called Turtle Bay and it felt like the most luxurious place I'd been in my entire life.

We couldn't wait to get out onto our surfboards together.

'This is where you and I belong,' you said to me as we paddled out on our boards. We'd only been in Hawaii twenty-four hours and your skin was already turning golden brown, whereas I felt so pale compared to all those Hawaiian babes. But you only had eyes for me. I will never forget the pure joy, the liberation of riding those waves that day.

Lying on the boards with our eyes closed, we listened to the surf, the crash and drag of the sea. Feeling the aqua reflections of light on water dappling our skin. The salty taste in our mouths, loving it every time we went under. Opening our eyes to see the magical underwater kingdom beneath the surface. Fish flickering by, the sea garden swaying on the bed, so luscious and wild, and the sea turtles slowly paddling past. The awe we felt watching them, as if they could impart some deep mysticism to us. In the ocean, we didn't feel human at all, but as if we belonged to another species, part mer.

Later, we rested on the beach, with the satisfied exhaustion of paddling, surfing and swimming underwater. At peace and at one, after we'd been spinning beneath the surface of the deep blue, staring into each other's eyes, tiny bubbles pluming from our mouths. You fell asleep, and I counted the bridge of sun freckles on your nose, admired your lashes – so long for a man – and your tender lips. I leant over and kissed you, and you grabbed me by the waist and rolled me in the sand. You hadn't been asleep at all, only pretending. We laughed, the two of us together, our bellies aching, as we pressed against each other.

In the dark, which descended early, we walked down the beach. The moon shone on the water, all the waves gentle now. We peeled off our clothes and waded in. Made love, tenderly, caressed by the soft tidal drag of water against our skin. The ocean was the beginning of our love, our marriage. But the ocean was also our end. Now I am frightened of the very place I always felt was mine. Because the ocean took you from me.

What were you hiding from me, Connor? Why were we never able to go back to your home and visit your grandmother, Rosemary? I hold the memory of my young, laughing, golden husband on his surfboard in Hawaii like an icon in my heart, but was that really who you were?

I remember the day after we went surfing, we took a hike into the rainforest. Let the trees close in around us, seduced by the colours and scents of all the huge luscious blooms. You wanted me to climb a small hill with you, helping me up the uneven ground when we neared the top. The view was incredible. Mist wafting through the treeline of the forest below us. The Pacific rolling into shore in the distance. We sat on a rock sharing a bottle of water, and you told me how you liked to climb mountains in Ireland.

You'd been so vague about your family back in Ireland coming to our wedding. I wondered if I should ask you about your grandmother, about your dead mother, and the father you'd always said you had no idea about – but I didn't want to break the beauty of the moment.

I am arriving in a foreign land on a quest for truth, Connor. But did I even ever know who you were?

Lily fidgeted in the airline seat and looked out the window again. They hadn't even taken off, and she was already a jumble of nerves. She took the packet of melatonin out of her bag. Her cousin Angie had said to take one just before they took off, and then get a glass of wine with the meal and that should knock her out for the whole journey. It was Angie who'd brought her to the airport. Her mom had gone crazy when Lily had told her she'd spent the money she'd given her on airline tickets to Ireland.

'But your dad isn't working, and nor are you,' her mom had said. 'Honey, we really need that money!'

'I need to get out of here,' Lily had said, the first sure feeling she'd had since Connor had been lost.

'Please forgive your father,' her mom had said. 'It wasn't his fault.'

'But it was, Mom,' Lily had spat at her mother.

She felt so hurt, so furious with her parents. Her dad for ignoring the weather warning, and her mom for standing up for him.

'You can't go to Ireland all on your own,' her dad had said to her. 'You've never even left mainland.'

'I have, remember I went to Oahu with Connor for my honeymoon? And I got my passport because I always meant to go further,' Lily said. 'I've always been the good daughter, working hard lobster fishing. Well, now I need a break.'

Her dad hadn't been able to look her in the eye. 'But why Ireland of all places, Lily?'

'Because I want to visit Connor's grandmother,' Lily had said. 'She needs to know what happened to her grandson, and I am not writing it in a letter.'

She had no idea of Rosemary's exact address, or second name. But how many Rosemarys could there be in Mullaghmore? She was definitely not going to mention the mysterious email to her parents. She was certain they would try to stop her going if she did.

'Look, you need to be with family right now,' her mom had said, her voice softening. 'The last thing you should do is go off on your own.'

'I won't change my mind,' Lily told her parents. 'I have to get away. I can't look out my window at that view any longer. At the ocean which took away my husband's life.'

'Running away is not the answer,' her father said. 'You're just putting off the inevitable.'

'I don't care,' Lily said. 'I need to get away from both of you, now.' She gave her dad a fierce look, but inside her heart was breaking. She missed her father so much. The man who stood before her was no longer the same person to her. It felt like he was pretending to care. He was a liar, responsible for Connor's death. Yet at the same time, she was frightened for him. What if he got found guilty of manslaughter?

'Take the bus then,' her mom had said tartly to her.

Her mom knew Lily hated buses, got travel sickness as soon as she sat down. A strange thing to happen to a fisher who never got seasick. But there it was: land and air travel made Lily queasy. 'I'm not driving you to the airport, and nor is your dad,' her mom had warned, hoping their refusal to transport Lily would stop her from going.

But all she'd done was to ring Angie for a ride.

As the sedatives Angie had given her began to take effect, Lily wondered whether she was running away or running towards the truth.

She woke up as the plane was landing. It was early morning in Dublin, and as she looked out of the small window, her chest tightened with anticipation. She'd actually done it. Flown across the Atlantic – and here she was in her husband's homeland. It was a grey day, and she could see it was raining, drops of water trailing down the outside of the airplane window. Her plan was to get a car rental and drive directly to the west of Ireland. It should only take her two or three hours. She'd slept the whole plane journey, so she felt okay, if a little groggy still. A strong black coffee would sort her out, then she'd get on the road.

Everything was so different. For a start, she had to drive on the other side of the road and use a shift gear. Luckily, she'd driven an old shift stick pickup of her father's a few times as a teenager, so it didn't take long for her to get used to it again.

At first there was motorway and that was fine, but it didn't last for long. Soon, she was turning off onto a smaller road, following her GPS directions towards Sligo. It was the narrowness of the roads which freaked her out, and how twisty they were, especially the closer she got to her destination. She had no idea what she was going to do when she got to Mullaghmore. But surely someone would have heard of Connor, and be able to direct her to his grandmother? She felt sick with nerves at the thought of having to tell her he was gone. Lily bit her lip, and tasted blood. The further she was away from home, the more illusory it was that Connor was gone forever. Her husband was fading, and the closer she came to Mullaghmore, the closer she came to the enigma of the man referred to in the mysterious email.

By the time she drove into the small town of Carrick-on-Shannon, Lily was so tired – despite the coffee in the airport – that she knew she had to take a break and eat something. She was just over an hour away from Mullaghmore, but the winding Irish roads meant she had to concentrate hard when she was behind the wheel. She parked the car on the outskirts of the town and walked back in, crossing a stone bridge over the River Shannon. It still felt so unreal that she was physically in Connor's homeland. Regret swept through her. She should be here with her husband, not on her own, broken-hearted and grieving. She took a breath, gulping down the tears. She couldn't start crying in the middle of the street in front of a bunch of strangers. She went into the first pub she could see, thankful for its dark interior. After ordering a coffee and a plate of smoked salmon and homemade brown bread, she sat down at a table in the corner and checked her phone for messages. A long one from her mom:

> *Hope your flight got in okay. Please let me know, Lily. I get you're real upset with me and your dad. But we only want what's best for you. You shouldn't be on your own right now. We should hear the outcome of the US Coast Guard's official report next week, and whether they'll drop charges or take*

*it forwards to trial. It would be good if you could be there
as part of the family. Love, Mom.*

Seriously? Fury coursed through her. If her mom was right
in front of her, Lily would be screaming her head off at her.
How dare she put that on her, when her dad was responsible for
Connor's death? The report was about his seaman's manslaughter
charge for the death of Connor, for *christsake*. What planet was
her mom on? She took a big gulp of coffee to try to steady her
irritation, but it didn't help. She'd never felt so angry in her entire
life. In fact, she was tempted to text a message back, and tell her
parents she never, *never* wanted to see them again. It took all
her restraint not to, and only because she knew it would make
Connor sad to know they were fighting.

Lily ate up her salmon and bread, then drained her coffee mug.
She went up to the bar to pay, but the bartender had disappeared.
Everything was so slow over here. She just wanted to get going.
Not only to find Connor's grandmother, but also to get to the
bottom of the mystery behind the threatening email. And then
what? Go back and be the dutiful daughter, working with her
daddy on fishing vessels for the rest of her life – or visiting her
father in prison for the manslaughter of her own husband? It was a
serious charge. He could even get more than three years, if found
guilty. She shoved an image of her dad in an orange overall out of
her head, connected back to her righteous anger at her parents.

'Hi, there!' she called out, and eventually, an old man ambled
out of the back room. 'I need to pay.'

She knew she was being abrupt, but she couldn't help it. She
had to get out of the pub, back on the road, before she broke
down completely.

She managed to keep it together until she got into the car.
Gripping the steering wheel, she gave out a low moan, and then

dropped her head on it. Tears began to stream out of her eyes. Her left arm ached, so red and sore. No matter what creams she put on it, the hives wouldn't go away. As if her body was screaming at her.

She couldn't do this. Who was she kidding? She hadn't just lost Connor, she'd lost her mom and dad, too. She had no one.

Come on, Lily. You're stronger than this.

It was as if Connor were sitting right next to her in the car. His voice felt so real inside her head. She slammed her hands on the steering wheel again.

'Don't you tell me that!' she shouted, not caring if people saw her shouting at herself inside her car. 'You lied to me for years, Connor!'

Connor again, in her head: *You're a warrior. I've always loved that you don't take shit from anyone.*

'But you've broken me!' she blazed. 'You left me, Connor! You left me.'

She slammed her hands again for a third time. The hard leather on the steering wheel hurt her palms, but she didn't care, because if she was feeling physical pain it distracted her from the pain in her heart. Then, as suddenly as her anger had swept through her, Lily was spent. She rested her head on the steering wheel, tears bubbling in her eyes.

'I just can't go on.' The words squeezed out of her mouth as if they were made of pins.

She lifted her head. Took one deep, shaky breath. She had to go on. Because she was all alone now. She just had to take one step at a time. The truth should always come out. No matter what the consequences.

Lily was calmer now. She felt as if a weight had been taken off her shoulders. There had been no one there to make her feel better. She had had to do it for herself. She wiped her face with a couple of tissues, took a sip of water from her bottle and checked Google Maps on her phone. There were three possible routes to Mullaghmore, but she selected the main road. It took her through the town of Sligo and then north, to a peninsula sticking out into the Atlantic Ocean. Mullaghmore was right on its edge.

After raining the whole way on her drive from the airport, the sun emerged from behind clouds and a rainbow filled the sky as Lily sped west. She negotiated the centre of Sligo with ease, crossing another bridge, and not long after leaving its suburbs, she began to see views of the Atlantic Ocean. The sight of the coast lifted her heart. The deep blue ocean soothed her as she lowered her window and inhaled deeply. Yes, she could smell the salty, seaweed tang of the ocean on the breeze, and it reminded her of home.

On the outskirts of the village, Lily saw the crescent of an empty beach with golden sands and rolling waves. She pulled in and parked. It was windy, with a fine drizzle – whether from rain or sea she wasn't sure – spraying her cheeks. She walked through the dunes and sea grass to reach the beach. Despite the cold, she had to take her boots off and feel the sand between her toes. She pushed her bare feet deep into the wet sand, feeling the satisfying weight of her body sinking, then lifted each foot up and walked towards the edge of the sea. To her right, she could see distant blue mountains, she guessed of Donegal. But then she looked straight ahead, across the cresting waves, knowing that on the other side of the ocean was Rockland and Maine, and her parents, lost and grieving too. She felt guilty for a moment, but then her anger returned. Not just at her parents, but at Connor for leaving her. She was the widow. The word made her shiver.

Spying a 'Vacant' sign outside a B&B in Mullaghmore with the appropriate name of *Seaview*, Lily pulled up and parked the car. The rain had returned, and despite the temperature being so much higher than back home, she felt cold as she walked up the drive and knocked on the door of the B&B. It was as if this damp drizzle had permeated her bones.

The door opened to reveal the smiling face of a woman with masses of curly black hair, and eyes the same colour as the ocean behind her.

'Good afternoon, are you looking for a room by any chance?' the woman asked.

'Yes,' Lily said, immediately feeling welcomed by the woman's friendly manner.

'Well now, we've plenty available,' the woman said, opening the door wide. 'My name's Noreen McMahon and you're very welcome.'

'Thank you,' Lily said, stepping across the threshold. 'I'm Lily.'

'Lovely to meet you, Lily,' Noreen said, bustling down the hallway. Lily followed her into a spacious lounge with spectacular views of the Atlantic Ocean. The room felt bright and airy with wooden floors, and big white walls covered in paintings of the sea.

'Would you prefer a room with a view of the sea, or at the back of the house, which is quieter, and less expensive?' Noreen asked.

Lily didn't even need to think about her choice.

The bedroom was quite large, with a big rectangular window looking out across the road to the beach she'd just been walking on. The sun was beginning to set behind the grey clouds, and shafts of golden light were beaming across the choppy sea.

'What a view,' Lily commented.

'I know, it's the best,' Noreen said, handing her the room key. 'So, you've your own en suite bathroom,' she continued, talking so fast, Lily was having problems keeping up. 'Breakfast is between seven and nine in the morning during the week, and eight and ten at the weekends. Are you just staying the one night?'

'Oh, no, maybe a few days?' Lily said, uncertainly.

Noreen gave her a curious look, but didn't push. 'Well now, I'll let you get settled in,' she said. 'Have you had any dinner?'

'No,' Lily said, realising that she was very hungry after her walk on the beach. 'Is there a pub or restaurant where I can get food?'

'The pub serves a good Irish stew, but you're welcome to join myself and my daughters for dinner.'

Lily felt a little awkward at the suggestion. 'I can't intrude on your family meal.'

'Not at all, it's just me and the girls,' Noreen said. 'They'll be delighted with the company. Someone other than their boring mam to talk to. Do you like fish?'

Lily smiled. 'Yes, I sure do.'

After Noreen left, Lily sat down on the bed and stared out of the window. She watched the sun setting, clouds lit up stacked orange and gold in the sky. She sat quite still until the sun was gone and darkness spread across the sky. She didn't move until she could only see faint glimmers of the sea caught in scattered moonlight from the crescent moon. She got up and closed the curtains, turning on the beside lamp. The room was all cream. Walls, carpets, and furniture. On the wall above the bed was a picture of a vase of lilies. She wanted to take it down. How she hated lilies.

Lily unzipped her suitcase and pulled out a sweater. She was freezing. She put her hand on the radiator, and to her surprise, it was hot, but the room still felt cold. On the bedside table there was a small card with the Wi-Fi code. Lily took out her phone and got connected to the internet before bringing up the email, which she had forwarded to her own address. She sat on the bed, the pillows propped behind her back and read it again.

Does your wife know who you really are, Connor Fitzgerald? I
don't want you to ever forget not one day goes by when I don't
want to get you back for what you did.

Lily stopped reading to scratch her arm. But the itching still
wouldn't go away.

You're not welcome in Mullaghmore ever again. So, don't ever
think you can come home with your new wife. Because if you
do, I swear I'll kill you.

The email was short, but every single word felt threatening.
Someone in this small village in Ireland must know who she was.
Could she even be in danger herself, perhaps, if this person was
monitoring her and Connor's lives? What had Connor done to
make someone want to kill him?

Lily hadn't driven around the village yet, but looking on a map
on her phone it appeared small. So, whoever it was, if they still lived
here, could be right next door, or down the street. Lily felt a clench
of anxiety in her stomach. Who had her husband really been?

Noreen's two daughters took after their mother with all the fast
talking, and, moreover, questions.

'Where're you from?' the younger one asked. 'My name's
Aisling, I'm twelve and I've lived in Mullaghmore all my life,'
she said proudly. Aisling had black curly hair and blue eyes like
her mother. She kept on staring at Lily, pushing her glasses up
the bridge of her nose, eyes huge behind them.

'Aisling, have some manners now,' Noreen said. The girls'
mother looked to be in her thirties, a young mother. She flitted
about between the kitchen and the dining room.

'It's fine,' Lily said, preferring to talk rather than to eat in awkward silence. 'I'm from America, Maine.'

'Is that on the north-east coast?' asked the other girl, whose name was Saoirse. She looked several years older than her sister, with long, straight red hair, and also wore glasses. As she spoke, she was texting on her phone, her eyes flicking up and down.

'That's right. Maine is north of New York and Boston, the last bit of the States before Canada. It's on the coast. Right by the ocean,' Lily said.

'Saoirse, would you put your phone away at the table?' Noreen asked her daughter.

Saoirse gave her mother a sullen look. 'Why?'

'Because it's rude,' Noreen said.

'Tell you what, I'll put it down, but on the table so I can still see it,' Saoirse bargained.

Noreen sighed and rolled her eyes at Lily. She was embarrassed, but clearly didn't want to lay down the law in front of her guest.

'So, you live on the other side of the Atlantic?' Aisling asked Lily.

'Yeah, that's right.'

'You could sail home if you wanted.'

'Well, it would take a real long time,' Lily said. 'But sure, yeah, I could.'

'So why are you here?' Aisling cocked her head on one side. 'All on your own?'

'Aisling is all about sailing,' Noreen talked over her daughter. 'During the summer she took lessons at the sailing club.'

'I want my own boat,' Aisling announced.

'My family has a boat,' Lily told Aisling, before realising in fact this wasn't true anymore.

'What's it called?' Aisling asked. 'Is it a girl? All boats are supposed to be girls.'

'My dad named her after me,' Lily told her, feeling an ache in her heart. '*Lily May.*'

The *Lily May*, their little fishing vessel, was gone for good. Smashed up into pieces by the fury of the Atlantic Ocean. Buried in the seabed, just like her husband.

'Oh, I want a boat named after me,' Aisling enthused.

'Ah sure, it would most likely be a dirty old rust bucket,' Saoirse teased her sister.

'Well, yours would be a manky rowboat with no oars,' Aisling countered.

Lily looked down at her dinner plate, at the pale pink flesh of her salmon steak, and her stomach turned. Her appetite for fish suddenly vanished. She turned to the tiny new potatoes, spearing one on a fork and popping it into her mouth.

'Saoirse, I told you not to look at your phone at the dinner table,' Noreen said to her daughter again.

'For God's sake, Mam.' Saoirse tossed her head in irritation, slamming the phone back down on the table and picking at her food, while giving her mother killer looks from under her eyelashes.

After a dessert of apple pie and fresh cream, Noreen's daughters cleared the plates and went to wash up, while their mother made a pot of tea. Lily could feel her jeans digging into her waist. Since Connor had died, she'd been sitting around a lot. Comfort eating. Not caring how she looked. She hadn't been out on a boat since, and the tough nature of their work meant she was usually lean. Noreen's food had been so good, though. The potatoes sweet and buttery, and the apple pie with cream melting in her mouth.

Noreen invited Lily to share the pot of tea with her while the girls disappeared into their bedrooms.

They had eaten in the conservatory, a small greenhouse-style extension on the side of the lounge, filled with house plants and a big oak table and chairs. She could see nothing outside the windows but black night, but she could hear the distant rise and fall of the sea. The sound was comforting.

'What brings you all the way to Mullaghmore?' Noreen asked Lily, pouring her out a cup of tea.

Lily considered spilling her story, but she couldn't bear to see pity in Noreen's eyes when she told her what had happened to her.

'Holiday,' Lily said, taking a sip of her tea and averting her eyes.

Clearly, it was a lie. Who went on a holiday to the west of Ireland at the beginning of winter, and on their own?

'How did you hear about Mullaghmore?' Noreen asked Lily, her face bright with interest.

'Oh, I just found it, I guess,' Lily said vaguely.

'It's a little off the beaten track,' Noreen said. 'Have you been out to Mullaghmore Head?'

Lily shook her head.

'Oh, it's quite stunning out there, you must pay it a visit, and Classiebawn Castle, too,' Noreen said. 'I could get one of the girls to show you around the village.'

'Oh, it's fine, thank you.' Lily didn't fancy either the constant chatter of Aisling or the surliness of Saoirse.

'We get a lot of tourists in the summer, but right now it's very quiet. I hope you'll not be bored.'

'Oh no, I like quiet,' Lily said.

After the chatter of dinner with the daughters, her conversation with Noreen now felt forced. She tried to hide a yawn, but caught Noreen looking at her.

'Sure, you must be exhausted.'

'Yeah, I guess I'm jet lagged,' Lily said, finishing her tea and standing up.

Back in her room, she turned out the beside lamp, pulled back the curtain and stared out the window. Out there, across the vast Atlantic, was home. But it wasn't home any more, because Connor was no longer there. She hugged her sides. Being here in Ireland was harder than she'd thought it would be. Everyone had the same accent as Connor, even a sort of look of him about them, around the mouth. The lips slightly parted, the ready smiles. Even the joking between Aisling and Saoirse reminded her of the way Connor had teased her sometimes.

Trailing back to bed, Lily got under the covers without even bothering to clean her teeth. She was tired now, from the journey, from her emotions.

As her eyes dropped, her thoughts returned to the author of the email. She wasn't going to give up until she found out who had written it, and why.

Chapter Twelve

Mullaghmore, 12th August 1992

Niamh watched from the doorway to the boathouse, hanging on to one of the old faded green double doors as Jesse worked. He was standing on a box and caulking the stern of the wooden boat with his back to her. She could see he put his whole body into what he was doing. Totally immersed and focused. Niamh found herself mesmerised by the muscles straining in his arms as he worked away with the caulking mallet.

As if sensing her presence, Jesse stopped what he was doing and stepped off the box. Turning around, he saw her standing at the door. She waved, gave him a smile, but he didn't smile back. In fact, his face looked taut.

Jesse put down his caulking mallet and wiped his hands with a cloth before walking towards her. She could see a fine spray of sawdust on his cheeks, and she wanted so badly to brush it off with her fingers.

'Hiya,' she said, feeling tongue-tied with nerves, and wishing she hadn't come down to the boatyard now. What should she say?

'Hey,' he said, but no more.

The silence was uneasy between them. Niamh felt her cheeks redden.

'So, sorry about what happened on Sunday,' she said, unable to look him in the eyes, staring down at the dirty boatyard floor.

'Yeah.' Jesse finally spoke up. 'That was weird.'

She looked up, surprised. She'd been expecting him to say sorry, too. There had been no reason for him to take off. Brendan had offered for them both to stay.

'What do you mean?' she asked, unable to keep the defensive note out of her voice.

'The whole thing,' Jesse said. 'I don't get it. Building the road, just so it would get blown up again.'

'That's not the point,' Niamh said, bristling, but Jesse had walked away and was washing his hands in the little sink in the corner of the boatyard.

She followed him, feeling a tight pinch of anger in her chest. She had come here today to say sorry for how things had gone on Sunday, but now she was shocked by his lack of empathy for the border community.

'Some of those people have to drive for an hour just to get to the other side of their own property, or visit their relatives,' she told him.

Jesse shrugged. 'Yeah, that's a pain, I get it. But rebuilding a road which gets blown up again the next day isn't going to fix the problem.'

She felt the heat rising in her cheeks. 'You wouldn't understand,' she said. 'You're not Irish.'

Jesse turned and looked into her eyes. She could see his disappointment in them. 'I didn't realise you were so political, Niamh,' he said. 'And I'm not.' He paused, still staring at her. His eyes looked even darker in the shadows of the boatyard. 'I really don't want to know about what's going on across in the north. It's got nothing to do with me.'

'How can you say that?' she said in a fury. 'Your father was Irish! So was mine, and he's dead because of the conflict!'

Jesse's face softened. 'I'm sorry, that was dumb of me,' he said, walking over to her, opening his hands wide as if in explanation.

'But we're from different worlds, you know, and your cousin Brendan was sure clear I wasn't welcome.'

Was he breaking up with her? Had they even been a couple in the first place? She wanted to shake Jesse up, she was so angry. Yet another part of her wanted his arms to wrap around her and help her forget everything. Like he'd been doing so well all summer. It made her more furious with herself than him.

'So is that it, then?' she said, crossing her arms defensively across her chest.

'It just got a bit heavy, is all,' Jesse said. 'You picked to stay with your cousin, not me.'

'But he's family,' Niamh blustered. 'His father's old and sick. I had to go see him.'

'Sure.' Jesse nodded. 'But you should have been straight with me before we set off, right?' He looked her directly in the eyes, and she flinched, because though he sounded calm, she could see he was angry, too.

'It's not my fault you were so stuck up,' she lashed out. 'Looking down your nose at Brendan and his friends.'

Jesse raised his eyebrows. 'That's not true, Niamh,' he said. His calmness was driving her mad. She wanted him to lose it. Shout at her. Tell her he was pissed off that she let him down. But he merely took a step back, placing his hand on the side of the boat, spreading his fingers upon its wooden curve. 'Brendan and his friends aren't my kind of people.'

'Well, then, nor am I, Jesse,' she said, turning on her heel, unable to look at him any longer.

She stormed out of the boat shed, hoping he'd call her back, or run after her, but nothing happened. She just kept walking to the top of the lane. When she got to the top, she took a quick look over her shoulder and was infuriated to see he had started work again on the boat. Not only that, she could hear him whistling.

Niamh stomped back home, ripping coarse stems of weeds from the hedgerows in her fury. Leaving a trail of them behind her on the road. She could feel a lump in her throat, tears beginning to well in her eyes, and she bit her lip hard to stop them. She was not going to cry. Not over this boy she hardly knew. Sure, they'd only been together a few weeks. He was too different from her, and it would have never worked. But while her head said one thing, her heart was hurting. She broke out into a run. She had to get home. The last thing she wanted was for someone local to see her so upset.

Inside her father's shed, Niamh curled up on the mattress by the window and buried her face in her arms. She couldn't stop the heaving sobs, her cheeks wet with tears that wouldn't stop. She was raging now. But not with Jesse, with herself. How could she have let her guard down? The relationship should have been a bit of fun, nothing heavy, like Jesse said. But she'd fallen for him.

She should have known things were too good to be true. She had learned nothing good lasts forever.

Chapter Thirteen

Mullaghmore, 15th November 2017

Just for one minute, when she opened her eyes first thing the next morning, Lily had forgotten. She'd always been a morning person, bright and cheery – unlike Connor, who could be quite moody first thing. In those first few seconds of consciousness, Lily stretched in the unfamiliar bed – where was she? – feeling refreshed and relaxed, before she suddenly slipped into despair. She was here in Mullaghmore, chasing the truth about her dead husband. Now she wanted to curl up in the bed and never get up. But she was among strangers and had to put a brave face on things. She took a gulp and tried to steady her breath. Today, she would find out who her husband really was.

When she checked her phone, she was astonished to see she'd slept for twelve hours, having fallen asleep at around eight in the evening. There was a missed call from her mom at around 10 p.m. which she hadn't heard. It was now the middle of the night back home. She'd have to wait until later to call her. Her thoughts immediately went to the Coast Guard's report. Had it been delivered early? Was there a case drawn up against her father? The idea of him going to trial seemed insane. He'd never so much as got a parking ticket his whole life.

Lily could hear sounds downstairs. The girls clattering up and down, calling down to their mother as they got ready for school. Lily took a shower, then dressed in her warmest clothes.

Blue jeans, and a pale grey cashmere sweater Connor had given her last Christmas. The rash on her left arm had calmed down after her long rest.

She went back into the bathroom and brushed her hair, tying it up into a ponytail, then changing her mind and taking the band off. She always had to have her hair tied up for work, but today she was going to let it fly free.

Downstairs, Aisling and Saoirse were sitting at the dining table, notebooks and pens littered across its surface. Aisling was scribbling in a notebook while eating cereal, and Saoirse was sitting back, scrolling through her phone while eating a piece of toast.

'Good morning!' Aisling said brightly. Saoirse glanced up at her and gave her small smile.

'Well hello, Lily.' Noreen emerged from the kitchen, rosy-cheeked and wearing a blue and white striped apron. 'How did you sleep?'

'Well, thanks,' Lily said. 'The bed was very comfortable.'

'That's grand,' Noreen said. 'Will you take a seat at the table now? Cup of tea or coffee?'

'Coffee, please.'

'Are you any good at maths?' Aisling asked Lily, as her mother went back into the kitchen to make Lily's coffee.

'Oh no, pretty bad,' Lily said.

'Well, you're no good then,' Aisling grumbled, chewing the end of her pencil.

'Don't be giving our guest such cheek, young lady.' Noreen tsked, coming back in with Lily's cup of coffee. 'So, what can I offer you, Lily?' Noreen asked, laying her place for her. 'There's full fry with eggs, bacon, sausages and toast, or you can have scrambled eggs on toast? Or we've lots of cereals, and porridge, too.'

'What about pancakes?' Aisling called out.

Saoirse rolled her eyes. 'She's obsessed with pancakes,' she said to Lily.

'I can make you pancakes too,' Noreen said, 'no bother.'

'But we don't have maple syrup,' Aisling said, frowning. 'She's American and you'll want maple syrup, right?'

'I can have them without,' Lily said.

'We have sugar, will that do?' Noreen suggested. 'Tastes good with a squeeze of lemon.'

'Sure, thanks.' Lily sat back at the table with her cup of coffee. Sunlight filtered through the glass roof and doors of the small conservatory as Lily admired all the foliage. Big pots of green ferns, spider plants trailing from shelves, and hanging baskets of brightly coloured winter blooms.

Aisling slapped her notebook shut.

'Done,' she said, looking triumphant, piling everything back in her bag. 'Mam, can I have a pancake too?' she called out.

'Okay, but don't be late again. Do you want one, Saoirse? Saoirse?'

The elder sister looked up from the phone.

'No, no.' She shook her head, getting up off her chair. 'I have to go.'

'Will you not wait for your sister, and walk to the bus together?'

Both girls pulled faces.

'Only if she hurries up,' Saoirse said. 'I'm not running for the bus like last time.'

As Lily took a sip of her coffee, she noticed Aisling staring at her hand holding the mug.

'Oh, are you left-handed?' Aisling asked. 'Because I am, too.'

'Yes,' Lily said, winking at her. 'All the best people are.'

'Is that your wedding ring?' Aisling asked, her gaze falling on the band of gold around Lily's ring finger. 'Where's your husband now? Why's he not on holiday with you?'

'Aisling, where's your manners?' Noreen said, bringing in a plate of pancakes. 'I'm so sorry. She doesn't think before she speaks, sometimes.'

'It's okay,' Lily said, her appetite waning as she felt Aisling's curious eyes on her wedding ring. She selected a pancake and placed it on her plate, squeezing a quarter of lemon over it. Aisling grabbed one after her.

Noreen sat down at the table and took a pancake. Lily noticed she was wearing a wedding ring, too.

'She's always asking guests private questions, so embarrassing,' Saoirse explained to Lily, sighing. 'It's because she wants everyone to know about Daddy and feel sorry for her.'

'That's not true.' Aisling went pink.

'Honest to God, you're mortifying,' Saoirse declared. 'Just so you have the heads-up, our dad is dead, okay?' Saoirse's eyes were sharp with emotion, and her shoulders hunched.

'Oh, I sure am sorry,' Lily said.

'Lily doesn't need to hear all this. Off to school, girls, you're going to be late,' Noreen said briskly, but Lily could hear the upset in her voice.

Aisling snatched up another pancake before running out the door, while Saoirse slipped her phone into her pocket and sauntered after her sister.

When both the girls were gone, Noreen took a big sigh.

'Oh, my goodness, sometimes I really feel I'm not doing too good a job.' Noreen turned to Lily. 'I do apologise.'

'They're great,' Lily said, nibbling on her pancake.

Noreen took a sip of her tea, and then sighed, clearly building up to something. 'Their daddy passed away three years ago, and well, it's been tough ever since,' she confided. 'The girls really miss him.'

Lily stopped eating. 'I'm so sorry,' she said.

'Finbar was only forty-one,' Noreen continued, her eyes swimming with tears. 'Too young. Sometimes we just feel like we have a great big hole in our home. Us girls need someone to look after, you know?'

Lily took a gulp of her coffee. Something about Noreen made it feel as if it would be so easy to talk to her. Easier than her own mother, for some reason. Was it because she might understand how Lily was feeling right now? Though Lily was terrified she might fall apart, she wanted so badly to tell someone.

'Actually,' she said, dredging up her own loss, 'my husband's dead, too.'

Noreen looked aghast. 'But you're so young!'

'It was an accident,' Lily explained, although in her head the phrase 'seaman's manslaughter' kept rolling over. She imagined how Noreen might react if she told her that her own father had been accused of killing her husband.

'I am so sorry,' Noreen said.

'Thanks,' Lily said, feeling tears begin to rise. 'I'm sorry, it's not been long.'

'Darling, you cry if you need to,' Noreen said, handing her a box of tissues. Lily wiped her eyes and blew her nose.

'So, how long has it been?' Noreen ventured.

'October,' Lily said.

'Last year?'

'No, just past,' Lily told her.

Noreen looked horrified. 'But that's only a few weeks ago. What are you doing here in Mullaghmore? Miles away from your family and friends? Oh my Lord, it's hardly a holiday now, is it?'

Lily shook her head. It felt so good to confide in someone, and maybe Noreen could help her.

'That's why I'm here,' she said. 'My husband was from Mullaghmore.'

'He was?' Noreen said slowly, looking at her in surprise. 'Well, I must have known him. Sure, we all know each other. What was his name?'

'Connor Fitzgerald.'

Lily saw it. A minute jolt, and a flicker across Noreen's eyes, before she spoke.

'Oh, no, I never heard of Connor Fitzgerald,' she said, looking uncomfortable – and to Lily's eyes, clearly lying.

'Are you sure?' Lily pushed the other woman. 'I really want to find his family. I know he's a maternal grandmother called Rosemary living here. But I don't know her second name.'

She saw Noreen hesitate, but then she shook her head again.

'No, sorry, no, he's not from these parts. I've never heard of Connor Fitzgerald or his grandmother. You must have it wrong.'

'Are you sure? His grandmother doesn't know he's passed away. I do need to find her.'

Noreen shook her head, biting her lip and not catching Lily's eye.

Lily was tempted to force Noreen further, accuse her of lying, but the other woman was already stacking their breakfast things up.

'I'm sorry, I've got to go out,' she said, stumbling out of the conservatory and back into the kitchen.

Lily sat at the table, feeling a little stunned by Noreen's reaction to the mention of Connor and his grandmother. She heard plates clattering in the kitchen and thought about following Noreen in, demanding she tell her everything she knew. That was how she would have done things in the old days. But before she had a chance, she heard the back door slam and saw Noreen walking fast down the drive and along the road into town.

It was all very strange indeed. But one thing Lily was sure of: Noreen knew exactly who Connor and his grandmother were.

Lily sat in the rental car, gripping the steering wheel. She felt so confused. Noreen and her daughters had been so welcoming, and yet as soon as she'd mentioned Connor's name, Noreen had changed. There was something bad the woman wasn't telling her. Lily sensed it. All she had to do was ask in the shop or the pub. Surely someone could tell her where she could find Connor's grandmother?

The rain was coming in off the Atlantic in sheets, lashing across the hood and the windscreen. She'd no inclination to get out of the warmth of the vehicle and traipse around the village yet. She turned the key to start up the engine and put the heating up full, as well as the de-mister. The ocean was calling to her. She needed to see more of this wild peninsula where her husband had been born and raised.

She drove along the coastal road around the head of the peninsula, stunned by the raw beauty of the coast. Back home in Downeast Maine, though their town was on the coast, an archipelago of small islands sheltered their little bay. Sometimes it wasn't possible to see just how wild it was far out to sea. Here, though, the land was a spit of rock thrown out into the Atlantic. Lily pulled up at a viewing point, astonished by the huge slabs of rock below, the frothing white waves crashing onto them. It was such a dramatic landscape. Breath-taking. She wished so much she was here with Connor, and that he was telling her a story about his childhood.

'Why did you have so few stories?' she asked him out loud. Was it her fault? Had their marriage always been about her, and her wants and needs, her family, her love of fishing?

But the sea was in Connor's blood too – you only had to take in this incredible view to understand that. In the distance, to her left, she saw the silhouette of a castle, looking lonely and abandoned. Behind it was a very distinctive-looking mountain. Flat-topped and blue. She looked it up on her phone. Ben Bulben. The name rang a faint bell. Yes, Connor had mentioned he'd climbed Ben Bulben once, she was sure of it.

Lily got out of the car. The wind was so strong, it nearly pushed her off her feet. Tucking her head down, her chin to her chest, she shoved into the wind and walked towards the cliffs. No one else was about. Just her and the wild sea, and her memories of Connor. If only they'd found a body, she could have had some kind of closure. Brought his ashes with her to Ireland, and thrown them out into the sea right here. But Connor was still lost in the Atlantic. Out in the big wide blue, all alone. The coastguards had been very clear with her. They would never find his body, because he had been lost so far out to sea. He would become part of the ocean. His flesh would fall away first, and eventually, his bones would come to rest on the bottom of the ocean floor.

The thought made her shiver. Her husband's bones, along with all the bones of other lost fishermen. She felt she should say something, a prayer, but she was beginning to doubt God, or anything divine at all. Fate and fortune. Being born under lucky stars. She wasn't lucky. In fact, she had to be one of the unluckiest wives out there. Widowed at twenty-four, childless, estranged from her parents, and no desire to ever set foot on a fishing boat again.

Hey, what's with the pity party, Lily?

'You left me!' she screamed out at the wind. 'Why didn't you tell my dad to turn the boat like I would have? Why'd you try to please him for me? Why?' she screamed again, the wind whipping tears from her eyes.

As she turned around to get back into the car, she realised that she and Connor never would have been in Mullaghmore together. There was some dark secret in this wild edge of the west of Ireland that her husband had never wanted her to find out. That was why he'd hidden the email from her. She should leave well enough alone. Pack up her things and go back home. But as she started up the car again, she knew she was never going to do that. She might never be able to bury her husband in a graveyard with a headstone, but she could gain some kind of closure by finding out who the man she married truly was.

Chapter Fourteen

Mullaghmore, Sligo, 21st August 1992

Summer was ending. As the long bright evenings began to fade earlier and earlier, Niamh's mam's light grew dimmer. Niamh sensed it coming. Like every year since her father's death, her mam's depression would arrive the week before his anniversary, and each day get progressively worse, so that on the actual date of his murder, she would be curled up in bed, monosyllabic. Over the years, Niamh had hoped it would get better. But it never had. She'd tried to talk to her mam about going to the doctor's. Getting some antidepressants. But she would protest, claiming no pills could fix her.

In the first three years following her father's murder, An Post had been very sympathetic, always getting in a temporary worker to cover her mam's round. But in the fourth year their patience had worn thin, and they requested she get grief counselling.

'Can you believe it?' her mam had given out to Niamh in one of her rare animated moments. She'd lit a cigarette, another activity she took up during her depressions, and took a long pull on it before proceeding. 'You don't get over a death like Cormac's. You never do! They're talking out of their arses.'

'They're just trying to help, Mam,' sixteen-year-old Niamh had said gently. More the parent than the child. 'Everyone's worried about you.'

'I'm just in mourning, is all,' her mam had said, hunching her shoulders and shaking her head as Niamh offered her a bowl of vegetable soup. That was another feature of the depressions. Her mam stopped eating all but the bare minimum. The weight fell off her, and it frightened Niamh how gaunt her mam would look after just a few weeks of this behaviour. No matter what Niamh made for her to eat, all her mam would nibble on was the odd slice of bread and butter with her homemade raspberry jam. Working through the jars every year, as if in memorial to the night her husband had been killed. Niamh, on the other hand, could no longer bear the taste or scent of raspberry jam because it brought back the horror of that night. Their sticky jam pots still soaking in the kitchen sink, the pots of fresh ripe red jam lined up on the table, and the scent of raspberries all around them, as she and her mam had clung to each other, sobbing at the bad news.

Ever since Niamh had learned to drive, five years ago now, she had taken over the post round for her mam on her bad days. It was simpler to deal with it quietly like this, and all the local postmistresses were sympathetic, and didn't let on to management. Nobody cared, as long as people got their post.

It was tiring for Niamh now, though, because she had to be up at five in the morning for the round, but most nights only got in from the bar around midnight at the earliest. She was only up for a lock-in at Murphy's on Friday or Saturday nights, when there were no postal deliveries the next day.

When the day of her father's anniversary dawned this year, unsurprisingly, her mam remained hidden under the covers. Ten years, and still Niamh was waiting for him to walk back in through the door with his fishing rod and tackle.

She brought a cup of tea in to her mam, but there was no convincing her to get up, so Niamh pulled on her mam's An Post shirt over her own jeans.

'Mam, I'm going to do your round,' she told her.

No answer. Niamh felt a little prick of fury. Part of her wanted to jump on the bed and yank the covers off her mam. She was being so selfish. But then, she knew it wasn't her fault. Her mam couldn't help her low moods.

Niamh was in bad form, feeling irritated and lonely. As she got into the An Post van, Pixie jumped onto the passenger seat. Against all regulations, Niamh pulled the door shut, letting the dog lick her hands as she turned on the ignition. She needed unconditional love today, even if it was from the dog.

The past nine days had been so bad. Mullaghmore was such a small community, Niamh had been certain she and Jesse would bump into each other, although the way things had been left she didn't know what she would say if they did. But the situation had never occurred. He was clearly avoiding her.

Each night at work, she'd hoped Jesse would come in to see her, but every time Joseph O'Reilly had arrived for his evening pint, he was alone. Last night, she hadn't been able to resist asking him about Jesse.

'Oh the lad's still working on that boat, *Grainne*,' Joseph said. 'He's obsessed with her.'

'In the dark?' Niamh asked.

'Well, he works until the light's totally gone, and then he goes to bed, so he can get up first thing in the morning,' Joseph told her. 'The boy puts me to shame, he's such a hard worker.'

Niamh turned the van around before driving out of the yard and on to the lane, yawning. Pixie gave a short sharp bark, making Niamh brake in surprise. Sitting on the drystone wall opposite her house was Jesse. As soon as he caught sight of her in the van, he got up and walked over. The sight of his tall, lean body, dark hair and beautiful face almost took her breath away. She wound down the window as the engine ticked over, her heart racing a little with anticipation. The scent of the new day rushed in the open window at her, the soft, lush damp of the late summer morning surrounding Jesse as he bent down.

'Hey,' he said. 'How you doing?'

She didn't know what to say back, completely thrown by his unexpected presence. Why was he sitting outside their house at five in the morning?

'I wanted to check you're okay,' he said, chewing his lip and frowning. 'Today,' he added, looking into her eyes.

'You remembered?' she asked, slowly realising why Jesse had made this visit today of all days.

'Sure I did.'

Niamh was blown away. She'd only mentioned the date of her father's death once to Jesse, as far as she remembered.

'So, are you okay?' he asked again.

'Yeah,' she said, blushing. 'Just, Mam isn't so good.'

'I heard,' he said.

They looked at each other. It hit her. Beneath all his aloofness, he did care about her.

'You want a lift to work?' she asked, feeling shy all of a sudden, not wanting to reveal her surge of feelings. 'You'll have to share the seat with Pixie.'

'Sure, no problem,' Jesse said, hopping into the passenger side of the van. Pixie wriggled in excitement before settling on Jesse's lap.

'I can't believe you remembered,' Niamh said again as they took off down the bumpy lane.

'I've always been good with dates,' Jesse said. 'It's my thing. Besides, I knew how important it was.'

She glanced over at him. He was looking down at Pixie, stroking her head and ears, much to the dog's delight. Niamh felt a sharp ache inside her belly. She wished his hands were touching her.

They drove in silence for a few minutes, before Jesse spoke up again.

'I've missed you,' he said, and now she felt his eyes on her as she drove. She didn't dare take her attention from the road, though she was longing to gaze into his eyes so badly.

'Me too,' she said in a small voice, as she swerved around a wild rabbit.

'I mean, what happened?' he said. 'We were having a lot of fun.'

'We were,' Niamh agreed. But she wished he'd said something more. Like he missed her because he loved her.

It didn't take long before she was pulling in by the boatyard. He couldn't just get out now and walk away. Surely something else had to be said? As if reading her mind, Jesse leant over and tucked a tendril of her hair behind her ear. She turned to face him.

Beyond the boatyard, out at sea, Niamh could hear fishing boats chugging out of the small harbour – but apart from the fishermen, everyone else was still tucked up in bed. It was so early, it felt like the whole world could be hers. Jesse leant in and kissed her softly on the lips, and she found herself kissing him back. Pixie pushed up between them, forcing them to separate.

'She's getting jealous,' Niamh joked.

'I think she's a little protective of you,' Jesse said, patting the dog.

'Say, the forecast for tomorrow is good; would you like to go out sailing in the afternoon?' Jesse asked. 'I've finished work on the *Grainne*. Joseph said I can take her out.'

'I hope not to test if she's seaworthy!' Niamh teased.

'No, she's totally safe,' Jesse said, proudly. 'It's my work, so she's going to be!'

'Not sure, I might have to be up early for the round, and then I'm working late in Murphy's,' Niamh said. 'I usually have a nap in the afternoon.'

'Well, you can have a lie-down on board…' Jesse's eyes glinted with mischief.

'I'm sure I can,' Niamh countered. 'But I doubt I'll get any sleep!'

Jesse had been right. The weather was perfect for sailing. Dry and warm with clear blue skies, the sea capped with light waves so he could let the sail out. Niamh had never been on a yacht before, and although it was small, it felt very grand to her. She'd tried to dress the part, in a pair of denim shorts and a stripy T-shirt, with an old panama hat belonging to her grandpa. She'd also brought a picnic: cheese sandwiches made with fresh batch bread, Tayto crisps, bottles of stout, and strawberries. As they set off, Niamh experienced a little flutter of nerves in her tummy. She had always been more a land-dweller than a sea-lover. Her safe place was the woods and bogs of their hinterland: hidden, mysterious and full of fairy lore. The sea was so open and exposed. But watching Jesse move about the boat, confident and lithe as a cat, she felt safe in his hands. She sat in the bow and surrendered to his expertise, feeling the spray of sea on her face, enchanted by the boat slicing through the blue ocean.

Jesse dropped anchor out in the middle of nowhere. When Niamh looked around, there were no other boats, and the coastline looked tiny and far away. Jesse spread a blanket on the deck as Niamh laid out their food and drink.

'What made you decide to work with wooden boats?' Niamh asked Jesse. She bit into her sandwich. 'I mean, aren't they dying out?'

'I've always loved sailing,' Jesse told her. 'When my dad and I were out on the ocean, I was fascinated by how it's possible to make this thing out of wood which will float and carry us.' He pressed his hand down onto the wooden deck of the *Grainne*. 'I love the shape of boats, and the beauty of the clinker design – simple, used for generations and yet still as effective.'

Niamh put her sandwich down and copied Jesse, pressing her hand onto the deck beside her and spreading her fingers.

'Doesn't she feel alive?' Jesse said to her, his eyes shining.

'I wouldn't go that far,' Niamh said, smiling back at him.

Jesse put his hand over hers and laced their fingers.

'What about now?' he said, looking into her eyes.

'Oh yeah, I can feel it now,' she said, hypnotised by him. He bent down and kissed her lips. The sun was behind him and for a second, she was dazzled by light – but in the next moment, the sun passed behind a cloud and she opened her eyes again. He was so close, she could see the texture of his skin, the tiny scar on the top of his lip, and the warmth in his brown eyes, their lashes long and thick.

'Are you tired?' Jesse asked her. 'Do you want to lie down?'

She nodded. He got another blanket, and pulled it over the two of them as he lay down next to her on the deck. She looked up at the blue sky, watching the seagulls circling, hopeful for food. This time she initiated, stroking his face, then his arms, and all the way down his body. She rolled on top of him, unbuttoning her shorts, and bringing the blanket up around her so they were wrapped up within it. They made love, slowly, meditatively, all the while looking directly into each other's eyes. Niamh knew she was losing herself in Jesse again. Dropping away all her guard. A voice in her head told her not to. But she just couldn't help herself. When she was with Jesse, she felt whole. As if he was bringing her back to who she really was. She squeezed her eyes shut. How could that be possible? There was no way back to before: deep down, she knew that. And yet the words tumbled out of her mouth before she could stop them:

'I love you.'

She saw him drink in what she'd just said. His cheeks flushed, the black of his pupils limitless, but he didn't respond.

Niamh shifted off his body and wrapped the blanket around her. She felt crushed. She had never said 'I love you' to any boy before. She picked up her bottle of stout and took a slug while looking out to sea. As always, once the sun began to fade, the cold set in. The boat's rocking on the water intensified.

'Hey, are you okay?' Jesse asked her, putting his arm around her shoulders. 'You're shivering.'

'It's just gone a bit cold, is all.'

Jesse reached up and put his palm to her cheek, so she turned her face to him. 'It's more than that. What's up?'

'Nothing, really,' she said, feeling herself blush.

'Niamh, come on, what is it?' He scrutinised her face.

'Okay, then, it's just… I said something to you, and, well… You didn't say it back.' She felt silly now.

Jesse said nothing for a moment, just looked at her, before reaching forward and stroking the length of her face. 'I've never met a girl like you before,' he said. The sea rocked the boat, and waves splashed against its sides. 'I just thought we were going to have a bit of fun, but it's more than that…'

'I know,' she whispered, looking at him from under her lashes.

'I'm so into you, Niamh,' Jesse said. 'It's just…'

'Just what?'

'My apprenticeship finishes in five days, and then I have to go back home to America.'

'Oh,' was all she could say.

'I told you right from the beginning, I'm on an apprentice-ship,' Jesse said, picking up on the look on her face. 'I've a job set up in a boatyard back home, and then I'm going to open my own yard, like I told you.' He looked flushed and guilty.

'It's fine, sure,' Niamh said in a small voice. She felt stupid for revealing her feelings, but she was also angry with Jesse. Why had he sought her out again when he was leaving so soon?

'Are you sure you're okay?'

'Yes, I told you,' she snapped. 'Forget it, okay? Let's go back, it's getting cold.'

Jesse hesitated, as if he wanted to say more. But what could he say? thought Niamh. He was leaving, and she was staying, of course. She would never escape.

Chapter Fifteen

Lily drove around the small roads of Sligo, making pictures in her head. The broken-down stone walls and boggy green fields were all part of her husband's childhood. The sorry-looking sheep and the herds of cows wandering on the beaches would have been common sights for Connor, growing up. That big sea with the crashing waves was his ocean. The same ocean as hers, just the other side of it.

Everything had been turned upside down. But Lily needed to find the truth. Find Connor's grandmother and the author of the email. Find out what the email had meant. Who had sent it?

The rain abated and the sun emerged as Lily drove along the coast road into Mullaghmore, past the sailing club Noreen had mentioned. She parked along the beachfront and got out of the car, already feeling a few curious looks as she walked back into the village centre. The first shop she came to was called 'Micky's Convenience Store'. She went inside. Her nerves were on edge, but she pushed them away.

There was a little old man sat up on a stool behind the counter. Surely he must know of Connor, or at least his grandmother?

'Good afternoon to you.' The man gave her a wide smile. Lily wondered if he was Micky, the namesake of the shop. 'How can I help you?'

'Good afternoon,' Lily said. 'I'm looking for someone by the name of Rosemary, whose grandson would be Connor Fitzgerald.'

There it was again: the pronounced flinch.

Micky gave her a good look up and down. 'Connor Fitzgerald is long gone from these parts.' His welcoming smile was gone, his expression chilly.

'I know,' Lily said, her voice almost a whisper. 'It's his grand-mother I'm looking for.'

'The whole family is bad news,' Micky said. 'Can't help you.'

It was the same story in the few other shops, and the pubs, too. Lily got more and more frustrated. No one wanted to talk about Connor Fitzgerald and his grandmother. In the last pub, she bought herself a packet of crisps and sat on the seawall, munching them angrily. She was just going to have to go back to the B&B and prise the information out of Noreen. She wouldn't leave, she decided, until the woman had told her everything she knew.

Back at the B&B, Lily marched down the corridor to the kitchen, but when she put her head around the door, Noreen wasn't there. It was just Aisling and Saoirse, sitting at the kitchen table. Aisling was doing her homework, and Saoirse was of course texting on her phone. The two sisters looked up in unison as she came in.

'Hi, girls, do you know where your mother is?' Lily asked them.

'Gone for messages to the shop,' Aisling told her. 'She'll be back soon.'

'Messages?'

'Shopping for food,' Saoirse clarified.

'Right,' Lily said, disappointed. She'd been so fired up. 'Do you know when she'll be back?'

'She's been gone a while, into Sligo, so I guess not long,' Saoirse said.

'Do you want a cup of tea?' Aisling asked Lily, as Saoirse got up to put the kettle on.

'Thanks,' Lily said. She couldn't help noticing the girls were so much more polite when their mother wasn't around, and seemed to get on perfectly. Both sisters still had their school uniforms on, but Saoirse had pulled her shirt out of the waistband of her skirt, and had a big cardigan on over the uniform, her glasses pushed up on top of her head. She had to be about sixteen or seventeen, Lily thought, feeling a stab of jealousy. Most likely she'd be off to college soon. By the time Lily was Saoirse's age, she'd been working full-time with her dad on the boats, and had dropped out of high school – much to her mom's fury. But the money had been so good, trapping lobster. What had Lily needed with more schooling?

'So, are you really on holidays?' Aisling asked Lily, as her sister placed a steaming cup of tea on the table in front of her.

'Don't be so rude, Aisling,' Saoirse gave out to her sister. 'That's Lily's private business.'

'It's okay,' Lily said. 'I told your mom this morning, anyway. I'm not here on holiday.' She took a sip of tea, staring down at the wooden kitchen table, tracing a whorl of its grain with her finger. 'I'm looking for my husband's grandmother. He grew up in Mullaghmore and he just passed away, so I need to find her.'

'But you're too young to be widowed!' Aisling blurted out.

'Jaysus, Aisling,' Saoirse said, looking mortified. 'Will you ever shut up?'

'It's okay,' Lily said, 'I know I'm young. He was fishing. Drowned in a storm.'

Aisling looked at her with round eyes, clearly desperate to say more, but holding back.

'I'm sorry,' said Saoirse. 'Our daddy died too, three years ago, from cancer.'

'That must have been real tough,' Lily said gently.

'I miss him every day,' Aisling said. 'But Mam says we have to do him proud. Carry on, like troopers.'

'Yeah,' Lily said sadly. 'What else can you do?'

'What's your husband's name?' Saoirse asked. 'If he was from Mullaghmore, Mammy must have heard of him.'

'Connor Fitzgerald.'

Saoirse frowned. 'I've heard the name; I'm sure I know it.'

'Well, there's a Connor Fitzgerald in my year at school, but he's only twelve, and he's not from Mullaghmore,' Aisling said brightly.

'Shut up, Aisling. Let me think,' Saoirse said, still frowning. 'Do you know anything about his grandmother?'

'Her name's Rosemary.'

Saoirse's face cleared. 'That's it! Rosemary Kelly's grandson was called Connor Fitzgerald. I never met him, but I heard all about him—'

'Saoirse, that's enough now!' Noreen came into the kitchen laden down with shopping bags, having clearly heard the tail end of the story.

'But Mammy, Lily's husband was Rosemary Kelly's grandson, right? Wasn't his name Connor Fitzgerald?'

'Enough,' Noreen admonished her daughter. 'Go on upstairs, girls, and leave us in peace.'

Saoirse looked furious, but obeyed her mother. She and Aisling gathered their books and bags and left Lily with Noreen.

'Would you like another cup of tea, Lily?' Noreen turned to her.

'No, I would not like another cup of tea,' Lily said firmly, annoyance rising. 'But I do need you to tell me what you know about my husband. His grandmother, too. I'm sick of people lying to me in this place.'

Noreen sidled away, looking shifty.

'The whole day, this town has been refusing to tell me anything about Connor or his grandmother,' Lily continued, hands on her hips. 'Every single shop and pub I went into, there were more of you people, lying to me. It's my right to know who my husband was. Now spit it out.'

Noreen clutched her hands, looking very worried indeed. She sat down at the kitchen table opposite Lily.

Lily felt a clench of nerves. What was this woman going to tell her? That her husband had been a serial killer? She looked that serious.

'I'm sorry I lied to you this morning.' Noreen's voice was gentle. 'But I felt raking up the past wouldn't make you feel any better. I do know who Connor Fitzgerald is. His grandmother, Rosemary Kelly, lives near Bunduff Lough, on her own in a cottage. She's a bit of a loner. I know you want to tell her about your husband, but I wouldn't go bothering her. Rosemary's had a lot of sadness in her life as it is. She's not quite right because of it. Away with the fairies, like.'

Lily didn't care if Rosemary Kelly was a lunatic. She needed to see her. It wasn't Noreen's place to tell her what to do.

'But where does she live exactly? Please can you tell me?'

'It really will do no good to go there,' Noreen repeated. 'Believe me, you're better off going home now. Being with your own family at a time like this.' Noreen turned her back on Lily and began to put her shopping away.

Lily was staggered by Noreen's attitude. She stalked out of the kitchen without another word. Back in her room, it felt as if the walls were closing in on her. She needed to get out, and besides, she was hungry. She certainly didn't want to eat with Noreen and her daughters again, not after the way Noreen had dismissed her. Lily sat down at the little dressing table and brushed her hair, which was a tangled mess after walking along the cliffs.

She applied a little make-up to pick herself up, but the face which stared back at her still looked washed out and miserable. Her black hair, which normally hung smooth and silky, was all messed up and frizzy because of the damp weather. She examined her sore arm, the skin still red and angry. She took a breath. So what if she looked like shit? She couldn't give a crap right now. She was going back into the village to get to the bottom of the mystery surrounding her husband.

Outside, the wind had dropped, but the drizzly rain had returned. She put her hood up and walked down the road into the village. In the mist, she could see boats bobbing up and down in the little walled harbour. The sound of the clinking rigging made her feel a little homesick. She passed the boats, heading into a pub which faced out onto the harbour. It was early still, and the bar was practically empty, but they served food. She ordered a vodka and Coke, and fish and chips.

While she ate her food, more locals came into the bar. Mostly guys. Like in Moll's Bar back home, these were working men, coming in for their daily pint before they headed home. The TV went on so they could all watch a soccer match, but even so, Lily could see some of the men glancing over at her. A stranger, and a woman. She didn't belong in here. Some of those men were Connor's age. Surely they would have known him?

She left her table, slipped onto a high stool at the counter and ordered another vodka and Coke. She could feel some of the men tense around her. Well, let them feel awkward. She had every right to sit up at this bar. Besides, she was used to the company of men, being the only woman who fished alongside the men at home. In fact, hearing the banter amongst the guys made her feel quite relaxed. Nobody got too personal. She looked up to watch the football game – which wasn't, as it turned out, soccer. The players looked a bit like they were playing hockey, but it was way wilder.

'Who d'you want to win?' A guy had sidled up beside her. He was extremely good-looking in a Colin Farrell way, with blue eyes, unruly black hair, and dark stubble.

'Oh, I don't know who's playing,' Lily said. 'In fact I don't even know what they're playing.'

The guy grinned at her. 'The great Irish sport of hurling,' he informed her.

'It looks very rough,' she commented, watching one of the players bash another. In America, they'd have helmets on at least, and so much padding they would all look like the Incredible Hulk.

'That it is,' her new companion agreed. 'Never took to it too much, preferring not to risk brain damage, but my brother over there, well, he used to play for the county.' He pointed to the back of a man in a blue checked shirt who was standing with his arms crossed, watching the game with a few of the others.

'So, who do you want to win?' Lily asked.

'Sligo, naturally,' the man said. 'The other team's Kilkenny, so it's not looking likely. Sure, we're getting battered.' He took a sip of his pint. 'My name's Daniel, by the way. Can I get you a drink?'

'Lily,' she said, draining her vodka and Coke. 'Okay. I've never drunk Guinness. Is it good?'

'Well now, I'm an Irishman so it's in my blood, but you'll get the best pint of the black stuff in the whole of Sligo in this here pub, so,' he said, waving over at the barman.

Lily had meant to have half a pint of Guinness – or a glass, as Daniel called it – but he was having none of it and insisted she have a pint. The first couple of sips of the drink made her feel better, numbing her heartache and confusion.

'Where're you from?' Daniel asked her.

'Rockland, a small fishing town on the coast of Maine,' Lily told him. 'How about you? Did you grow up here?'

'Spent my whole life in this godforsaken boghole,' Daniel said, taking another slug of his pint. He drank fast, and Lily found herself doing the same to keep up with him.

'I wouldn't call it a godforsaken boghole,' Lily said. 'It's so beautiful here.'

'More beautiful than Maine?'

'Well, not more, just different,' she said. 'I guess our towns are prettier, especially our houses, but your landscape is very dramatic.'

'Did you grow up in your little town in Maine, Lily?'

'Yeah, I sure did,' she said.

'And what do you do back in Rockland?' Daniel asked.

Was he flirting with her? Really, she didn't care if he was or not. She'd no interest in him, but it was good to talk to someone who didn't know her sad story. 'I lobster fish,' Lily said. 'Been doing that my whole life.'

'For real?' Daniel said, looking impressed.

'Yeah, I'm the only woman who does it in our town. It's mostly the guys, but I always loved going out with my dad, so I just carried on from there.'

'Cool,' Daniel said, ordering them more pints. 'I have to say, I do love crustaceans.'

Lily raised her eyebrows. Was he trying to be funny? 'What about you?'

Daniel shrugged. 'I work on the family farm.'

'What kind of farm is it?'

'It's a pig farm,' Daniel said, looking a bit rueful.

'Oh,' Lily said. She'd never liked eating pork, and found the idea of a pig farm rather unpleasant.

'But, Lily, I'm not a pig farmer in my heart,' Daniel said. 'I'll have you know, I used to be in a band.'

'What did you play?'

'I was the lead singer,' Daniel said. 'And you know, we were quite good, back in the day.'

The hurling game ended. As Daniel had predicted, Sligo had lost. As the bar began to empty out, Daniel's brother came over to join them.

'Hey, this is Lily, Sean,' Daniel introduced her. 'Lily is from Maine.'

Sean gave her a distinctly unfriendly look, before turning to his brother. 'Come on, Daniel, we've to be up early tomorrow morning.'

'Ah, you go on, Sean, I'll be up shortly.'

Sean frowned. 'Don't drive, will you?'

'No, sir.' Daniel gave a mock salute. 'I shall get Jimmy, our local taxi driver, to chariot me home.'

Lily wasn't imagining it – there was a distinct chill between the two brothers.

After Sean had left, Lily made to leave. 'I think I should be going, too,' she said. 'I've had way too much to drink.'

'Ah sure, let's have one for the road,' Daniel persuaded her.

Was it the last drink which tipped her over the edge? One minute, Lily was about to go, and the next, when she looked at her phone, an hour had passed. There were two missed calls: one from her mom and the other from her dad. Damn, she'd meant to ring her mom back earlier – but she couldn't very well do it now, drunk. As for her dad, she still didn't want to talk to him.

'What brings you to Mullaghmore at the shittiest time of year?' Daniel asked her.

Lily considered lying, but she'd come all this way to find Connor's family, and Daniel might have known him. They were around the same age. The fact that Noreen had told her it would do her no good to find out the truth made her feel even more determined to do just that.

'I'm looking for my husband's family,' she said.

'Oh.' Daniel, though very drunk, looked a bit taken back. 'Sorry, I'd assumed you weren't married.'

She raised her hand, showed him her ring.

'Right,' he said. 'Well now, sorry for shamelessly flirting with you all night. But where's your husband?'

Lily leant forward, teetering on the high stool. Every time she told someone Connor was dead, it felt like it was less real. 'He died. That's why I'm here, because I need to find his grandmother and tell her what's happened to her grandson.' Her words were all slurred together.

'Oh fuck, sorry,' Daniel said, looking very uncomfortable.

'Would you have heard of Connor Fitzgerald?' Lily asked.

There it was again, the same flinch she'd seen in Noreen earlier: the flicker of recognition in the eyes, and then shut down.

'Nope, can't say I have,' said Daniel, draining his pint. 'Are you sure he's from these parts?'

'Yes,' Lily said. 'Yes, I'm sure. What about his grandmother? Rosemary Kelly?'

'No, nope,' Daniel said, slipping off his stool, his gaze suddenly shifty. 'Don't know her. Look, Lily, they're closing up the bar. We'd best be going.'

'Ah God, already?' she said, slumping her elbows on the bar.

'Well, come on, so.' Daniel tugged at her gently. 'I feel responsible for getting you hammered. I'd best walk you back to your B&B before I call upon the services of Jimmy.'

It had stopped raining and the moon lit a path as they made their way down the road and past the harbour. The ocean was silvery with moonlight.

'See how beautiful the ocean can be,' Lily said 'And then, bam – all of sudden, she's a bitch. Swallows you up. That's what happened to Connor, you know? He was drowned and they never found his body.'

'Sorry, that's rough, Lily,' Daniel said, taking her arm as she swayed.

'Connor told me nothing about his family in Ireland. Like, zero.'

'Maybe there's a good reason for that,' Daniel suggested.

Lily stopped walking, stared up at the stars. She had never felt so desolate. 'I miss him so much,' she said. 'Real bad. I don't know how to live without him.' The stars were shifting above her head. All the Guinness and vodka she'd drunk was making her feel as if she had become detached from herself. She tottered forward, slamming into Daniel, who took her by the shoulders to straighten her up.

Before she knew it, she and Daniel were kissing. She wasn't sure whether he had made the first move, or she had. For a moment, she tried to lose herself in the arms of another man. He'd slipped his hand inside her coat, placing it on her left breast, as if feeling her heart, and it was turning her on. Part of her wanted to let her body go, so her mind could be lost, too – but then she felt his other hand move to her waist, and all of a sudden it felt so wrong. She pushed him away.

'No, no. What am I doing?'

'I'm sorry,' Daniel said, stepping back so his face was in darkness. 'I shouldn't have taken advantage. It's just… You're very beautiful.'

'No, no,' Lily said, hiccupping, waving her hands at him to get him away.

'I'm really sorry to tell you this. But oh God, Lily, you should leave Mullaghmore. My brother Sean's not someone to be messed with.'

'What do you mean? Why would I be messing with Sean? What's he got to do with this?' Lily pushed through the fog of her inebriation to take in what Daniel was saying. 'You've got to tell me… Did you know Connor?'

But Daniel just shook his head at her.

'I'm sorry,' he said again, before turning around and walking away.

Lily was frozen in shock. Knew she should run after him, demand he explain what he meant – but all she could think about was the fact she'd kissed another man. Besides, she could hardly walk, let alone run after Daniel.

As she stood there, a car came flying towards her, its headlights blinding her. She jumped out of its way just in time. Had the driver seen her? The car went tearing on down the road; she couldn't even make out what kind it was. Feeling a little uneasy on the dark road all alone now, she staggered as fast as she could back up the steep hill to the B&B.

Fumbling with the key, breathless, she managed to open the front door as quietly as possible. The last thing she wanted was to wake Noreen up and for her to see her drunk.

Inside her bedroom, she curled up on top of the covers, shivering, not even bothering to get undressed. She hugged her sides, trying to make herself as small as possible. She ached for Connor's touch. No other man felt the same. She felt sick at herself for having kissed Daniel. But what had his warning meant? In particular, his reference to his hostile brother, Sean? What had Connor left behind, and what had she walked into?

Chapter Sixteen

Mullaghmore, 23rd August 1992

The day after the boat trip with Jesse, Niamh's mam got out of bed. As if the passing of her husband's anniversary had lifted the weight off her shoulders for another year. While Niamh was making her 5 a.m. cup of tea, feeling even more exhausted than the day before, her mam appeared in the kitchen, dressed in her An Post uniform. Without a word, she took the van keys off the dresser – much to Niamh's relief. Kissing her daughter on the head, she left the cottage wordlessly, after which Niamh trooped back upstairs with Pixie at her heels. The two of them got onto her bed and Niamh crashed out immediately, Pixie curled up next to her.

That afternoon and the next, Niamh's mam was still quiet, shut away in the front room, scribbling on pieces of paper. Niamh could hear the typewriter clacking as she made dinner. But by Tuesday, her mam had totally rallied. When Niamh got up at lunchtime, she found her mam standing at the stove, making lentil soup.

'I haven't seen the American boy in a while,' her mam commented, putting a bowl of the spicy soup down in front of Niamh.

'He's leaving,' Niamh told her mam, her voice tight with emotion. 'In two days.'

'Ah that's an awful pity,' her mam said, giving her a sympathetic look. 'But why don't you make the most of it? What are you doing, moping here with me?'

After their boat trip, Niamh had tried to put distance between herself and Jesse. She'd opened up her heart to him, only to discover her feelings were pointless. He was leaving. As soon as they'd hit dry land, she'd broken it off with him. *Just as well*, she kept telling herself. It would never have worked out. The trip up north had clearly shown that. Yet at night, she couldn't sleep for thinking of him.

Now her mam was back on form, she wanted to make it up to Niamh, see her daughter happy. 'Well, Niamh, you may as well make the most of his last two days, don't you think?' she said, ladling her own soup into a bowl. 'Go on down to that boatyard of Joseph O'Reilly's and say a proper goodbye.'

Niamh blushed. Her mam could be so strange sometimes. Very modern in her ideas, and yet resolute in her fidelity to her dead husband. The two of them were women who felt keenly. Her mam, of all people, knew that. And yet here she was, pushing her daughter out of the door towards heartache.

It was a wet August day, rain bucketing down, dripping off all the dense foliage as Niamh drove down the laneway towards Mullaghmore. She'd no idea what she was going to say to Jesse when she saw him, but her mam had a point. Things hadn't ended right between them.

Jesse wasn't in the boatyard. Niamh felt a little stab of panic as she knocked on Joseph's door. Had he left already? There was no sign of his bike. Jesse still wasn't coming into Murphy's and anyway, she'd been off the past two nights.

'Well hello, Niamh,' Joseph said as he opened the door. 'How are you? How's your mam?'

'Grand, thanks,' Niamh said, feeling a little awkward. 'Is Jesse home?'

'Ah no, he's gone to sell his bike,' Joseph said. 'I'm about to pick him up. He just rang me. Want to come?'

'Well, I could go get him myself,' Niamh suggested, indicating her old Toyota Corolla.

'I didn't know you had a car now, Niamh,' Joseph said.

'My father's cousin gave it to me,' Niamh said. 'I've just got it registered down south.'

'Well, it would be great so if you could go get him,' Joseph said. 'I've a lot of work. Especially now the lad is off back home.'

Jesse had found a buyer for his bike in Strandhill, on the other side of Sligo. Joseph told Niamh which pub he was waiting in, giving her a wink as he did so. Mortified, Niamh wondered if Joseph had ever seen her sneaking into Jesse's attic bedroom – or even worse, heard them.

The drive took Niamh along the coast, the sea obscured by grey clouds and mist as the rain swept in off the Atlantic. She could smell it, though, even from inside the old Toyota. The scent of seaweed, and the dampness of sea grass and wet sand dunes falling all the way down to stony strands. It settled her nerves a little as she kept taking deep breaths in.

She pulled in on the seafront at Strandhill. The car park was deserted. She sat for a moment, looking at the surf crashing upon the shore. One lone surfer in a wetsuit was struggling to ride the waves. Her heart was thumping in her chest. What if Jesse was over her already?

She needn't have been so anxious. As soon as Jesse looked up from his corner table in the bar and saw her walking towards him, he gave her a huge smile.

'Hope you don't mind, I told Joseph I'd come get you,' she said.

'Not at all,' Jesse said, beaming.

'Look,' Niamh said, standing in front of him. 'I know you're heading off in two days, but let's just make the most of it.'

'Sure.' Jesse stood up, holding out his hand to her.

It felt so good to be in his arms again. She inhaled his scent deeply, taking in his presence, letting her skin awaken with his touch.

They drove to Mayo, even further south and away from home. Through the Iron Mountains and along the ragged coast, until they were out on a spit of land. The rain had stopped, and late afternoon sun burst through the clouds. Niamh parked the car and they looked down at the changing colours of the sea. The clouds' reflections moved across the surface of the water, and Niamh imagined they were whales or fantastical sea creatures emerging from the depths beneath.

They got out of the car. Ran down to the beach together, then walked its length holding hands, letting the wind sweep past them.

Later, down the dead end of a tiny boreen, hidden from view by overgrown hedgerows, they made love in Niamh's car. The two of them entwined under a tweed blanket on the back seat, Jesse cradling her head, looking at her with adoration. Niamh tried to imprint the memory in her mind. What was it her mam sometimes said to her? *Everything passes.* Joy. Grief. But her mam had held on tight to her grief all these years – why couldn't Niamh possess this joy for a little bit longer?

As the light faded and they pulled their jeans back on, Niamh couldn't help feeling a little cheated. It just wasn't fair that he was leaving. But there was no point blaming Jesse.

'You got anything to eat?' Jesse asked her as he buttoned up his shirt, his dark hair tousled.

She clambered into the front of the car and opened up the glove compartment. Finding a KitKat, she broke it in half. 'Here you go, dinner for two,' she said, trying to sound cheerful.

Jesse joined her in the front of the car and they munched on their chocolate.

'Say, why don't you come out to Cape Cod?' Jesse said as he polished off his last bite of KitKat.

'I can't afford the flight on my wages.'

'I've some money, I can buy your flights,' Jesse suggested. 'You'll get work in a bar easy back home. They love the Irish accent.'

Niamh turned to him in astonishment. This was the last thing she had expected Jesse to say. 'I thought this was supposed to be casual?' she said, spreading her hands to indicate the two of them. 'You made that clear the other day.'

Jesse looked at her from under his dark lashes, and his expression made her stomach clench with desire. 'I know.' He paused and chewed his lip. 'But I sure have missed you these the past few days. And, well, I guess I do love you, too.'

She was so shocked, she just stared at him open-mouthed.

'I'm sorry if I hurt you,' he said, picking up her hand. 'But come to America with me, Niamh.'

'What, now?' She looked at him, incredulous.

'Yes, why not? We can go to the travel agency in Sligo tomorrow. Get your tickets and then take the train together up to Dublin. My flight is the following evening.'

'A friend's sister lives in Dublin, we can stay the night with her,' Niamh found herself saying.

Jesse grabbed both her hands, looking excited. 'So you'll come?'

Niamh was dizzy with confusion. 'Don't I need a visa?'

'We can get you a holiday one at the American Embassy in Dublin,' Jesse said. 'I rang them up.'

'You did?' Niamh whispered in awe. 'But my job?'

'Come on, Niamh,' Jesse cajoled her. 'You can do better than Murphy's.'

She wanted to say yes so badly, but ever present in her mind lurked the thought of Brendan and Tadhg. They had family in America. Could she really get away from it all? Would Tadhg send people after her? Surely not – she wasn't important enough, was she? Of course they'd let her go.

'So, is it a yes?' Jesse was saying, squeezing her hands, looking so much younger than his age. Like a kid excited for Christmas.

'What about my mam?' Niamh said, feeling the weight of her mother's moods pressing down on her.

'She won't hold you back, surely?' Jesse said. 'Your mom is cool.'

'She needs me.' Niamh struggled, too loyal to tell Jesse about her mam's terrible depressions. How would she cope without her daughter? And yet Jesse was right. She knew her mam would be the first to tell her to go. Live her life. Get away from the past, from Ireland. Had she even suspected this might happen? Was that why she'd sent Niamh off to see Jesse today?

'Niamh,' Jesse said, pressing her hand to his lips. 'You need to get out of here.'

She looked into his eyes, and knew he was right.

Chapter Seventeen

Mullaghmore, 16th November 2017

It felt as if she'd never had such a bad hangover in her entire life. Halfway through the night, Lily stumbled across her bedroom and into the bathroom to throw up. Feeling a little better for this, she drank glass after glass of water from the bathroom tap and brushed her teeth, only to throw up again. The vomiting continued for an hour or more, until eventually, spent, she curled up in bed and fell unconscious.

When she woke, shame swept across her and she burst into tears. She pulled the covers over her head and tried to quieten her sobbing. She didn't want Noreen or her girls to hear her.

As the tears began to slow, she clenched her jaw. She couldn't give up. In her heart, she knew she'd never lay her husband to rest unless she did all she could to find his grandmother. She emerged from the bed and reached for her phone. Her mom had left a voicemail when she'd called last night, and she hadn't listened to it yet.

'Hi, Lily.' Her mom's voice came down the phone. 'Hope you find what you're looking for.' Pause. 'We're getting the Coast Guard report any day. Things are real tough here right now. Your father is very low. We need you home, Lily, as soon as you can.'

Her mom's message enraged her. Lily nearly threw her phone against the wall in frustration. It felt like her parents had ganged up on her.

The other missed call was from her dad, but he'd left no message. It didn't surprise her. Her dad never left voicemails.

She crawled out of bed, groaning. She was never, ever going to drink again.

Noreen was alone in the kitchen. The girls had already gone to school.

'What can I get you?' Noreen asked, looking at Lily a little nervously. 'Full fry? Scrambled eggs?'

Lily still felt annoyed about Noreen's refusal to tell her where Rosemary lived the previous day. But she was also starving.

'Scrambled eggs, please,' she said, sitting down at the table, scratching her itchy arm.

Noreen gave her a curious look. 'I didn't hear you come in,' she said. 'Did you have a good night?'

'Not really.' Lily grimaced. 'I went to the pub and drank too much Guinness.'

'Well, no harm,' Noreen said, clearly trying to break yesterday's tension as she mixed a bowl of eggs with a fork.

'I met some locals,' Lily said, determined to interrogate Noreen further, despite the fact she was feeling so rough. 'A guy called Daniel and his brother. I think Daniel knew Connor, but he wouldn't tell me anything, either.'

Noreen turned around, despite the fact the pan was spitting oil. 'Would that be Daniel Malone and his brother, Sean?'

'I don't know what their second name was. But yeah, his brother was called Sean. Daniel had dark hair, was a bit messy-looking with stubble, and Sean was very big. Thinning hair.'

Noreen chewed her lip, looking very serious indeed. 'Oh dear,' she said, turning back to the pan.

After Noreen put down Lily's breakfast plate, crammed with eggs and toast, she sat opposite her at the kitchen table.

'I've been thinking about it all night,' Noreen said, frowning. 'I'm going to tell you why it's best never to mention the name Connor Fitzgerald around here. Especially to the Malone brothers.'

Lily's heart leapt in her chest – finally, she was going to find out the truth. But Noreen looked deeply troubled.

'I'm sorry to tell you this, Lily, because you seem to be a lovely girl, and clearly Connor must have turned his life around when he met you, but…' Noreen paused, licked her lips and looked nervous.

'You can tell me,' Lily said firmly, putting her knife and fork down. Her appetite had suddenly vanished. 'The reason I'm here – aside from trying to find Rosemary – is because I got this email. It was warning Connor to never come back here. Threatening to kill him if he did. I need to know what it's all about.'

'The name Connor Fitzgerald is not popular around here,' Noreen told her. 'He was a bit of a wild teenager, constantly getting into a bit of bother. Rosemary couldn't control him in the least.'

Lily listened, astonished. The Connor she knew had been extremely law-abiding.

'I think they were both in their final year at school,' Noreen continued, 'so they would have been about seventeen when they started dating – much to the disapproval of the Malone father. According to him, Eve was a diligent, hard-working student until she met Connor. He was a bad influence, distracting her away from her studies by getting her stoned and taking her to late-night raves at the weekend.'

Lily sat in stunned silence. It wasn't that she hadn't expected Connor to have girlfriends before her – but he had never, not once in all their time together, mentioned a girl called Eve. She began to feel a bad sense of foreboding. Did she really want to know the rest of the story? But it was too late now.

Noreen ploughed on. 'I remember seeing them in a gang on the beach drinking cans of beer, and building fires at night-time. There was Eve and Connor of course, then also Eve's brother, Daniel, the Armstrong boy, and Maggie Leahy.'

Lily tensed with surprise. Daniel had told her a barefaced lie last night. Not only had he known Connor, he had actually been his friend.

'What did Eve look like?' Lily found herself asking Noreen.

'Small and slight, with fair hair.'

The opposite of Lily, who was nearly the same height as Connor and sturdy from all her fishing years.

'Are you sure you want to hear this?' Noreen asked, looking shrewdly at Lily's expression.

Lily nodded. 'Just tell me everything you know,' she said.

'Well, Eve got pregnant.'

Lily's heart froze inside of her. Noreen paused, as if wondering whether to say something else, but then she pressed on with the story.

'As I said, her father was dead against Connor. But when it came to his daughter being an unwed mother, well, he wasn't having that. The Malones think they're above the rest of us, but really they're just pig farmers who've made a lot of money. They have a big Dallas-style ranch just outside of town. Anyway, there was holy war over it. In the end, Connor married Eve to keep the peace. Although Rosemary, his grandmother, went wild. There was a story she went down to the Malone house and was shouting at Mr Malone out in the yard, that it would all end in tears if those two kids got married.'

Lily put her hand on her chest. She could barely breathe with shock. Connor had been married to someone else. But worse than that – he had a child out there somewhere? How could he not have told her all of this?

Noreen put her hand on hers. 'I can see you're very shocked, darling, but I'm sorry to tell you, there's more to the story.'

Lily removed her hand. She didn't like Noreen calling her 'darling', either. They weren't friends.

'I remember seeing Connor and Eve together, and they were not a happy couple,' Noreen said. 'Mismatched. Well, the only thing they liked in common was drinking and partying. Which Eve continued to do when she was pregnant. Her family insist on painting a picture of this meek, studious girl they say she was before she met Connor, but I think in many ways she was more a tearaway than him.'

Noreen paused. Clearly struggling to continue with the story, she wrapped her cardigan around her tighter.

'But where's Eve now? And the child?' Lily asked, shakily. This was the last thing she was expecting to find in Connor's homeland: another wife and a child. His child. How could he have abandoned them?

'It's not what you're thinking, Lily,' Noreen said, clearly reading her face. 'Something happened. Something terrible.'

Lily went rigid with anticipation, her breath shallow in her chest as Noreen continued.

'Eve would have been about five months pregnant, and she was still gadding about. To be fair to her, she hadn't even hit her eighteenth birthday, and she wanted to have fun before she got tied down with the baby. She and Connor went to a party, and word has it, he got drunk. But still, he got in their car to drive them home.' Noreen shook her head, looking sorrowful. 'No one really knows how it happened, Lily, but Connor crashed the car. Eve and her baby were killed.'

'Oh my God,' Lily said, bringing her hands to her face in shock.

'It was a terrible business altogether, as you can imagine. Connor ended up in court, accused of drunk driving. As a juvenile he got a fine, and banned from driving for four years.'

Lily's mouth fell open in horror. How could she have had no idea at all about her husband's past?

'And of course, as you've worked out, the two brothers you met in the pub – Daniel and Sean Malone – were Eve's brothers. When Connor got back from his court appearance, Sean Malone beat him up and made threats in front of a rake of people. He had the whole GAA behind him.'

'What's the GAA?' Lily asked.

'It stands for Gaelic Athletic Association,' Noreen told her. 'All the young lads around here are part of it. It can be very tribal,' she explained. 'I believe Connor had no choice but to leave.'

Lily thought of the game she'd been watching in the pub the night she'd met Daniel and Sean. How wild and fierce the players had seemed, without any protection from each other as they'd swung their sticks.

Noreen reached over and squeezed her hand. 'I know it's a lot to take in,' she said.

'But what about Rosemary?' Lily whispered, clutching on to the one piece of information she knew about Connor's past. 'Could she not have helped Connor?'

'Poor Rosemary, I see her in the shops now and again. Terrible sad for her. You see, when Connor was up in court on the charge, and had admitted it, Rosemary was still claiming he was innocent. Back she went to the Malone's yard, shouting that her grandson would never drink drive. Eve's father blackened her name in the community for that.' Noreen sighed. 'She keeps to herself. Hides away in her house by the lake. I heard she was receiving hate mail, being called a murderer's grandmother and such. I don't know why she hasn't moved further away by now.'

Lily stood up, pushing her unfinished breakfast away. 'Please can you tell me where she lives? I need to speak with her.'

Noreen gave her a considered look, and then pulled out a notepad and pen from the kitchen drawer. 'Her house doesn't have a name or number, that's how it is around here, but it's on the road right by Bunduff Lough. It's a stone cottage with a green door.' Noreen drew a little map on the piece of paper and handed it to Lily. 'Are you all right, darling? Are you sure you don't want a cup of tea first, just to take it all in?'

'Thanks for telling me, I appreciate it,' Lily said. It was hard to believe everything that Noreen had just told her. 'I don't know if I'll go see her but right now I need some air.'

It was raining, but Lily didn't care. She needed to walk without stopping. The rain lashed into her, and within minutes her jeans were soaked, rain streaming down her face and dripping off the end of her hood. Her sneakers squelched as she walked. She hadn't even thought to put on her boots. She walked through the village, past the boats and the pub she was in last night, and kept on walking, out the other side and round the headland. Waves crashed against the coast alongside her as she put her head down and into the rain. Her heart was beating so fast. How could Connor have kept such a huge lie from her for the whole of their marriage? No wonder he hadn't wanted children. Part of her was so angry with him, furious. He'd hidden a whole part of his life from her, and she had shown him everything in her life. He had been part of her family. Had he not loved her enough to confide in her? Shame followed in closely upon her anger. Was it her fault? Had she been so forbidding, he couldn't tell her? Their marriage had always been about her – Connor living in her hometown, supporting her work as a fisher, finally agreeing to go for a baby because she'd wanted it. But he'd known all along he could have kids, when they'd been suffering from fertility problems, and he'd never told her. She swung between anger at him, and then desperate sadness.

Lily kept on walking. She felt sick as she remembered that she'd kissed Daniel, Eve's brother, last night. And she'd met Sean, who she now guessed was the author of the horrible email. How had Sean found out where Connor was living, after all those years? How had he known that Connor had married Lily? Clearly, the Malones blamed Connor for Eve's death. But as she kept turning it over in her mind, Lily began to feel that something was a little off with Noreen's story. She found it so hard to believe Connor would have done such a reckless thing as drink-drive with his pregnant wife in the car. Someone didn't change that much, surely? It just didn't fit. Had he been so very different in Ireland?

Maybe he had, she told herself. He'd just been a kid, after all. Maybe he had made a terrible mistake, and Eve's death had been a tragic accident.

She walked in a loop back to the B&B. The rain was behind her now, pushing her forwards. She thought of her daddy. She needed him so badly right now – he always knew what to do in a crisis. At least he had done, before the fateful storm. And finding out this terrible secret after losing her husband was the biggest crisis she'd faced in her life. But she wasn't talking to her dad. Because of what had happened. Besides, it was still the middle of the night back home. Her dad was being accused of seaman's manslaughter for the death of Connor – but that had been an accident too. He hadn't meant for Connor to die. He was wracked with guilt. Was she being too harsh on her dad?

What would Connor think? She knew instinctively, he would have forgiven her father. Connor had been the least judgemental man she'd ever met. Now she knew why.

When she got back to the B&B, Lily was relieved to discover Noreen had gone out. She stood dripping in the hall, pulling off her wet sneakers. As she did so, she saw a letter on the mat. To her surprise, it was addressed to her: *Mrs Lily Fitzgerald*. It wasn't stamped. She ripped open the envelope.

Go home. Raking up the past and asking questions about Connor Fitzgerald will do you no good. For your own safety, leave Mullaghmore and never come back.

Lily stormed upstairs and threw the letter down on her bed. It made her furious. She was not going to be bullied like her husband had been all those years ago. She reckoned it was the surly Sean Malone who'd dropped the letter in. Well, he wasn't going to intimidate her.

Lily picked up the map that Noreen had given her to Rosemary Kelly's cottage. It was about time she met Connor's grandmother.

Chapter Eighteen

Mullaghmore, 25th August 1992

As Niamh pulled into the yard, she was surprised to see the light on downstairs in the house. It was midweek, and her mam would usually have gone to bed hours ago, but as she walked in the back door, she heard voices coming from the front room.

Sitting in her father's old armchair, cradling a mug of tea between her hands was Brendan's girlfriend, Deirdre. Niamh's whole body tensed with the shock of the girl's presence in their house.

'Well, there you are,' her mam said, her voice hoarse with tiredness. 'Poor Deirdre here has been waiting hours for you.'

'Sorry for the bother, Mrs Kelly,' Deirdre said politely, as she balanced her mug on the arm of the chair. 'Sure, it's not Niamh's fault, I was only passing by, so I was.'

Her mam turned to Niamh and eyed her suspiciously. Deirdre's Derry accent was hard to ignore. 'You never told me you'd met Deirdre before, Niamh?'

'Years ago, with Brendan,' Niamh said quickly.

Her mam narrowed her eyes, but asked no more. 'I see,' she said. 'Well, I'm off to bed. Make our guest welcome, won't you, Niamh?'

As soon as her mam had left the room, Deirdre's manner changed. She stood up, leaving the mug of tea balancing on the chair. 'I've been waiting hours, so I have,' she complained.

'Where the hell did you come from?' Niamh said. 'How did you get here?'

'Brendan dropped me off, but he didn't come in,' Deirdre said, taking out her cigarettes and lighting one, but not offering the packet to Niamh. 'Thought your mam would ask him too many questions.' Deirdre gave Niamh a slow smile, but her eyes were cold.

Niamh was furious. How dare Brendan dump his girlfriend at her house in the middle of the night!

Deirdre turned to her, flicking her long blond hair off her shoulders. 'We've got to go now,' she said, taking a drag off her cigarette, before stubbing it out half-smoked in the Connemara marble ashtray Niamh's mam kept on the mantelpiece, but never used.

'Go where? Why?' Niamh asked, feeling a creeping dread.

'Catch yourself on.' Deirdre frowned at her. 'You know why,' she said, as she went out the door and into the kitchen.

'Can you not just take the car on your own?' Niamh said, throwing Deirdre the keys of the Toyota. Of course, this was payback for Niamh having taken the car from Tadhg. 'I don't want to go anywhere with you right now,' she complained. 'I've been driving all day.'

Deirdre raised her eyebrows. 'Wise up,' she said. 'Mind, we're two girls, heading back from visiting our fellas down south.'

'Are you telling me I have to drive across the border, now?' Niamh said in horror. She was so tired from her day with Jesse. They'd driven for hours, and all she wanted was to get into bed. Besides, tomorrow, she was supposed to be leaving with Jesse. She needed to talk to her mam about it, which meant she would have to get up early tomorrow, before her mam went to work. And then she had to pack. It had all seemed so easy earlier today, planning her adventure with Jesse – but now the whole idea of it began to overwhelm her.

'Not tonight,' Deirdre said. 'We've to go get a wee something first.' She lowered her voice. 'We'll drive over tomorrow. Bring it to South Armagh. You can leave me there.'

'South Armagh!' Niamh cried out in dismay. The round trip was at least four hours. How would she be able to do that and make the meeting with Jesse at the travel agency in the afternoon?

Deirdre put her head on one side, giving Niamh a hard judgemental stare. 'Don't start me,' she snarled. 'It's the deal now you've the wee car.'

'But I've plans tomorrow…' Niamh began.

'Well, cancel them,' Deirdre interrupted. 'Nothing is more important than this.' She stepped forward, gripped Niamh's hands, and shoved the cold hard metal of the car keys into Niamh's clenched fists. Her hold was strong, surprising for such a slight girl.

'Watch yourself, Niamh; I told Brendan you'd be ascared, but he insisted you were up to it,' Deirdre hissed at Niamh. 'Are you going to let your cousin down? Do you want to make *them* raging with you?'

Niamh shook her head. The mention of the anonymous *them* sent a shiver down her spine.

'Come on,' Deirdre said, opening the back door and blasting Niamh with cool air. Pixie came scampering over, but Niamh instructed her back to her cushion. Grabbing her leather jacket off the chair, she followed Deirdre out of the door. Her heart was heavy with dread, and her legs shaky.

Deirdre made her drive for miles. Niamh was amazed the girl knew the backroads so well. Even Niamh was confused after about thirty minutes, and it was her own county.

'Take a left here,' Deirdre instructed, as they turned down a tiny boreen. 'Turn the lights off.'

'But I can't see,' Niamh complained.

'Keep going, slow,' Deirdre said. 'I'll tell you when to stop.'

The car bumped down the boggy track until Deirdre put a cold hand on Niamh's knee. 'Now,' she said.

Niamh came to a halt and turned off the engine, as the car ticked over. Her hips were stiff from sitting in the car so long, and her eyes were sore from tiredness, but fear kept her alert.

Deirdre opened the door of the car and got out, before leaning back in. 'Wait here,' she said to Niamh. She pulled a torch from her pocket and turned it on.

Niamh watched Deirdre walking away from the car. The small beam of light from her torch illuminated her figure as she strode down the boreen, until the dark shadows swallowed her up. Niamh waited. She had no idea where she was, or how she'd get home. Who was Deirdre meeting and why? She didn't want to think about it.

Her hands were still clutching the steering wheel. She took them off and unclenched her fingers. Her palms were sweaty with nerves. What should she do?

A voice inside her head told her to go. Drive away, and never come back. But if Niamh deserted Deirdre now, there could be repercussions for her mam. Could she persuade her mam to run away with her to America? They didn't have the money for the ticket, though, and her mam would never leave Pixie behind.

Her only choice was to wait for Deirdre to come back. To bring her to South Armagh tomorrow, after talking to her Mam, then race back to Sligo to meet Jesse at the travel agency. Niamh closed her eyes, wishing she were anywhere else but here on the bog, in the middle of nowhere. An owl hooted, and she heard a cow lowing in the distance. She shivered in her jacket, biting the nail of her thumb down to the skin.

She must have dozed off, because all of a sudden her face was blasted with light.

'Wake up, you eejit,' Deirdre said, getting into the passenger side. 'Move it.'

Niamh turned the car on and reversed down the narrow lane until she found a place to turn.

'We'll go to yours until daybreak,' Deirdre told her.

They headed back the way they'd come. As Niamh drove, she wondered what Deirdre had collected and put in the boot. Whom had she met, out on the dark bog in the middle of the night? She looked so harmless with her blond hair, dimpled cheeks and soft hourglass figure, and yet she was clearly as tough as old boots.

Back home, Niamh gave Deirdre a blanket and showed her the mattress in the shed. 'Probably better if you sleep here,' she said, not caring much how comfortable her unwelcome guest was.

'We'll head at first light,' Deirdre warned her.

They slept in. Niamh hadn't even heard her mam get up. It felt like she'd only just dropped off to sleep, and Deirdre was shaking her awake. She was so surprised to see her kneeling on her bed, she couldn't even tell her to get out of her bedroom.

'Come on,' Deirdre said, and Niamh detected panic in the girl's eyes. 'We've need to get on.'

Niamh hated being bossed around by Brendan's girlfriend, but she didn't know what else to do. One last job, she told herself. Then she'd be gone with Jesse.

'Do you want something to eat?' Niamh asked Deirdre, as she pulled on her jeans.

'No time,' the other girl said, legging it down the stairs.

'So which way should I go?' Niamh asked as they headed off down the road. It was nine-thirty in the morning. Still early, and enough time for her to get back to talk to her Mam before heading into Sligo to meet Jesse at the travel agency. The morning was glorious. Bright and golden, the leaves glistening with dew, and the land fragrant with late summer.

'Whatever way,' Deirdre said, looking at her face in her compact while applying her signature red lipstick.

'Okay,' Niamh said, trying to remember the quickest route to South Armagh. 'What town are we headed for?'

'Crossmaglen. Mind, we're muckers,' Deirdre said, snapping her compact shut.

Not ever, Niamh wanted to say out loud. *We will never be friends.*

'Your name is Lucy, I'm Nancy,' Deirdre told her.

'What if they ask for ID?'

'Say you forgot it, and smile at the Brits,' Deirdre said with confidence. 'I do it all the time.'

'What's in the boot?' Niamh asked.

'Don't start me,' the other girl replied, with a clip to her voice.

Within the hour, they were slowing down at a checkpoint. Tension shivered down Niamh's spine. She'd no idea what was in the boot, but she guessed it must be guns. What would happen if they were caught?

She clasped her hands in her lap to stop them from shaking. The soldier peered in the driving window.

'All right, girls? Where you off to?' His eyes skimmed over Niamh to focus on Deirdre.

'We're visiting my granny in Enniskillen,' Deirdre said, her voice transformed, Derry accent gone, soft and girlish. Niamh looked across at her as she flicked her fair hair, and pouted with red lips. How could she do it?

The soldier looked back at Niamh. She tried her best to smile too, but he clearly smelt the fear coming off her.

''Fraid I'm going to have to ask you girls to get out the car.'
The soldier indicated, with his gun pointing downward. 'We're
doing random checks today. Nothing to worry about.'

Thick terror choked Niamh's throat as she got out.

She glanced over at Deirdre, who had wandered over to the
other soldier and was transfixing him with her cleavage.

'Isn't it a grand day?' she said to him.

'Yeah,' he replied, still staring at her tits. 'At least it isn't bloody
raining.'

Under instruction of the first soldier, Niamh unlocked the
boot with trembling hands. He ordered her to step back. He
pulled back the carpet, took out the spare wheel and had a
good look. To Niamh's astonishment, there was no bag of guns
hidden underneath. Relief washed through her. She thought
she might faint.

'Okay, girls, ta very much,' the squaddie said. 'On you go.'

As soon as they were round the bend, and the soldiers had
disappeared in the distance, Deirdre began to laugh.

'What the fuck!' Niamh said, turning to her.

'The Brits are such dickos!' Deirdre gloated, the expression on
her face transformed from innocent to contemptuous.

'Can you tell me why I am smuggling an empty car across the
border?' Niamh said, furious.

'It's not empty, eejit,' Deirdre said. 'The Brits looked in the
wrong place.'

Niamh glanced over as Deirdre patted the door beside her.

'They're in the door panels,' Deirdre said.

'What's in the door panels?' Niamh asked, but even as she
said it, she felt the cold realisation of what she had just smuggled
across the border. Explosives.

*

Hours later. After the longest morning of her life, Niamh was heading back home. She felt sick and tired down to the pit of her belly. Deirdre had directed her to a rundown old farmhouse in the Catholic heartland of South Armagh.

Two men Niamh had never seen before in her life had emerged from the farmhouse as they'd pulled up. No introductions were made. Better they didn't know each other's names.

There had been no sign of Brendan. Even more surprising, one of the men had kissed Deirdre on the cheek. Was he a relative? Evidently not, Niamh had realised, when she saw Deirdre kiss the stranger back on the lips. The air felt charged with danger, and dark secrets.

The second man, tall with fair hair and a hard face, had told Niamh to go for a walk and come back in an hour.

She had wandered in the boggy woods, glancing at her watch as the minutes ticked by. She and Jesse had to meet at the travel agency in Sligo at three o'clock in the afternoon. It was already nearly one o'clock. There was no way she'd make it. Her plans with Jesse seemed so trite, in comparison to what she was actually involved in. She'd stopped walking, putting her hand on her thumping heart. Had she just smuggled explosives across the border? It didn't seem real.

But when she returned to the farmhouse and walked in through the back door, the first thing she saw was Deirdre carefully handling the packs as if they were newborn babies. As she placed them on the wooden kitchen table, the fair man whipped around, a gun in his hand. Niamh gave a small scream in fright.

'You should have knocked,' the man said gruffly, lowering the gun.

Niamh took a step back in shock. Until now, everything she'd done for Brendan had been hidden. She'd never seen a weapon, even. But this was all horribly real.

At last, the other man – Deirdre's second boyfriend or lover – had told her she could leave.

Niamh had walked out the farmhouse without so much as goodbye to any of them. She was so angry. It felt as if she'd been kidnapped. Brendan and Tadhg had forced her to cross a line, and she'd never forgive them.

She slammed her foot down, not caring if the car revved loudly, and tore off out the yard of the farmhouse and down the narrow lanes.

Before long she was stuck behind a tractor, desperate as she glanced at her watch, realising she had long missed the time of her meeting with Jesse at the travel agency in Sligo. All she could do was aim to get back before the Sligo train departed for Dublin. She was going to have to go straight to the station, tell Jesse she'd go up to Dublin the next day, and meet him in the evening at the airport. She needed to talk to her mam. Tell her she was leaving.

It had to be the most twisty road she'd ever driven along, bend after hairpin bend. As soon as the road straightened out, a car would appear in the other direction and she'd have to hang back. With ditches on either side of the road, there was no place for the tractor to pull in for her to overtake it. By the time the road widened enough for her to finally speed past, glaring at the old fellow sitting up with his collie in the tractor's cab, there was a whole line of cars behind her. She put her foot down and sped down the road – a little fast, granted, but she was running out of time.

The white Toyota bounced along the road. She'd already gone through the checkpoint, and even though the roads were in a worse state, she felt so much better south of the border. She pushed the surreal events of the past twenty-four hours out of her head. All she needed to focus on now was getting to Jesse before the train left.

At last, she was in Sligo. Niamh tore down the main street, grateful not many were about, and into the train station car park. She could see the train was in the platform, ready for departure. She had just two minutes. Niamh jumped out of the car, ran into the station and onto the platform, feeling dizzy and sick with anticipation.

Jesse hadn't boarded the train yet. He was standing right by the door, his rucksack off his back and ready to load. As he saw her, she could see the confliction of anger and relief on his face.

'What happened to you?' he asked, as she ran up him. 'I waited for you at the travel agency for hours.'

'I'm sorry,' she gushed. 'Something happened.'

'Where's your stuff?' Jesse asked her, noticing Niamh didn't even have a handbag with her. Just the car keys, still clutched in her hand.

'I need to talk to my mam,' she said. 'I haven't had a chance yet.'

'Have you changed your mind?' Jesse asked, as the guard called at them to get on the train.

'No! It's just, I have to tell her,' Niamh said. 'But she'll want me to get out of here.' She paused to catch her breath. 'Give me the plane ticket and I'll meet you in Dublin tomorrow. At the embassy, to get my visa.'

'I thought you'd bailed,' Jesse said, as the guard yelled at them again. 'I'm sorry, Niamh, I didn't buy the ticket. It's a lot of money, and I thought you weren't coming.'

He took a step up onto the train.

'Maybe we should wait, you know,' he said, turning to her. 'Come out in a few weeks. I can send you the money.'

Her heart fell. She could see in his eyes that he didn't believe in her.

'Look, get off the train now. We'll go together, tomorrow,' Niamh begged.

But Jesse stayed put as the guard slammed the door shut between them. She stood on the platform, looking up at him.

'I can't do that,' he said, leaning out the window. 'But I'll call you.'

'Please, just get off the train,' Niamh said, panic rising. 'We can go get the ticket now. We'll still make the plane if we get the early train.'

'You can't run away on your mom like that, Niamh,' Jesse said, all rational now, when it was he who had asked her to go in the first place. 'There's no rush.'

The whistle blew, and Niamh saw the guard jump on.

'No, Jesse,' she whispered, but the train began to move. She reached out for him and he touched her hand. For just a few seconds, the tips of their fingers connected, before the train picked up speed and Niamh fell back as she jogged to keep up.

She could see the goodbye in his gaze and she wanted to scream with fury. *Come back! Don't leave me here!*

But in the next moment, the train had left the station and she was abandoned on the platform. They hadn't even kissed goodbye.

He was gone. A spot of rain landed on her face. As she made her way back to the car, it began raining in earnest. The air smelt earthy. She looked up at the sky, letting the raindrops trail down her cheeks. She could see the leaves on the trees were already turning. Summer was well and truly over.

Despite her exhaustion, she didn't drive straight home. In fact, she drove past the top of their lane, on into Mullaghmore, and down to the harbour. She sat in her car, looking out at the lines of rain and the moored boats. Remembering Jesse in the sailing boat, the day he'd taken her out.

She closed her eyes, conjuring up his scent and touch.

It felt impossible to consider she would never see him again. She clutched at a tiny bit of hope. Maybe he really would send her the money for a ticket and she could go out in a few weeks. It wouldn't be so rushed, and she could ease her mam into it. Niamh was worried about her depression.

But in her heart, Niamh knew Jesse wouldn't be sending any ticket money. She had seen the goodbye in his eyes. He had lost faith in her when she'd stood him up at the travel agency.

She bit her lip, pushing back the tears, then reversed and turned the car, heading back towards home. As she turned down their little laneway, she began to feel dizzy again, like she had in the train station. It was no wonder – she hadn't eaten anything since the night before, and she'd had hardly any sleep. She'd been driving constantly for hours, and her stressful experience with Deirdre was bound to have had a big effect on her.

No sooner than she was in the front door, she was overwhelmed with nausea. She made it to the bathroom just in time before throwing up. Though there was hardly anything to throw up, because she hadn't eaten. She felt awful.

As she sat back on her heels, a thought occurred to her. She began to count back the days and weeks, and cold realisation flooded her entire body. She wasn't sick from exhaustion. She was pregnant.

Chapter Nineteen

Mullaghmore, 16th November 2017

Lily parked at the top of the lane. She wanted to imagine herself walking in Connor's footsteps to his grandmother's house. She pulled her coat tight about her, but left her hood down. The rain had stopped, although the air was cold and damp. It smelt so different from home here. Not so far from the sea, and yet all scent of it gone. Around her were muddy fields, trees, and ditches thick with undergrowth. There was so much green and earth in Ireland.

The lane was full of potholes brimming with rainwater. Lily walked right through them, seeing Connor as a little boy running through them too. It had always irked her he'd had no pictures of himself as a boy, whereas he'd been made to sit down by her parents and look through photograph album after photograph album of her as a child. She was an only child, so of course her parents had obsessively documented everything in her life – from her first steps, to her first days out lobstering with her father. But Lily had not seen one picture of Connor. Would Connor's grandmother have pictures of him as a child? Could she handle seeing them?

Lily wasn't sure what to expect. Noreen had intimated that Rosemary Kelly was a strange and reclusive figure, but she hadn't come all this way for nothing. There were no other houses down the narrow lane, so Lily knew Rosemary's had to be the only cottage facing her. A grey stone cottage with shuttered windows, a green door, and a wild garden.

Lily walked up to the front door and knocked. Waited. Knocked again, but nobody came. She walked around to the back of the house. The yard was empty, but she could see tyre tracks in fresh mud. Clearly, Connor's grandmother wasn't in. There was no shutter on the back window, and Lily peered into it, but the cottage was full of shadows. She couldn't see anything, apart from a crystal hanging in the window.

On a whim, she put her hand on the back door and turned the handle. To her surprise, the door opened. She stood on the doorstep, not sure what to do.

'Hello there,' she called out, pushing the door open a bit more. 'Hey, is anyone home?'

No answer. She took a step onto the doormat. It was as if she just couldn't stop herself. She had come so far that she couldn't walk away now. Another step, and then she was inside. She held her breath, taking in the tiny cottage kitchen. She had been expecting a sad, miserable interior, suited to an outcast old lady, but the downstairs of Rosemary Kelly's cottage was the exact opposite. A slate floor covered in bright rugs, a big kitchen dresser packed with cheerful crockery, and on the wall, paintings full of energy and light. She liked them, which surprised her as Lily had never liked modern art. This might have been the kitchen table which Connor would have sat at as a little boy. She placed her hand on its worn surface, feeling emotion swell up within her.

Lily lifted her hand and pressed it to her chest. She was dying to go upstairs, but she was aware she was trespassing. How would it look to Connor's grandmother if she came back and found her already inside her home? She should come back later.

It was as she was turning towards the door to leave that she saw it, and was unable to stop herself from crying out in shock.

There, on one of the shelves of the kitchen dresser, was a framed photograph of Lily and Connor on their wedding day. Lily picked it up and stared at the picture, her eyes misting with tears. They looked so blissfully ignorant of what lay ahead. She traced her finger, outlining Connor's face: the big, open smile, his eyes so bright with life. The two of them together under the willow tree back home, and behind them, the blue ocean. Lily remembered squeezing into her white dress, all frothy and lacy, and how she'd felt like a princess as her daddy had walked her down the aisle. Her daddy had told her he couldn't be happier for her. Lily closed her eyes, letting the tears trail down her cheeks. She missed Connor so much, but she also missed her daddy. The storm had taken them both from her.

She put the picture back down on the dresser. Rosemary Kelly knew about her. Connor hadn't hidden his life in Maine from his grandmother unlike the secrets he had kept from Lily. The knowledge that Connor hadn't trusted her with the truth about Eve and the baby really hurt. Had he thought she was too judgemental to cope with the truth?

Lily walked briskly back down the lane. The last thing she wanted was to run into Connor's grandmother while she was feeling so raw and upset. She'd return later.

Back in the rental car, she turned the key and started the engine. She was struggling to fit her Connor with this other Connor, who'd got into a car drunk and killed his pregnant wife with his own recklessness. But then, everyone had a dark side. Look at her father. Because he'd been greedy to get as many lobsters as possible, he'd risked Ryan and Connor's lives. Her daddy, who she'd idolised her whole life, had been responsible for Connor's death. She wasn't sure how she'd ever get past this fact and return to any kind of normal life back home.

*

There was another letter waiting for her on the hall table of the B&B. Lily tore into the envelope, tension rippling through her body.

Leave the past well alone, Lily Fitzgerald. Go home before you regret it.

Lily's anger flared up again. No way was she going to be intimidated. Besides, this second letter only served to fuel her suspicion that she hadn't had the whole story from Noreen. Connor was dead; why would any of the Malones care about Lily being in Mullaghmore? Unless there was something they were trying to keep from her.

Without thinking, she shoved the letter in her coat pocket and went back out again, down the hill into town. If the brothers weren't in the pub, she'd find out where they lived and drive on out there. But as she walked back into the same dim pub as the night before, she saw the Malones sitting up at the bar, eating sandwiches. Sean had a glass of Coke, but she could see Daniel was already at the Guinness. When he caught sight of Lily, he had the decency to blush. She gritted her teeth. She would not be embarrassed. He had deceived her, got her drunk, and tried to take advantage of her, all along keeping from her that his sister had been married to Connor.

She pulled the letter out of her pocket and tapped Sean on the shoulder. Lily had worked with brawnier fishermen than him and been treated as an equal. She had held the respect of every guy in her fishing community, and she wasn't going to let this bastard get the better of her or run her out of town.

Sean turned round and looked down at her. As soon as she saw the expression on his face, it was clear he knew exactly who she was.

'If you've something to say to me, you should have the balls to do it in person,' she said, waving the letter in his face. 'I won't be intimidated by your pathetic threats.'

Sean's cheeks turned a deep shade of reddish purple. It was clear to Lily that she had poked the bear, but she didn't care any more. She'd had enough of men and their lies.

'Don't know what you're talking about, you mad bitch,' he said.

'Admit it,' Lily said. 'You know I'm Connor Fitzgerald's wife, and you sent me those letters warning me to get out of town, but I won't – not until I get to the bottom of things.'

'Wife? Don't you mean widow?' Sean sneered at her. 'You're Connor's widow.' He got off his stool and towered over her. Bits of bread were stuck between his teeth, and his breath smelled. 'I don't give a shit about what you're doing here,' he said.

'What about the letters?' Lily waved them in Sean's face again. Daniel got off his stool, taking an uncertain step towards her and his brother. She felt a shiver of repulsion. How could she have let this man kiss her last night? In daylight, she could see he had the face of a heavy drinker: red, bloodshot eyes and thick jowls.

'I didn't send you any letters, you crazy woman,' Sean said, but then his eyes narrowed. 'I did send your husband an email though, warning him not to ever set foot here again. Else I would kill him.' His tone was so harsh, so laced with hatred, it made Lily step back. 'But I don't need to now,' he said, giving her a cruel smile, 'because Daniel here told me what you confided in him. Connor's dead anyways. Good riddance. I hope he rots in Hell.'

Before she could stop herself, Lily's arm shot out and she gave Sean a resounding slap on the face. But instead of getting angry or hitting her back, he just started to laugh at her.

'Hey, what's going on?' said the barman, coming over.

Lily went again for Sean, but Daniel caught her arm.

'Come on, now, Lily, calm down,' Daniel said, before twisting around to Sean. 'Have you no heart, Sean? The girl's in mourning.'

'Well, she's better off without that bastard, Connor Fitzgerald,' Sean said, sitting back up on his stool and taking a sip of his Coke.

'He was my husband!' Lily started to go for Sean again, but Daniel dragged her away. She was furious with him, too.

'Eve was my sister, too, you know,' Sean snarled back at her.

'Come on,' Daniel said, veins bulging in his forehead with the effort of restraining Lily. 'Come on, let's go; you don't want Ted to ring the guards, now.'

'Yeah, off you go now,' Sean heckled them. 'Pair of losers.'

Before she knew it, Daniel had pushed her out of the pub, and they were standing on the street outside. She was still furious.

'I won't have him saying things like that about Connor,' said Lily.

'Leave it,' Daniel said, putting a hand on her arm. 'You'll get nowhere with my brother. He hated Connor even before he married Eve.'

Lily turned on Daniel. 'And you,' she said, her eyes blazing. 'Kissing me, when all along you knew who Connor was, and who I was!'

'I'm sorry,' Daniel said, looking shaky. 'I was drunk!'

'Your brother can't threaten me like that, send letters,' Lily continued to rant. 'I'll go to the police.'

'It wasn't him,' Daniel said, shoving his hands in his pockets, and looking sheepish. 'I sent you the letters.'

'But why would you threaten me on the one hand, and try to get off with me on the other?'

'I was scared the truth would come out. I thought it was safer for you just to get out of here…' Daniel petered out.

'What exactly is the truth?' Lily pushed, determined not to let up, despite the fact Daniel wouldn't meet her gaze.

'Look, let's go somewhere else for a drink. The hotel bar down at the pier?'

'Only if you tell me what's going on,' Lily said.

The last thing she wanted was to have a drink with Daniel Malone, but she also needed to know why he had sent her letters. Were there more secrets about Connor she didn't know?

Daniel ordered himself a fresh pint of Guinness, while Lily got a black coffee. She watched Daniel's hand shaking slightly as he took a sip of Guinness. Again, she wondered how she'd found him attractive the night before.

'Right, then, tell me what it is,' Lily said, her tone hostile. It was mortifying that she'd let this man touch her, when she'd only been widowed less than a month.

Daniel looked doleful, with big puppy eyes, clearly a look he thought worked on women – but she was no way falling for it.

'Come on, spit it out,' she said. 'Why did you send me the letters?'

'I'm sorry about the letters,' he began, shaking his head. 'I got scared.'

Lily took a sip of her coffee. It tasted particularly bitter. She tore open a sachet of sugar and poured it into the black liquid.

'Go on,' she said, her whole body tense with anticipation.

'Sean always hated Connor, even before Eve died,' Daniel said. 'Eve and Sean were twins, you see. Grew up inseparable. I came along one year later, and it never really felt like I got a look in.'

Lily waited impatiently while Daniel downed some of his pint.

'You've heard of my father? The Malones own a lot of land around here, as well as the pig farm,' Daniel told her. 'My father was a bit of a bastard to us when we were kids. Used to hit me and Sean a lot – although never Eve. She was the apple of his eye. My mam was very religious, and Eve was sent to a convent school.

'Sean blames himself for Eve ending up with Connor. He joined the Irish army at sixteen and went abroad to serve with the UN. Eve really missed him. That's when she began to go off the rails. Started hanging out with Maggie and her friends, who were a bit older. But it was great for me for a while because with Sean gone, Eve would bring me with her. It's funny because they were twins and so close, but Sean never touched drugs, and honestly I think my sister spent most of her sixteenth year stoned.'

Daniel sighed, pushing his messy hair back off his forehead. Lily could see he was sweating, although it was far from warm in the hotel bar.

'The night Connor and Eve got together, Maggie had organised a big rave in an empty hangar in Leitrim on her friend's farm, and everyone was invited. Kids came from all over Ireland; it was deadly. I remember me and Eve getting dressed up together. She had on a tight little black dress and hid it under a baggy jumper and jeans. We told our parents we were going to a study group.' Daniel smiled at the memory. 'As if,' he continued. 'But it was while we were waiting for our ride to the rave on a road near his grandmother's house that Connor walked past us. We all knew who he was. The kid with no mother or father. He was in the year above me at school. But I guess Eve hadn't seen him since national school.

'Eve asked Connor for a cigarette, and then she asked him if he wanted to share a joint. Next thing, he was squeezing in the van with all the rest of us.' Daniel paused and took another gulp of his Guinness. 'Such a night that was! But the point is, everyone says Connor led Eve astray, but it's just not true.' Daniel looked up, his eyes watery. Lily wasn't sure if it was from the drink or if he was actually close to tears.

'The three of us used to hang out a lot, you know,' Daniel said. 'I always liked Connor. He was sound. The sensible one out of the three of us. Kept an eye on Eve, and me too, if we got too high on E. Stopped me from going too far.'

It hurt Lily to hear Daniel talking about a Connor she had never known. The young teenage Connor, going to parties and raves. But being a little bit sensible, still.

'I loved my sister, really, but she could be difficult, always wanting to be the centre of attention,' Daniel continued. 'I could tell she liked having Connor around, but she wasn't that into him. Like, she had *lots* of fellas on the go.'

Lily leant forward elbows on the table, surprised.

'I don't know why everyone in this town talks about my sister as if she was some kind of angel and Connor Fitzgerald was the Devil tempting her into bad ways, because if anything, it was the other way around,' Daniel mused. 'Probably because of Connor's mother, you know, and her reputation.'

Lily pricked up her ears. 'What *about* Connor's mother?' she asked.

'That's a whole other story, isn't it? All those rumours must have truth in them.' Daniel clearly assumed Connor had told Lily all about his mother, and she was too embarrassed to reveal how little she knew about her husband's family, so she said nothing. She waited, her body tense, sensing Daniel was building up to some kind of revelation.

'So, look, what everyone thinks happened that night when Eve and the baby were killed – it isn't the truth.'

'What do you mean?' Lily shot back.

Daniel lifted his Guinness back up to his lips. He'd already finished half his pint. 'I was with Eve and Connor at the party.

Connor was trying to persuade Eve not to drink because she was pregnant, but she was telling Connor to fuck off.' Daniel shook his head. 'She was so angry she was having a child. She really didn't want one.'

'Why didn't she have an abortion?'

'Because it's still illegal in Ireland, though probably not for much longer. It's a big deal, especially in the countryside. And then I think on some level, my sister thought a baby would help her be a better person. But once she started getting big, she regretted her decision.'

'Did Connor and Eve love each other?' Lily asked Daniel.

He shrugged. 'They were so young. But I'm pretty sure Connor must have been in love with my sister because he put up with so much from her. As for Eve…' Daniel sighed. 'I don't think so, though there were moments when she could be very tender with him. Protective, almost. But as the pregnancy advanced, she got angrier and angrier.'

Lily felt a twist of pain in her belly. Eve Malone had got pregnant so easily with Connor, whereas she had been trying for months. And yet Eve hadn't wanted their baby. It seemed so unfair.

'Anyway, it was some rave,' Daniel continued. 'A West Brit kid whose parents were away had put up an invite on Facebook.' He sniggered. 'Man, he was mobbed. There was, like, an actual ballroom. And a DJ, and everyone sharing E like candy. The music was loud and heavy, and we all got dancing, but Christ, what the fuck was Eve doing there five months pregnant?' Daniel shook his head mournfully. 'I should have stopped her from going. But my sister was not one to be told what to do. At first, she wasn't drinking, or taking anything. I remember seeing her and Connor dancing in the ballroom, and he was spinning her slowly around the floor. She looked happy. Calm, and sober. But then I lost sight of them. I was busy networking, so to speak.'

Daniel stopped talking for a moment. Looking down at his hands as they gripped his pint glass. 'I guess I probably overindulged. When I caught up with Connor and Eve again, they were having a terrible row. She was blind drunk, staggering around, and accusing Connor of sleeping with Maggie – which was insane, because Maggie is gay. I remember Connor saying we should call a taxi to bring us home, and I said I'd come with them as I wanted a lift.' Daniel licked his lips nervously. 'I was dealing hash and ecstasy at the time and I needed a lift to another rave to sell some gear.'

'Go on,' Lily said, tension searing through her body. Unable to drink her coffee.

'Eve said the taxi was too expensive. She got in Connor's car to drive, said she was fine.' Daniel was unable to look Lily in the eyes. 'It's all a bit hazy because I was so off my head, but I'm pretty sure Connor tried to stop her and she said if he didn't get in, she'd drive off without him. So he did, and I got in the back.'

'Are you telling me that on the night of the crash, it was Eve who was driving, not Connor?' Lily asked in a low voice. It felt as if the whole bar had gone very still, all noise fading into the background. Her complete focus was on Daniel and what he was saying. He looked really terrible now. His face grey, and the look in his eyes desperate.

Daniel closed his eyes. 'You know, I only remember the crash in my dreams.' He opened his eyes again, red with drink. 'I couldn't remember what really happened for years, not until I was clean.'

Lily raised her eyebrows as he lifted the pint to his lips.

'From drugs,' Daniel clarified. 'I gave all that up.'

'Just tell me what happened,' Lily demanded.

'It was all so fast,' Daniel said. 'Eve was racing down the road, and Connor was telling her to slow down, pull over, to let him drive because at least he wasn't so drunk. But she just kept going faster, and shouting at him: "Are you scared now, Connor Fitzgerald, have I got the fear of God into you now?"'

Daniel placed his hands either side of his empty pint glass, staring into it as if it were a screen replaying the events of that night.

'Eve was laughing. Wild, the way she used to. And looking over her shoulder at me. Asking me if I wanted her to turn up the music on the radio. Even though I was totally high, I remember thinking she was out of control. Connor was beside her, shouting at her to look at the road and trying to grab hold of the steering wheel to keep us going straight. But she kept pushing him away and the car was swerving. Next thing I remember, we were out of control, the car was skidding and Eve was slamming on the brakes and her laughter had gone hysterical. The road came up to meet us, and there was a big bang and a terrible crunching noise as we slammed into a ditch. Eve was screaming that our dad would kill her, that she couldn't get done for drink driving. She was going mental. So, Connor told her to get out the car, and he'd say he was driving. He'd take the rap for it, so she didn't lose her licence. But he made her promise she'd stop drinking, and she said she would. They both looked okay to me. Like, they had a bit of blood on their faces, and Eve said her head hurt, but I had to get out of there because I had a big bag of hash and another bag of ecstasy on me. So I ran away before the Gardai came...' Daniel's voice petered out. 'I thought Eve would cover for me like always. I didn't realise...' His voice faltered, and he looked up at Lily with pleading eyes. 'I wouldn't have run away if I'd known...'

Lily's whole body had gone cold. 'Let me just get this straight. It was your sister Eve who crashed the car, not Connor?'

Daniel nodded. 'But Connor told the Gardai it was him when they came, so Eve wouldn't get in trouble. I mean, no one was hurt – that was what they thought. They took them to hospital to check them over, and then, and then…'

It was as if Daniel couldn't bring himself to say the words. He took a big breath, and now Lily could see tears loading in his eyes.

'Eve went into some kind of seizure because of a head injury, and my God, she died. They tried to deliver the baby, but it was too early. Like I said, she was only five months gone. I heard Connor went wild in the hospital, they had to sedate him. And then he was arrested. By the time my parents had turned up, Connor had been carted off to the Gardai station. Lucky for him, because my father would have killed him with his bare hands. I only heard about it the next day. Can you imagine how I felt?' Daniel looked at Lily with pleading eyes. But she didn't care about Daniel. All she wanted to hear about was Connor.

'But why didn't you speak up?' Lily asked. 'Tell everyone it was Eve who was driving, and Connor was innocent?'

'Because Connor kept insisting, he *had* been driving,' Daniel said. 'I don't know why he kept saying it. Why would anyone believe me, when Connor himself was saying he was to blame? He was under eighteen so he didn't get sent down, but he lost his licence, and he couldn't stay in Mullaghmore. My brother Sean wanted to kill him.'

'All these years,' Lily whispered. 'How could you let everyone think that of Connor?'

'Because he wasn't here.' Daniel gave a small shrug. 'He took the blame, all because Eve was screaming after the accident about getting into trouble with our father. It really fucked me up. My brother wanted me to help him beat up Connor, but Connor had been my friend. I refused, so Sean beat me up, and then went and beat up Connor on his own.' Daniel gave a sad little hiccup.

It was all so tragic. Lily's heart ached for Connor. How she wished he'd confided in her about his past. 'What about his poor grandmother?'

'Sure, Rosemary Kelly never believed Connor was guilty,' Daniel said, almost defensive. 'I remember seeing her standing outside my parents' house, hollering that her grandson was innocent. They had to call the Gardai on her.'

Lily sat back on her chair. She was still so hurt that Connor had never told her about his past, but to know he hadn't been responsible for the death of Eve and their unborn child made her feel as if a weight had lifted from her shoulders.

'I don't know why he didn't tell the guards Eve had been driving,' Daniel said again. 'Or that I was in the car too. But he never did.'

Lily nodded. That was her Connor. Protecting others. Looking after others, even if their decisions were poor. Like how Ryan had said Connor had backed up her dad's decision to head into the storm, despite the fact it ended up costing him his life. She guessed Connor had blamed himself for Eve's death. She was sure he would have believed he was guilty because he felt he should have stopped her from driving. But he hadn't been the one behind the wheel. That was the important thing to Lily. He had been lucky he'd been under eighteen and not sent to prison, but it had still ruined his life in Ireland. When she'd met him in Rockland it would have been four years later. No wonder he had so happily laid down foundations with her. He'd been without a home for so long by then.

The light had dimmed already in the hotel bar, and Daniel almost seemed to be sinking into the shadows. His pint was finished up, but Lily wasn't going to buy him another.

'Do you think your brother Sean is still having his lunch?' she asked him.

'Probably back home on the farm by now,' Daniel said. 'Sean left the army after Eve was killed. Came home to work with my dad. Keep an eye on me.' Daniel grimaced.

'Come on,' Lily said, standing up. 'I'm going to drop you back home, and you're going to tell your brother the truth.'

Daniel went pale.

'But what does it matter if you're going back to America?' he said weakly.

Lily looked at Daniel in disgust. 'This place is part of my husband's legacy, and his grandmother lives here. How do you think it's been for her, all these years?' Despite never having met her, Lily felt very protective of Rosemary Kelly. She was the only link Lily had left with Connor. As they stood up to go, something occurred to Lily. 'How did Sean know about me and Connor?'

'I don't know exactly, but I think Connor's grandmother told a friend of our Mam,' Daniel told her. 'News spreads fast in a place like Mullaghmore. Sean wanted to make sure Connor never came back. My brother can be very intimidating.'

'I'm not frightened of your brother, Daniel,' Lily said.

And indeed, Lily didn't give Sean a second thought as she drove Daniel back home. What she was thinking about were all those secrets Connor had kept from her for the whole of their marriage. Lily could let the hurt of that go, though, because she'd loved him. And if you really loved someone, shouldn't you be able to forgive them anything?

Chapter Twenty

Mullaghmore, 26th September 1992

Niamh sat on her bed, holding the ferry ticket to Wales in her shaking hands. She was certain she'd made the right choice, but she was still terrified. Wishing she didn't have to take this journey completely alone. But there was no way she could tell her mam. Although Rosemary could be very open-minded about lots of things, Niamh knew the idea of her daughter going for an abortion would break her heart. She'd try to stop her. Probably promise to help bring up the baby. But Niamh wasn't ready to be a mother, especially not a single mother. Once she'd decided she was going to have an abortion, she wanted to do it as soon as possible. She had wanted to tell Jesse – but he had never called her up as he'd promised. She had no number for him, and no address. All she knew was he lived in a boatyard in Cape Cod. She missed Jesse. The pregnancy could have been a way to guilt him into coming back or sending for her. But she didn't want to be with anyone on those terms.

She folded up the ferry ticket and put it in her handbag. She had booked a room in a B&B in Hammersmith, close to the abortion clinic. Her plan was to drive to the ferry port and take the night boat. She would sleep for a few hours in the car in Holyhead, then drive all the way across Wales and England to arrive in London tomorrow afternoon. She wasn't looking forward to the ferry. She was feeling queasy enough as it was. Throwing up at all times of day. She found it particularly hard if she forgot to eat anything for breakfast, and the stink of cigarette smoke in the bar at night made her feel vile. It was all she could do not to puke in front of punters as they lit up.

Niamh checked the contents of her bag again. A couple of changes of clothes, big knickers, and a wad of sanitary pads.

She bit her lip. She wasn't going to cry, and she wasn't going to overthink this. She just had to get on with it.

She went downstairs to make some sandwiches for the journey. Her mam was in the kitchen.

'Your trip is all very sudden.'

'Well, I thought it was high time I caught up with Teresa,' Niamh lied. 'She says she's having such a grand time in London.'

Her mam came up behind her, put her arms around Niamh's waist, and hugged her.

'I'll miss you, darling,' she said. 'But you deserve to have some fun.'

She could feel her mam's sympathy. She thought Niamh was down because Jesse had left. If only she knew the whole truth.

'I'll only be gone a few days.' Niamh looked away from her mam, so she wouldn't see the tears beginning to bud in her eyes.

Her mam picked up the van keys from the dresser. 'I'd best be going; folks complain if they don't get their post until five in the afternoon.'

'Sure, they're well used to you, Mammy,' Niamh said, as a voice inside her screamed to stop her mam from leaving. To tell her what had happened. How frightened she was.

'Have a safe trip, darling.'

After her mam was gone, Niamh stood at the kitchen counter, toying with her toast as she stared out of the window. She should be getting on the road soon, but something made her reluctant. She looked out at the overgrown back garden. It was only a month since Jesse had left, but summer was well and truly over. The leaves were slipping from the trees to become a multi-coloured mulch on the ground. Niamh opened the back door and inhaled the scent of the wet land, the dripping foliage, as she walked across the garden towards her dad's old shed. The grass was still heavy with dew, and her black DMs made footprints in the damp green.

Inside the murky interior of the shed, she sat on the old mattress, closing her eyes and remembering Jesse. It seemed like a dream. A magic kingdom of love that she'd slipped into for a few weeks – and now she was returned to hard reality.

Niamh heard a car pulling up outside in the yard. Had her mam forgotten something? But as she opened the shed door, she saw Brendan getting out of his car. Anxiety flooded her whole body. He couldn't have picked a worse time to turn up.

Brendan took a seat at the kitchen table while Niamh put the kettle on.

'Brendan, I'm away to London for a few days,' she said, turning to him, hearing her voice all high and panicked. 'I have to leave soon. You never let me know you were coming.'

She hadn't seen her cousin since the day after the road rally festival, although she'd spoken to him on the phone. When they'd spoken, she'd still been angry about the nightmare experience of smuggling the explosives with Deirdre. But she'd decided not to say anything, because she had no one else to turn to for money for the ferry ticket and the abortion. She'd told him that she and Mam had got behind with the bills. Anyway, she felt he owed her.

'Is that what you needed the money for?' Brendan asked her now, as she placed a mug of steaming tea in front of him. She felt him scrutinising her face, and she tried not to look him in the eyes. He knew her so well. 'You desperately needed to borrow three hundred pounds because you're going on a little holiday?'

She could hear the disbelief in his voice, but she said nothing. Made herself a cup of tea instead. She was going to be under pressure to make the ferry if Brendan didn't budge soon.

'Where's the American? Shouldn't he be funding your trip to London?' Brendan said in a cold voice.

Niamh went very still, her tea bag dripping off the teaspoon onto the kitchen counter. She didn't dare turn around, but she felt Brendan standing up behind her. Staring at the back of her.

'I know why you needed the money, Niamh,' he said in a low voice.

She turned around, shaking her head. 'Don't tell Mammy,' she whispered.

'Ah God, Niamh,' Brendan said. To her surprise, his expression was kind.

'He never called me. Jesse. It was just a fling to him, clearly,' she confided.

'But Niamh, have you really thought this through?'

'Of course I have,' she said with conviction. 'I'm not ready to have a baby. Not on my own.'

'But your mam would help you,' Brendan said. 'You'll not need to worry about money. Me and Dad will help you out.'

'That's good of you. But this is what's right for me.' Niamh put her mug of tea down. 'You can't give me handouts. What would Deirdre say?' She couldn't keep the bitchy tone out of her voice.

Brendan pushed the red curls from his forehead, a deep flush reddening his pale freckled cheeks.

'Sure, Deirdre and I broke up weeks ago. Just after the road rally. Haven't seen her since then.'

'But…' Niamh shook her head. 'She said that you dropped her to mine, four weeks ago.'

Brendan frowned. 'What? Deirdre came here?'

'Yes, she turned up late at night,' Niamh told him, seeing surprise in Brendan's eyes. 'Brendan, did you not know?'

'No,' he said, looking annoyed now.

'So, you didn't know I had to drive her to South Armagh, with a load of explosives in the door panels of my car?' Niamh hissed, her body beginning to shake at the horror of the memory.

'What the fuck?' Brendan said, looking furious. 'I told her you were strictly for pickups down south! You weren't to cross the border. The bitch!'

'Well, it's done now,' Niamh said, crossing her arms. 'I don't want to think about it again.'

'I'm sorry, Niamh,' Brendan said, and he really looked it. 'She was clearly trying to get back at me.' He paused, his expression lifting. 'But then again, you did it.' He smiled. 'I'm proud of you.'

'Don't be,' Niamh said in a harsh whisper. 'I was terrified.'

They stood in silence for a while. 'Look, I've got to go,' Niamh said, tipping the rest of her tea down the sink. 'I'll miss the ferry.'

Brendan reached out and put his hand on her arm. 'Niamh, you can't go today,' he said. 'I need your help with something.'

She spun around. 'For fuck's sake, Brendan!'

'Look, I'm not trying to change your mind, but we need to move some guns.' His voice was calm, despite what he was saying. 'We've a tip-off someone snitched.'

'Can't you go on your own?'

'My northern reg draws too much attention,' he said. 'We need to take your car.'

'No,' Niamh spat. 'I'm all booked in. I have to go.'

'I promise I'll bring you myself, tomorrow,' he said. 'We'll change the ferry ticket, the appointment. I'll make the calls.'

'Please don't stop me!' Niamh wailed. 'This is so hard!'

But the look in Brendan's blue eyes was determined. 'I am not the one stopping you,' he said. 'You have to do this with me today. We've orders.'

'I don't want to any more,' Niamh whispered, tears of frustration rolling down her cheeks.

'This is what you signed up for, Niamh,' Brendan said, though his voice was soft as he took her hands and pulled her into his chest. She sobbed against him, letting all the disappointment, all the fear and anger stream out of her.

Brendan stroked her hair. 'Look, you might still make your appointment even,' he said. 'We'll do this job, and then I'll drive us to Dublin. I'll get us plane tickets and I'll come with you.'

'You can't afford all that.' Niamh stepped back, wiping the tears away with the back of her hands.

'I can, I promise,' Brendan said. 'I'm going with you because you shouldn't be alone.'

Niamh's body sagged with relief. 'Thanks, Brendan,' she said in a small voice.

'We're family,' he said, bending down and kissing her on the lips.

The years fell away, and she was back with Brendan in the dark woods, sharing furtive kisses, bonded by secrets and lies.

Chapter Twenty-One

Mullaghmore, 16th November 2017

Lily dropped Daniel off at the top of the laneway down to the Malone pig farm.

'I'm sorry,' Daniel said as he got out of her car.

Lily didn't reply. She didn't know for sure if Daniel would confess the whole truth about Eve's death to Sean, but right now she wanted to meet Connor's grandmother. The need consumed her. As she drove away from the Malone pig farm, she pushed away thoughts of Connor and Eve walking these laneways as teenagers, making love in hidden, secret places. Eve had been Connor's first love, and she knew that was special, but Lily had been the love of his life. She had to always remind herself of this, hold it close and precious.

She followed the road out of town, back towards Rosemary Kelly's small cottage. As she pulled up outside, she saw an old Toyota Corolla parked in the yard and heard a dog barking. She turned off the engine, and took a breath. This was going to be hard. She wasn't quite sure what she was going to say, or how.

Lily got out the car and retraced the steps she had taken earlier that day. It felt like the axis of the whole of her life had been altered during those few hours. She walked past the old tumble-down shed, its roof sunk in and covered in ivy. The scent of wildflowers was strong, and she caught the soothing aroma of lavender from a tub of it near the green cottage door. Even the house looked a little different now. More tinged with tragedy and loss. The grey of the stone a little gloomier, streaked by the shadows of the afternoon.

Lily took a breath. She was exhausted, but she couldn't endure one more day without telling Rosemary what had happened to her grandson. She lifted her hand and knocked on the door.

The woman who opened it was not in the least how Lily had imagined her. Connor had given Lily the impression his grandmother was a frail old woman who couldn't travel to America for their wedding, but the person who opened the door was far from frail. Tall and lean, with short white hair and elegant features, she looked to be in her early seventies. Neither did she look grandmother material, dressed as she was in a pair of purple yoga pants and matching top, with big silver hoops in her ears and a long silver chain with a stone pendant around her neck. A brown and white spaniel jumped up at her heels before bounding out through the door.

Rosemary stared at Lily, her eyes wide open in surprise, the colour drained from her cheeks in shock. 'Is it you? Lily? Connor's American wife?'

Lily felt completely wrong-footed. Rosemary had recognised her and knew all about her. But of course, she reminded herself, the wedding picture on her dresser had indicated this would be the case.

'Is it you, Lily?' Rosemary asked again, clearly shaken.

'Yes, hello,' Lily said. 'Sorry not to call ahead.'

'That's no problem,' Rosemary said. 'Surprise visitors are always welcome. No, it's so wonderful to see you.' Rosemary held out her hands, and instinctively Lily took them. 'But where's Connor?' She looked past her, scanning the yard.

Lily's throat was tightening. 'Can I come in, Mrs Kelly?' she asked in a hoarse voice.

'Call me Rosemary!' Connor's grandmother said, then whistled and called out, 'Willie!' for the spaniel, who came tearing back into the house with a stick in his mouth, brushing past Lily in furry excitement.

Rosemary led Lily into the cosy kitchen, and she caught the scent of freshly baked bread. 'Would you like a cup of tea, and a slice of my soda bread with jam?'

'Okay, sure, thanks,' Lily said, feeling awkward, but anything to put off what she had to tell Rosemary Kelly. She sat down at the same beautiful oak table she had placed her hand on before. 'You're different from what I expected. Connor never told me much about you, Rosemary,' Lily admitted.

'Did he not? Ah, the terror, and the two of you getting married so sudden-like.'

Lily took in Rosemary's words. Clearly Connor had been keen to keep his grandmother and Lily apart because of the story about Eve Malone.

'Connor didn't want me to visit you in America,' Rosemary said, as if sensing Lily's thoughts. 'He had a new life. I respected that, though it hurt.' She handed Lily a steaming cup of tea, and a plate of soda bread still warm from the oven. She pushed a platter of butter towards her, along with a knife and a jar of jam.

'Rhubarb,' she announced. 'Made it myself last summer.'

'Thank you,' Lily said, not wanting to eat at all now. How was she going to tell Connor's grandmother what had happened to him? Not only that, Rosemary had missed her grandson's memorial. Lily felt a dart of anger towards Connor. All these secrets.

'I said to him, last time we talked, that a baby will bring us all together,' Rosemary continued.

'A baby?' Lily's voice came out in a shocked hush.

'Yes, he told me that the two of you are trying for a baby,' Rosemary said. 'So good, my dear – I mean, after all that awful business with the Malone girl.'

Lily was beginning to feel a little overwhelmed. It was clear Connor had had more phone contact with Rosemary than he'd let on to Lily because how else would she know they'd been trying for a baby? Rosemary was so open, as if she'd known Lily all her life. Evidently, she had no idea Connor had kept so many secrets from his wife.

'Where *is* Connor?' Rosemary asked her. 'Why's he not with you? Is everything okay? I have been wondering. He hasn't called for over a month.'

Lily swallowed. 'Rosemary, please would you come sit down with me?'

Rosemary sat down at the table, suddenly very still and attentive. Willie had calmed down too, dropping his gnawed stick on the kitchen floor, and pushed his snout onto Rosemary's lap, sensing something was wrong.

Lily took a breath. 'The reason I'm here,' she began, taking another breath, because it was so hard to say the words. 'The reason I came to see you, Rosemary, is because Connor passed away.'

There was a stunned silence.

'Excuse me, what did you say?' Rosemary said, her voice high-pitched with fear. 'I don't think I heard you right.'

Lily forced herself to look into Rosemary's eyes, now panic-stricken. 'Connor is gone,' she said, her voice hoarse with emotion, unable to stop the tears coming.

Rosemary leapt up from the table as the spaniel barked in fright. 'No, no,' she said, looking wild-eyed. 'Not my little boy.'

It was all Lily could do to hold it together. One deep breath after another. 'It was an accident,' she said. 'There was a storm. Connor was out fishing with my dad, and he got swept overboard.'

Rosemary couldn't speak. Lily was truly worried she'd have a heart attack. She stood up and put her arms around the older woman, though they were strangers to each other. Lily led her into the front room and made her sit on a sofa.

'Take a breath,' she whispered. 'That's it.'

Rosemary put her hand on her heart and looked into Lily's eyes. 'I knew,' she whispered, her eyes shining with pain. 'Tried to fool myself that my instincts were wrong, but I just knew something was wrong when he didn't call.' She shook her head. 'What day did he die? When was it? Tell me, darling, what happened?'

It was dark by the time Lily had finished telling Rosemary about the terrible night of the storm, omitting the fact her father had been responsible. Twice, she'd broken down crying, and Rosemary had put her arms around her, letting her weep in a way she never had with her mom.

Although it had been so painful to tell Connor's grandmother that he was gone for good, Lily also felt a sense of release by telling her about it. She was tired, too. So much had happened in just one day.

'I'm grateful you came to tell me in person, Lily,' Rosemary said. 'It must have been hard for you to come here, knowing what everyone believes about what Connor did.'

'I know the truth,' Lily said. 'I ran into the Malone brothers, and Daniel told me what really happened. He was there that night. It was Eve who was driving.'

'I knew it!' Rosemary said, triumphant. 'Connor refused to admit it to me, but I knew he wasn't guilty.' Tears were shining in her eyes. 'It was a terrible business, just terrible. He had to leave because he was an outcast here in Mullaghmore. But then he found you. He phoned and told me all about you, Lily. How you were the best thing that had ever happened to him.'

'When we were together, I felt like I knew Connor inside out, as if we were parts of each other. But after he was gone, it began to feel like there was so much I didn't know,' Lily said. 'I came here to tell you about what happened, but also because I was trying to find out who he really was.'

'Sure, you knew him already, darling,' Rosemary said patting her hand. 'He was a good boy, a great man.'

'But why did he never tell me much about you?' Lily asked. 'And his parents? He just told me his mom died and that he never knew his father, but I know nothing more.'

'There's not so much to tell,' Rosemary said, looking away. 'It was me who raised Connor. Mother and father to him.' She sighed. 'His father ran a boatyard in Cape Cod. Not too far from you, I believe?'

'Oh my God,' Lily said, as the impact of one more secret swept through her. Was the whole reason she had ended up with Connor because he had been looking for his roots?

'But you see, his dad never knew about him.' Rosemary shook her head. 'Connor told me he got cold feet. Afraid his father wouldn't want to meet him.'

'I wish he'd told me,' Lily said. 'It's so sad. And what about his mother?' she asked, hesitantly, aware it must be a sensitive subject. Poor Rosemary, to have lost both her daughter and grandson.

Rosemary's face dropped. 'Poor Niamh,' she said, her voice flat. 'Families should stick together when bad things happen to them. But ours fell apart.'

Rosemary's words hit a nerve for Lily. 'I'm sorry to hear that,' she said. 'The same has happened back home, since Connor was drowned.'

'How's that?' Rosemary asked her.

Lily exhaled. It was easy to talk to Rosemary. 'You know I said Connor was only covering for me on the boat because I had an appointment with a fertility specialist that day? He should have been at home. It was his day off. And… I guess my dad forgot how inexperienced Connor was.'

As Lily explained to Rosemary how her family had been split by Connor's loss, she realised her anger was no longer lodged tight in her body. She didn't know why, but it was gone. When she thought about her father now, her main emotion was one of concern.

'Like I told you, there was a big storm and my dad didn't turn back in time,' Lily said. 'If my dad hadn't tried to carry on, Connor wouldn't have got tangled up in the lobster trap line. He wouldn't have gone overboard.'

Rosemary was seated opposite her on a floor cushion, her legs crossed and her head tilted, listening intently. Lily pressed her hands together, and Rosemary closed her own hands over hers. Lily could see the tears wavering in her eyes.

'Now my dad's being accused of seaman's manslaughter for Connor's death. He could face up to three years in jail.'

'Oh my goodness,' Rosemary said, in astonishment. 'But surely it was an accident?'

'It doesn't matter. As captain of the boat, my dad was responsible, and if he made a negligent decision than he's to blame.'

Lily couldn't help thinking about her parents back home. She missed them so much.

She had drunk too much wine to drive back to Seaview. Besides, Rosemary insisted she stay overnight. After giving the B&B a quick call to let Noreen know she'd be back in the morning to check out, and managing to avoid her curious questions, Lily returned to Rosemary in the kitchen.

'I think we need to eat some food to soak up all the alcohol,' Rosemary said to Lily, waving a leek in her hand.

'Good idea, can I help?'

'Sure.'

Rosemary sat Lily at the table with a chopping board and a pile of vegetables. Lily didn't have the heart to tell Rosemary she wasn't a fan of eggplant or zucchini. She'd just not have to be so picky and eat it to be polite. Rosemary told her she'd been a lifelong vegetarian, was indeed a vegan now. This fact surprised Lily, because Connor's speciality had been cooking fish.

'He did always love the sea,' Rosemary said. 'What a great surfer he was! We have the best waves here in Mullaghmore, and Connor used to hang out with the surfing crowd. They were a little free-spirited, but no harm in them.' Rosemary paused, and Lily looked up from her chopping board to see the older woman's face cloud over. 'But then he started going out with the pig farmer's daughter,' she said with disdain. 'She changed Connor. That girl was his ruination.'

'What was Eve Malone like?' Lily couldn't stop herself from asking.

'A selfish little madam.' Rosemary's voice had hardened. 'She led Connor astray. He was so kind-hearted, and Eve took advantage of him.' Rosemary sniffed. 'Still, one shouldn't speak ill of the dead.'

They continued to chop vegetables in silence for a few minutes. Lily was desperate to ask more about Connor's mother.

'Can I ask too, what was Niamh like?' Lily ventured, unable to hold back any longer.

Rosemary stopped chopping garlic, her whole body still. 'My daughter's story is tragic and complicated, Lily,' Rosemary told her.

Lily looked up at Connor's grandmother. What she read in her expression was deep regret, a look just like Lily's father's when last she'd seen him.

Chapter Twenty-Two

Mullaghmore, 13th May 1994

Her mam was awake when she got home. Sitting up at the kitchen table, baby Connor cradled in her arms, asleep.

'Where were you?' her mam whispered.

Niamh turned her back to her, pulled off her muddy boots, and kicked them over to the back door. She was annoyed that her mam was spying on her. 'I couldn't sleep. Went for a walk,' she lied.

'I heard you come back in the car.'

'Yeah,' she said. 'I drove to somewhere to go for a walk.'

'You can't just go off in the middle of night, Niamh.' Her mam's voice was low, warning. 'What about Connor?'

'Well, you're here!' Niamh snapped. She was so tired now, and her mam was making her feel guilty. Why couldn't she have been asleep in bed when Niamh returned, like all the times before?

'He's your child,' her mam said, standing up and passing the sleeping bundle over to Niamh. 'You know I adore him, but it's you he wants when he wakes up.'

Niamh took Connor and saw his eyelids flutter as she held him tight to her chest, feeling the rise and fall of his chest against her body. She loved her son, of course she did. But sometimes she felt so trapped, like a cornered animal. It made her angry, and defensive. Short-tempered with her mam, who had been so brilliant ever since the day she'd told her she was pregnant.

One clear positive consequence of Niamh having Connor was his effect on her mam. A year had passed since he was born, during which Rosemary had not had one low period, not one day missed from her work because she couldn't get out of bed. Niamh saw the joy on her mam's face when she held her grandchild. She had been obsessed with him from the moment he'd been born.

It had been different for Niamh. She'd struggled for weeks. Her bonding with her baby son hadn't been as immediate as it had been for her mam. In her darkest moments, when Connor was crying from colic, Niamh hadn't slept all night, and Brendan was ringing her with instructions, Niamh wondered what would have happened if she had gone through with the abortion. Or even, if she had chased Jesse out to America, not waiting for a phone call.

She had never told Jesse. She'd meant to go down to Joseph O'Reilly and ask him if he had the contact details for his old apprentice so she could write to him. But during her pregnancy she hadn't wanted to force Jesse to be with her, and any kind of decision-making had felt overwhelming, especially at the end.

Once Connor had arrived, she should have written to Jesse with a picture of their baby but she still didn't have his address. Now she was too embarrassed to ask Joseph because so much time had passed. As weeks had turned to months it had got harder. And she'd never heard from Jesse, not once. That was her excuse. He hadn't wanted her. So why would he want their son?

It was Brendan who had supported her and Connor. Although this was a fact her mam didn't know: oblivious it was Brendan who had bought the car seat, the baby carrier and the cot. Believing Niamh's lies that it was old friends from school, who'd clubbed together and bought her some things. On the odd occasion she answered the phone to Brendan, her mam would narrow her eyes and purse her lips. Afterwards, she would tell Niamh yet again that she didn't like her hanging around with Brendan and Tadhg.

'They're not good people,' she warned her daughter.

Her mam had never asked her about Deirdre's appearance in their house in the middle of the night. It was as if she'd blanked it from her mind. Sometimes, Niamh wondered: did her mam suspect? Especially now she'd caught her creeping back in at night?

If she did suspect something, she never let on. Strangely, this hurt Niamh.

Niamh carried Connor up the stairs now, and put him down in his cot at the bottom of her bed. He stirred for a second, and she stroked his soft dark hair, the same colour as his dad's. She wondered what kind of little boy he would become. Would he be asking about his daddy? What would she tell him? And what kind of man would Connor become? She knew with certainty she didn't want him mixed up in her kind of life. But surely by then, things would be better? There was so much talk of a ceasefire between the Republicans and the Loyalists in the north. Niamh was praying for it to happen. It would be her liberation.

She was tired of the secrets. Tired of driving out to meet Brendan in the woods, or on the bogs at night-time. Hunting for the latest stash of guns, and moving them either to another location, or back to her shed. Or, on several occasions, she'd driven them over the border herself, each time as terrifying as the last. She was waiting for the day the soldiers would stop her and give the car a good search. Waiting for the day she'd not return to her son.

Had Brendan lied to her when he'd promised he'd bring her to London for the abortion that day? She didn't think so. But as they'd driven off in her car to move the bag of guns, he'd told her again she wasn't alone, that if she kept the baby, he and Tadhg would help her out.

'Mam won't want your help,' Niamh had said, wavering.

'Don't tell her we're helping, then,' Brendan had said, putting a hand on her knee. 'You've secrets from her as it is. One more makes no difference.'

The question of what to do was in her mind the whole time as they lugged the bags – two of them – across the bog, and into the boot of the car. Niamh wasn't even thinking about what she was moving, or what would happen if they were seen.

As she and Brendan had driven along empty bog roads, the skies loaded with dark clouds, spots of rain splattering the windscreen, the idea of going to London had begun to fade. Brendan would have her back. Like he always had.

After burying the guns in a new spot in a bleak, blasted corner of bog, hidden from view by scraggy bushes and spindly birch trees, she and Brendan had had to walk for an hour across the marshy land back to the car. They had to pick their way gingerly across, and the effort of concentrating on avoiding sink holes had made Niamh feel dizzy and sick. All of sudden, she'd been consumed by nausea. She'd bent over, throwing up on the dark, fecund earth. Brendan knelt down by her side.

'You okay?' he asked, gently lifting her hair away from her face and holding it back.

'Yeah,' she gasped, heaving again. Afterwards, she fell back on her haunches, feeling weak and tearful.

Brendan pulled a small bottle of water out of his coat pocket and handed it to her. 'Here you go,' he said. 'Take a sip.'

She gulped the water down. Took a breath. 'I don't know what to do,' she said to Brendan, looking into his searing blue eyes. So different from Jesse's brown eyes, with their long lashes and dreamy appeal. Brendan's lashes were so fair you couldn't see them, and his eyes were the colour of blue flames.

'Whatever you decide, Niamh, I'll support you,' Brendan said. 'I told you, I'll go with you.'

'But abortion's a sin,' she whispered.

'Ah, come on,' Brendan said, squatting down on the bog next to her. 'You know that's a load of bollocks made up by misogynists!'

This made her laugh. The release felt good. She clutched his hands, which were warm. Her own were freezing.

'And if you decide to keep it, I'll stick by you,' he said.

'Thanks,' she whispered, knowing he meant every word.

'It'll be okay,' Brendan said, helping her up. He took her hand and they headed back across the bog together.

This was the problem. Brendan had been true to his word. Stuck by her side the whole time since Connor was born. Not just supporting her materially, but also emotionally. After Deirdre, he'd never introduced her to another girlfriend. At times, Niamh caught him watching her, and a part of her worried. She loved Brendan, but she wasn't in love with him.

There had been three occasions now since Connor had been born, when she'd felt so lonely that she'd gone to Brendan.

The first time, Connor had been just over six months old. Niamh had called Brendan on a weekday morning, and asked him to meet her in a couple of hours. She'd driven along the coast to a deserted cove, with Connor chirping away in the back seat. Brendan had got there first. She'd seen him as she'd pulled up, leaning against the bonnet of his car in his long coat, smoking a cigarette. It had been cold. The sea had lashed onto the empty beach, and the wind had whipped past her.

'What's up?' he'd asked her as she'd walked towards him.

But he'd known. He'd been able to see quite clearly in her eyes what she needed. Niamh said nothing, just grabbed his hand and pulled him towards her.

'What about the baby?' Brendan had asked.

'He's fallen asleep.'

They'd both glanced over. True enough, Connor's eyes were closed.

'Come on, it's freezing,' Brendan had said, opening the back door of his car.

They'd clambered inside, burying themselves under a blanket, as Niamh had pulled off her jeans. It had been urgent, intense, and nothing like the sex she'd had with Jesse. Afterwards, she had felt like screaming, because she still missed Jesse so much – but she couldn't tell Brendan that. He had smiled, stroking the side of her face.

'We're a great team, Niamh,' he'd whispered to her, tracing his hand down her cheek. 'You and me, eh?'

On her drive home, Niamh had immediately regretted her actions. Being with Brendan had only intensified how lonely she felt. She'd slammed her hands on the steering wheel in frustration.

And yet they had met again, at her instigation, two more times over the past few months. Brendan had never asked her to say she loved him, or to be his girlfriend or wife. He just gave her sex when Niamh had found herself getting in deeper and deeper. She had wanted her freedom from the fight for a united Ireland so badly, and yet now she was even more involved than ever before. She even had a codename: The Boatman's Wife. She hated it. Not just because she wasn't married, or because Jesse had been a boatman, but because of what it symbolised. The Boatman was a mythical figure, Brendan had told her. Like the ferryman who brought the dead across the River Styx to Hades.

'So, you're saying I'm an agent of death,' Niamh had said, taking a drag on the joint before passing it back to him.

'Well, what else do you think these guns are for?' Brendan had replied, flicking the butt into a puddle of bog water before taking off across the fields. She had watched him move so fast, like a creature of the night, lithe and quick. When she was with

Brendan, she felt safe. But once he was gone, the fear descended. Her hands had trembled as she'd hefted the hold-all of guns onto her shoulder and lugged them back to the car. Pulling out the floor of the boot, she'd hidden them where the spare tyre should have been, and put the carpet back over them.

His words had stuck in her head on the drive back home. She had tried not to think about the consequences of what she'd been doing over the years. This was where she belonged, and Brendan and Tadhg were part of who she was.

Brendan might not ask for her love, but he had her whole life in the palm of his hand.

Chapter Twenty-Three

Mullaghmore, 16th November 2017

As Lily and Rosemary ate dinner, finishing off a bottle of wine, Lily imagined Connor sitting at this very table, refusing to eat his grandmother's vegan casserole and frying up a pan of kippers instead. She imagined Connor at the age of nine or ten, sitting up at the table, uniform askew, his cheeks sticky from his grandmother's rhubarb jam on bread. This had been his home, where he had grown up into the man she had fallen in love with.

The vegetables melted in Lily's mouth; the casserole was divine. She had never tasted such fresh vegetables before.

'This is so delicious,' she enthused.

'Thank you, darling,' Rosemary said. 'Most of the vegetables came from the garden. I store them in the shed. Too much for me on my own, so it takes ages to get through them. And my secret ingredient is seaweed – dulse to be specific, which I collect myself.'

'Oh yes!' Lily said enthusiastically, delighted at the evidence Connor had shared something with her about his time with his grandmother. 'Connor told me you harvested seaweed together.' She put down her spoon and rubbed her arm again. It was so itchy. Angry and red. Driving her crazy, especially since she'd forgotten her medicated cream.

'Is your arm all right?' Rosemary asked her.

'Oh yeah,' Lily said. 'I've very sensitive skin. When I'm stressed, I get really bad rashes.'

'Remind me after dinner,' Rosemary said to her. 'I've something which might help with that.' She topped up their wine glasses. 'So, you asked me about what happened to Niamh, Connor's mother.'

'Yes, if it's not too painful for you,' Lily said gently.

'I can honestly say I'm not quite sure what has happened to my daughter by now,' Rosemary said.

'Sorry, I don't understand. What do you mean?' Lily asked, looking at Rosemary's troubled face.

'I've given up on her ever coming back, but that's my fault.'

Lily nearly choked on her vegetables. She put her fork down and took a sip of the wine. 'I'm real confused, Rosemary, because Connor told me his mother was dead.'

A dark look loaded Rosemary's eyes. 'It was easier to tell him that when he was tiny; she vanished overnight. But when he was older, I told him the truth. I guess he chose to keep it simple and tell people she was dead. I tried to explain to Connor, but he was so angry. Said she'd abandoned him. That his mother was dead to him. But it was me who told her to go.' Rosemary shook her head. 'Connor never knew that, Lily. I didn't want him to hate me.' Her voice cracked. 'I was wild with rage. What she did, what she'd been doing, was so terrible that I believed at the time she wasn't a fit mother. Connor was so tiny and vulnerable.'

Rosemary clasped her hands, shaking her head slowly. 'But I never meant for her to stay away forever. I guess that's my punishment.'

'Do you know where she is now?' Lily asked Rosemary. She couldn't help feeling a flash of anger on Connor's behalf. Why had Rosemary banished her own daughter and separated her from her child? What could ever make someone do that?

'I think somewhere in the States, maybe Arizona,' Rosemary said. 'She used to call me up, the first year she left. But then she just vanished.' She put her knife and fork down on her plate, her appetite clearly gone. 'To be estranged from your child is a terrible burden to bear, Lily.'

Lily watched Rosemary as she got up and left the room, returning a few minutes later with two photograph albums. Waves of sorrow and joy washed over Lily as she looked through all of the pictures of Connor with his mother and grandmother as a baby, and then just with Rosemary later on. Niamh had been a very striking woman, with dark red hair and green eyes.

The photograph albums then took Lily even further back, to before Connor was born. Pictures of Niamh as a little girl with her mother and father, within whose face Lily could see shadows of Connor. One picture, Rosemary paused on. It was a group photograph by a lough, and by the fashion it looked to be about the late eighties. Lily recognised Niamh and her parents, but not the other family.

'That's my husband's cousin, Tadhg, and his wife Mary, along with their youngest, Brendan.' Rosemary looked over at Lily. 'Thereby hangs a very sad story.' She pressed her finger down on Brendan, her voice suddenly hard. 'He's the reason I had to send my Niamh away.'

'Will you tell me why?' Lily ventured, rubbing her itchy arm again.

Slowly, she was piecing parts of the puzzle of her husband together. She realised now that for the picture to be complete, she needed to know all about Niamh, too. She had been with Connor for the first year of his life. What could have happened which had made Rosemary ask her to leave her son behind?

Chapter Twenty-Four

Mullaghmore, 27th May 1994

As she drove up to the checkpoint crossing, Niamh took a deep breath and glanced at Connor in the rear-view mirror. He was chewing on his toy bunny, cheeks red and shiny.

As she ground to a halt, a soldier leant in, winking at Connor. He looked younger than Niamh, with a thick mop of curly blond hair and even white teeth.

'What age is the young one?'

'Just over a year,' Niamh said tightly.

'Ah, same as my nephew.' The soldier smiled at her. 'They're fun at that age, right?'

'Yeah,' Niamh said, doing her best to put on an act. *Please God, let him shut up*, she prayed.

At last, the soldier waved her on, and Niamh accelerated as smoothly as she could without drawing any more attention to herself. Her body was rigid with fear and guilt. What kind of mother used their baby as a cover to smuggle guns? She could hear Brendan's justification inside her head.

This is a war, Niamh. Nothing will change without violence.

But I don't want civilians to die, Niamh countered in her mind.

She could see him. In those dark woods, framed by ghostly white birch trees. She could smell him. So different from Jesse's scent of salt and sea. Brendan's power was drawn from the bleeding earth, heavy and overpowering. Brendan, putting his hands on her shoulders and looking into her eyes. All the times she had felt the pain of their ancestors blazing in his heart. Knew, without a doubt, he was willing to die for them. She had been once, too, but she wasn't willing to give the life of her child.

Remember, your own father was killed, Niamh. Brendan's voice again, as she drove along the roads of the north. Her cousin would never let her forget.

As Niamh drove into the yard at Tadhg's house, she saw Brendan's car parked out front, but no sign of him. Usually he was waiting for her outside. Sitting on a pile of old tractor tyres, smoking a cigarette in his long coat, no matter what the season.

Niamh got out of the car, leaving Connor in his car seat despite his little chubby arms reaching out to her. She didn't want to linger, so walked quickly towards the house. The air felt thick, and she got the sense of something being wrong. That was it. The woods were silent behind the house, as if all the birds had flown away. No dog was barking. Where was Patch? He never strayed far from Tadhg.

She pushed open the front door, then let out a roar as she saw Patch lying in a pool of blood on the hall rug. White fear descended on her. She rushed into the kitchen, and what she saw there caused her to let out a wail right from the pit of her belly.

They were both dead. Tadhg had been shot in the face, sitting in his armchair by the Aga. Brendan had clearly tried to fight back. He was shot all over. Blood oozed from his chest, his back, pooled across the floor. A river of blood. 'Oh God, Brendan!' She fell on her knees, not caring about the blood seeping into her jeans, and reached down to check his pulse. Of course, he was dead. But his hand was still warm. Unmarred by the blood. She brought it to her face. Held it there.

'No!' she screamed. 'Brendan, no!' Tears flooded her face, dripping off her chin. She felt as if her heart would crack open. She raised her face to the ceiling. 'Please,' she begged. 'Please, come back.'

Brendan had been her constant. As she squeezed his limp hand, she realised the fact it was still warm meant that whoever had done this was still close by. She let Brendan's hand go. Quickly, she closed the lids of his eyes, and got up. There was blood all over her legs, but she didn't have time to clean up. She knew well enough to get out. As she stood up, she turned her head away. She couldn't bear to look at Tadhg's blasted face again.

She rushed down the hall, slipping on the blood, giving a hiccup of grief as she stepped over poor Patch. Why the dog?

She ran back across the yard, relief washing through her to see Connor still strapped in, and crying for her.

'I'm coming, darling,' she called out to him.

But she could feel eyes on her. A shiver ran down her spine. She spun around in the yard, but she couldn't see anyone. Yet she felt it. The impending doom, as sure as the dark clouds covering the sun, plunging the yard in shadow.

A murder of crows took off from the dense spruce wood at the back of the house, cawing. Were they coming for her?

Niamh jumped in the driving seat, barely closing the door before she tore off down the road.

Connor began to scream, picking up her fear.

'It's okay,' Niamh said to him, pulling on all her inner strength and calm. 'It's okay, baby.' But she was thinking of her father. He'd been shot, too, left on the side of the road like a dog. Was this her fate?

Connor's crying intensified into full-blown wailing. Niamh glanced in the rear-view mirror and saw his face red and scrunched up.

'It's okay, baby, it's okay,' she crooned. She wasn't going to stop. She knew exactly where she was going, and what she needed to do.

By the side of Lough Melvin, Niamh pulled up. She placated Connor with his soother before getting out of the car. She walked around to the back of the car, opened the boot, and took out the spare pair of jeans she kept in the back. She pulled off her bloody pair and dropped them on the ground. Had the presence of mind to put on the gloves she kept in the back, too. Then she lifted up the carpet and pulled out the hold-all, shoving the bloody jeans into the bag. She lugged it over to the edge of the shore, and picked up a couple of heavy stones, putting them in the bag for good measure.

She went as far out as possible onto a rocky ledge, swung the bag back and forth and threw it as far as she could. It sank immediately, as the surface of the lake rippled outwards.

Chapter Twenty-Five

Mullaghmore to Maine, 21st November 2017

Connor,

We are halfway over the Atlantic, halfway between your home and mine, and I am sitting next to your grandmother on the plane. She's shown me album after album of pictures of you. I've even seen your wedding picture with Eve Malone. She was very beautiful, but I can see in your eyes that you weren't happy. Your expression is so different from our wedding pictures. So yes, I am taking that. I look at your big smile on our special day and I know in my heart you loved me. But Connor, why did you lie? Every day, I find out a little bit more about you before me, and it hurts to discover there's so much I didn't know. I can't stop staring at the photos of you as a baby with your mom. She was so young, with her long red hair – I've seen strands of that colour in yours. When I stayed in your grandmother's house, I slept in your bedroom. All around me was you as a little boy. The faded wallpaper with little blue airplanes on it, and the shelves filled with childhood books. I found a battered copy of The Call of the Wild, *my all-time favourite book. I love Buck, and how he felt different among dogs. A wolf at heart. I opened the book, and inside you had written your name in spidery, childish handwriting:*

'Connor Fitzgerald, aged 11.'

I gave a little cry and clutched the book to my chest.

I've so many questions. Why is it Rosemary said you were excited we were trying for a family, and yet you never told me this? But the biggest question is about your mother. Why did you never tell me she was in fact alive, not dead? We could have gone and found her together.

Your grandmother has helped me, Connor. Even my arm has stopped itching. Rosemary said the rash was caused by my body reacting to the stress of your loss. Before I went to bed, she poured me a bath. I watched her fill the steaming water with strands of seaweed she told me she'd gathered herself. It was just like you told me.

Once I got into the bath, sank into the warm water, beneath the salty aroma of the ocean, I could detect the soothing scent of rose geranium. Rosemary had claimed it would help my sore skin too.

It worked. The seaweed bath, the rose geranium oil, your grandmother's nurturing presence. Later, as I lay in your childhood bed, my body surrendered. I let myself cry until your bedsheets were wet with my tears. I knew I had to go back home but it was going to be so hard seeing all the places we were once together.

In your bed, looking around your room at things belonging to you, my darling Connor, the boy with no father, I remembered the first time my dad took you out on the Lily May. *We'd been married about three months when Dad finally accepted you as my husband. Once he did so he was all in.*

I remembered watching my dad standing next to you as you tried to negotiate exiting the harbour. His hand on yours helping you steer, and then stepping back to let you take control on your own. Telling you, 'As soon as we're clear, open it up, and we can see what we can do.'

*We. That's what he had said. Including you in the family.
I guess, my dad came to love you like a son. I think you
knew that, didn't you?*

*I left Maine because I was so angry with my dad. I
couldn't look at him, Connor, because I blamed him for
your death. But he and Mom lost you too. Now when I
think about it all the rage is gone. I'm grieving and all I
need is them so bad.*

*I am writing all this down for myself. Afterwards, like
all the other letters I've written you since you've been lost, I'll
tear it up into little pieces and burn it, so that all my words
to you become ashes. It's a small ritual of departure, of saying
goodbye from me to you. At first when they never found your
body, I desperately wanted them to, so we could have a coffin
and I could cling to it and let out all my grief. I wanted
to have an urn of ashes to carry all the way to Ireland and
throw into the wind off the edge of Mullaghmore Head. But
all I have are the letters I've been writing you every day. All
my anger, regret, and love, love, love for a man I will never
be able to hold again.*

*I look out the airplane window, and we begin to descend
to land. We are flying above the ocean. I watch the steady
motion of the waves, relentlessly pushing in towards land,
and pulling away. They move in rhythm to my breath. All
I can do from now on is just breathe, in and out, just like
our wide blue Atlantic Ocean.*

Chapter Twenty-Six

Sedona, Arizona, 15th August 1998

Niamh had travelled as far away from the sea as she could go, to a place so different from home. As soon as she got out of the truck in Sedona and surveyed the arid landscape, red boulders, and cloudless blue sky, she decided to stop running and stay put for a while. The landscape felt so alien. Here, she hoped she could forget about who she was.

Yet still the green fields, the rolling waves of the Atlantic Ocean, haunted her. In the face of every baby, she saw Connor.

She could never forget that terrible day. She'd driven like a zombie back towards the checkpoint with Connor screaming in the back of the car. She'd pulled in and placated him with a biscuit, and a drink of milk in his beaker. Tears had streamed down her cheeks, and Connor had grabbed on to her hair, tugging it. His big brown eyes had been hooked on her; her own fear reflected in them.

She'd held him tight. Hugged him fiercely, his heart beating fast against her chest. She'd inhaled the scent of his soft hair, felt his cheeks damp from their tears mixed together. Gradually, she'd began to calm down. All that mattered was protecting Connor.

By the time she reached the checkpoint, Connor was already asleep. The soldiers waved her on without stopping her.

As she neared her home, speeding around the twists and turns of the country roads, bumping through potholes and not caring if she damaged her car, Niamh knew what she must do. Leave.

Take Connor, and hopefully her mother, and leave Ireland. Now was the time to go get Jesse's address from Joseph O'Reilly. Pride had stopped her before, but their situation was desperate.

The bad feeling came upon her again as she passed the graveyard where her daddy was buried. Her body tensed with dread as she pulled into the drive and saw a strange car parked next to her mam's An Post van. Its registration plate was northern.

She began to shake uncontrollably. Should she drive away? But what about her mam?

Niamh took a breath, and got out of the car. She unstrapped Connor, who was fast asleep, and gently lifted him up. He stirred, wrapping his arms around her neck, and sticking his thumb in his mouth.

The back door was open, and to Niamh's relief, Pixie came trotting across the kitchen to greet her before retreating to her basket. But she could sense the tension as she pushed open the door into the front room. Her mam was sitting on her father's chair, rigid and pale. On the couch opposite was Deirdre and the man she'd been kissing the day Niamh had driven her across the border with the explosives. He had an AK-47 laid across his lap. The same type of gun as the ones Niamh smuggled.

'Well, there she is,' Deirdre said, raising her eyebrows at Niamh. 'Johnny and I've been waiting with your mam a wee while, so we have.'

Niamh wanted to rush at her and scratch her eyes out. Brendan was dead. Tadhg was dead. But her eyes were on the AK-47, which the man was cradling in his lap.

'What're you doing here?' Niamh managed to ask.

'Johnny and I want the guns, Niamh, then we'll be on our way, so we will,' Deirdre said.

Niamh sensed her mam's head turn, the heat of her gaze. Connor was a dead weight in her arms. But she wasn't letting go of him.

'I don't have them,' she said.

Deirdre gave her a cold stare. She had the eyes of a lizard.

'I left them with Brendan.'

She heard her mam's gasp of disapproval. But all Niamh could think about was Brendan's shot-up body. Had it been Johnny who'd done the deed?

'Sure, you know that's bollocks,' Deirdre said evenly.

Silence pooled around Niamh. She should be protecting her mam and Connor, but she was also raging. She let her gaze drop to the gun and then stared back at Deirdre. She wanted Deirdre to say it out loud, to say why she knew Brendan couldn't have the guns.

Eventually, Johnny stood up impatiently, waving his AK-47 around. 'Where's the fucking bag of guns, girl?'

Her mam shrank back in her chair.

'It's okay, Mammy,' Niamh said, handing her mam Connor, although she dared not look her in the face. Things were far from okay. 'I told you, Brendan has them,' she said, glowering at Johnny.

He grimaced and spat on her mother's carpet. 'That's a fucking lie,' he said.

Deirdre stood up, put her hand on Johnny's arm. 'Brendan and Tadhg are informers, Niamh, as bad as the Brits, and by association you're implicated.'

'They weren't traitors,' Niamh flared up. 'You butchered them for nothing.'

Her mam gave a tiny scream, but Niamh began to lose possession of herself. 'None of us are traitors. We've always been loyal. My father was killed because of the Cause.'

Deirdre remained calm. Took out a packet of cigarettes and lit one, before throwing the pack to Johnny. 'We're not going to hurt you, or your mam, or the wain,' she said. 'We'll go on a wee dander, Niamh, and we'll get the guns.' She began walking out of the front room, and Niamh followed her.

'No, Niamh,' her mam said in a strangled voice. 'Don't go with them.'

'It's okay, Mammy,' Niamh said. 'Just mind Connor, will you?'

Outside the house, the sun had emerged and Niamh was blasted by glorious sunlight. Deirdre and Johnny began marching towards Niamh's car.

'After I found Brendan and Tadhg, I threw the guns away,' Niamh called out to them. 'In Lough Melvin.'

'Why'd you do that, you waste of space?' Deirdre said icily, turning around.

'Because I didn't know who had killed them,' Niamh said, truthfully. 'I thought it was the loyalists. I thought they might get the guns off me—'

'Far enough,' Johnny interrupted, as he opened her boot to check. 'Yeah, empty.'

'There's a ledge of rock, right by the first bit of lake you come to, and I threw them from there,' Niamh said.

Johnny turned to Deirdre. 'Come on, let's go see if we can fish them out.' He strode over to their car, lifting up the back seat and concealing his gun beneath it.

'You killed them, didn't you?' Niamh pushed, her voice high and hysterical. She tugged on Deirdre's arm, and the blond girl spun around, flicking her hand off as if Niamh were a piece of dirt.

'Don't start me, Niamh. Your family were informers. Touts. The whole lot of you scum,' she hissed.

But Niamh could see it in her eyes. Deirdre was lost in her fury, coiled up in her rigid beliefs so tight that she'd just killed a man she'd once made love to.

After they'd driven off, Niamh stood in the yard, swaying. The sun had gone back behind a cloud, and her whole world looked unreal, in sharp relief. Deep, dark shadows and hard edges.

As soon as she came back into the front room, her mam let out a cry. Connor was awake now. Crawling on the carpet and playing with his little green tractor.

Her mam jumped up and grabbed her, hugging her tight. 'Thank God, thank God,' she kept saying. In the next second, she stepped back and slapped Niamh hard on her cheek, making her eyes smart. Her relief had given way to pure anger. 'You stupid, stupid little girl,' she hissed. 'You could have got us all killed!'

Niamh stepped back in shock. She had never seen her mother so angry before.

'I told you to stay away from Tadhg and Brendan,' her mam shouted at her. 'Tadhg is the reason your father is dead! They're bad people.'

'No,' Niamh whispered. 'They were my family. And they just got murdered!'

'Because you never, never get involved, Niamh!' her mam screeched. 'Anyone with any sense knows that around here. Your father knew it. But he was soft on his cousin Tadhg.'

'Brendan was there for me when Daddy died,' Niamh retaliated. 'You were so caught up in your own loss; I was all alone.'

'My husband had just been murdered!' her mam gave out.

Their voices had risen to such an extent that Connor looked up at the both of them with worried eyes, while Pixie ran into the room, barking at the two women.

'He was my daddy too!' Niamh screamed back. 'You got into your bed, and you just fucking abandoned me. Brendan was the only one who cared. And he's dead, Mam!' Niamh let out a wail, so that Connor began to cry again.

'I was there for you!' Her mother refused to believe her. 'I looked after you. Fed you. Clothed you. I've always looked after you. Never a word about you getting pregnant with that American boy's baby – but Niamh, this is unforgiveable.'

Cold realisation began creeping down Niamh's spine. As her child continued to cry, it was her mother who bent down and picked him up. Connor immediately stopped crying, soothed by his granny's touch.

'Your father would be turning in his grave,' her mam said in a quieter voice. 'You're not fit to be a mother.'

Niamh had stopped crying. She wiped her sleeve over her wet eyes. Her whole body felt a shiver of grief. She looked at her child, nestling into her mother. They belonged together. Her mam was right. She didn't deserve Connor.

Years had passed living in America in a daze, as Niamh numbly existed through each day. She'd hitched her way across the States to end up in this small town in Arizona. Got a job as a chambermaid in one of the tourist resorts. The first year, she spent all her spare money on phone calls to Ireland, ringing her mam to hear the sound of Connor's laughter in the background.

'Where are you, Niamh?' her mam asked.

But she didn't tell her. 'You were right,' Niamh replied, her heart breaking all the same. 'I'm a danger to you all. I have to stay away.'

Her mam didn't reply immediately, because it was clear she agreed.

'But Mam, do you forgive me?' Niamh begged.

'No, Niamh,' her mam said in a quiet voice. 'I can't. You put Connor's life at risk. I can't forgive you for that.'

'I know you're taking the best care of him,' Niamh said, before tears prevented her from saying any more.

It wasn't her mam's fault. She had done this to herself.

Niamh stopped calling. The years passed. Connor was better off without her. She knew her mam was a better mother than she could ever have been. Connor gave her mam purpose. Her child had banished her mother's grief, but now Niamh was drowning in loss.

At night, it took her hours to fall asleep. She'd hug her sides, aching for her baby boy. Either shivering from the air con, or if she turned it off, bathed in sweat. How could she ever get through such pain? When she did fall asleep, she'd have the nightmare. Walking into Tadhg's house, seeing Brendan all shot up. Tadhg's face gone, and the dog dead in the hall. Patch the dog would morph into her father. Why had they had to shoot the dog, too? Her own people. That was the terrible thing. Every morning, she felt such outrage. Tadhg and Brendan would never have informed on their own.

Often, she'd wake in the middle of the night, panting and sweating with fear. Imagining she heard sounds outside. Had Deirdre and Johnny come for her? All the way to Arizona? Of course not, she wasn't important enough. Just the gunrunner, The Boatman's Wife, with her instruments of death. But a gun had killed Tadhg and Brendan. She knew in her heart she was as bad as any other terrorist. She might not have pulled any triggers, but she was part of the cycle of violence.

Niamh tried praying to God on her knees at night, but it didn't make her feel any better. So then she went to some of the churches in Arizona. They were all evangelical, which reminded her of the narrowmindedness of some of the Loyalists, so she stopped going to church, too. She'd been raised a Catholic, but God had never felt real to her, and her mother had hated their parish priest in Mullaghmore. Sedona was a hub of New Age healing and Niamh turned to other forms of spirituality to try to ease her pain. She tried all sorts of things: visiting the energy vortexes of all four sites of Sedona natural healing at Airport Mesa, Bell Rock, Cathedral Rock and Boynton Canyon. Although the exertion of the hikes up these big red boulders of ancient rock made her feel momentarily better, it wasn't long before her heartache returned. She went to chakra balancing workshops and guided vision journeys with shaman healers, but when it came down to sharing circles, she couldn't tell any other soul who she really was, what she'd done. It was just too horrific. In the end, she told those who would listen that her family had died in a fire back in Ireland. Then they either left her alone, embarrassed to be in the company of such sadness and tragedy, or did their best to try to help her find peace through laying hands, or chanting. But how could they truly help her when what she had told them was a lie? A couple of times, Niamh had considered psychic readings, but she had been afraid of what the reader would tell her: not just the past, but also her future. Would she never see her son again?

It was only when she started painting that she began to feel anything close to okay. Quite by chance, she'd come across an art store on a drive to Flagstaff. On a whim, she'd spent all her wages that week on watercolour paper, paints and pencils. Driving back, she'd turned down a small track into the Oak Creek Canyon, and walked down to the rushing creek with her art materials in a tote bag. She'd spent her afternoon off painting by the water, immersing herself in the sensation of all the colours she could see and feel. At last, she had felt peace, and forgotten her loss – if just for a moment.

For the first time in all her years in America, she thought of Jesse. Could she contact him? She had no idea how she would begin to tell him about all that had happened, let alone that he had a child.

It was later on the same day that Niamh saw the news. What happened had been so awful, the tragedy had spread worldwide. An IRA bomb had gone off in the town of Omagh, north of the border, killing twenty-nine innocent people, both Protestants and Catholics. One of them had been a woman, pregnant with twins.

A tsunami of shame descended upon her as Niamh sat at the bar in Sedona and watched the footage of the devastated town centre in Omagh. She remembered the explosives she'd smuggled across the border in the door panels of her car. She hadn't wanted to do it, but she hadn't been brave enough to say no. To walk away. Now she'd been banished and was even more of an exile than she would have been if she'd refused in the first place.

Niamh was bereft of all she'd ever believed in. As she sat at the bar in Sedona, downing Bloody Marys, a man with dark leathery skin and long white hair slid up on a high stool next to her. He homed right in on her, as if sensing how lost she was. Later, Niamh couldn't even remember how they got talking. Just that Bob was sympathising with her torment over what had happened in Omagh. She got so drunk, she told him a lot. It seemed perfect. A stranger who she'd never see again. She let nearly all of it out. Bob was quite captivated by her story, and sympathetic to her guilt.

'Hey,' he said to her. 'I can help you.'

'What do you mean?' Niamh asked, stirring her Bloody Mary with the celery stick before taking a crunching bite.

'You can always make up for your past, if you dedicate your life to universal good now,' Bob suggested. His eyes were bright blue, like Brendan's, and had a spark in them like a child's, despite his age.

*

The next day, Niamh packed in her job. She stood outside the resort with her one rucksack slung on her back, and her tote bag of painting things, waiting for Bob to pick her up. She was a little wary of what she'd agreed to, but it couldn't be any worse than how life had been so far. Bob trundled up in his pickup a few minutes later, looking like an Arizona cowboy. But he was far from the tradition of the Wild West. As they drove out of Sedona city limits and into the desert, giant saguaro cacti marking their route, Bob filled Niamh in on his story.

'Was most of my twenties in India,' he told Niamh. 'Thought I'd spend the rest of my life there.'

Niamh glanced across at his weathered face, wondering how long ago that must have been.

'But my guru told me I needed to come back home. Start my own ashram here in Arizona.' His voice was gentle, like a balm, and as Niamh listened to Bob speak, she felt a sense of calm she'd never experienced before.

'You're not alone, Niamh,' he said, as they drove through the desert. The road was a straight line through red earth, blue sky and vast emptiness. 'There are others like you,' Bob said to her. 'Seeking forgiveness and faith, looking for a reason to live.'

Chapter Twenty-Seven

Rockland, Maine, 22nd November 2017

Lily had thought about asking her parents to collect her and Rosemary from Logan Airport, but in the end, she decided they'd take the bus. Rosemary was excited to look out the window at all the little New England towns and snow-laden houses.

'My, your snow is so thick!' she kept remarking every time they passed a dug-out pile of snow like a tiny hill of crystals.

From the bus stop in Rockland, they took a taxi to Lily's house. She had been nervous about walking in the door again after being away, but it was easier with Rosemary by her side. The older woman was interested in every little detail she showed her, so Lily could focus on looking after Rosemary rather than her own tumult of emotions.

'So where did Connor like to sit?' Rosemary asked her, pointing at the chairs.

'That one's his,' Lily said, indicating the soft green armchair by the fireplace.

'Can I?' Rosemary asked.

'Of course.'

Rosemary sat down in the armchair with her hands on the rests and closed her eyes. Lily saw the emotions pass over her face: loss, sadness, but happy memories, too.

'That felt good,' Rosemary said when she opened her eyes again.

Lily left Rosemary at her house while she headed across the lawn to her parents'. The snow was pristine and untouched between the two houses, although someone had shovelled the driveway clear in front of her home. Most likely her dad. Lily could feel her mom's eyes on her as she made her way across. The sun was beginning to set, the snow taking on tones of dreamy blue. Rockland had never looked so quaint, with smoke spiralling out of chimneys, and icicles fringing the roof of her parents' house.

Rather than go in the back way, Lily made her way around to the front of the house. Before she went inside, she took a moment to look down at the bay. Stretches of broken ice edged the coastline, the trees laden with the weight of white snow. The winter had been the season she'd loved with Connor. Snuggling in for the coldest months, when they were able to take pause together, before readying for the spring fishing season, and the busy summer and fall weeks for both of them. Winter had always begun with her birthday on the first day of December, the beginning of advent and the build-up to Christmas. Memories of Connor slammed back into her consciousness, making her feel breathless. His loss still felt so raw, despite her trip to Ireland. And yet, there was a slight easing of her despair. A gift had come her way in his loss. Rosemary, his grandmother.

For now, though, she needed make things right with her parents. There was still a part of her which hurt at what her dad had done and her Mom not supporting her over him. She turned as the front door flung open and her mom waved for her to come in. She'd lost weight on her face, but she looked happy. They hugged on the doorstep, then Lily followed her mom into the hall and tugged off her snowy boots.

Lily's daddy was standing in the doorway of the living room, holding on to the door frame. There were big black shadows under his eyes, and the texture of his weather-beaten skin was even more lined than she remembered.

'Oh Lily, it's so good to see you,' her dad said, shifting nervously.

'You too, Daddy,' Lily said. Despite everything her heart lurched at the sight of her broken father. She went straight over and put her arms around him. She felt the tension in his body release as he hugged her back.

'We missed you so much, honey,' her mom said.

'I missed you too, Mom,' Lily said back. She looked at her mom, knowing a part of her would always struggle to understand why she had sided with Lily's dad over her daughter's feelings – but what was the point of breaking up her family with resentments and recriminations? The regret she'd witnessed in Rosemary's tale of loss was enough to warn her to let go and try to understand her mom.

'Honey, we've just heard,' her mom said, excited. 'Tell her, Jack, tell her.'

'The Coast Guard report came in and they're dropping all charges!' her dad said.

'That's so great, Dad,' Lily said, relief washing through her.

'The coastguard who interviewed your father and Ryan came to the conclusion that although your father was a little slow in turning back after the weather warnings had been transmitted, the storm itself had been unforeseen earlier in the day,' her mom raced on. 'Jack will get his licence back, and the insurance will come through soon, so we can get a new boat.'

'What happened was ruled an accident,' Lily's dad told her.

'I'm glad, Daddy.'

Lily paused as she and her father looked at each other. The unspoken words passing between them. They both knew the truth. Her father's mistake had cost Connor's life. But Lily suppressed the feelings of blame because she knew if she let them take her over they might destroy everything she had in the world.

'Really, I couldn't bear the thought of you going to jail,' she said instead. 'Connor wouldn't have wanted that.'

'Oh, Lily May,' her dad said. 'I thought I'd lost you forever.'

Lily could see the pain her father had been in ever since the accident, but she couldn't find any more words to say. They stood for a moment in silence.

'Come and have some lobster and corn chowder with us, Lily,' her mom intervened. 'It's your special recipe.'

'Well, I've a bit of a surprise,' Lily said. 'I brought back Connor's grandmother, Rosemary.'

Her parents were stunned; it took them a moment to take in the information.

'Connor's Irish grandmother is here, in Maine?' her mom said, astonished.

'Yeah, she's quite a character,' Lily said.

'Well, go back and get her,' her dad said, already looking so much more like his old self.

'Yes,' her mom said, opening up drawers and pulling out one more place setting.

Her father followed her back down the hall to where she'd left her boots.

'I'm so sorry, Lily,' her daddy said to her as she was pulling them on. Lily reached out her hand to steady herself, and her dad bent down so she could put it on his shoulder.

'I'm sorry too, Daddy,' Lily said, straightening up.

'I loved that boy.' Her dad's voice went hoarse.

'I know, Daddy.'

The words were weighted with sadness. She felt her father beside her but for now she couldn't give him the solace he needed. It would take time. She opened the back door and stepped outside.

*

They sat around the kitchen table devouring her mom's creamy lobster and corn chowder, although as a vegan, Rosemary had politely declined. Her mom had looked at Rosemary as if she'd told her she was an alien when she'd clarified that she ate no meat, fish or dairy products.

'Don't worry about me,' Rosemary declared. 'This homemade bread is just delicious with a spot of your crunchy peanut butter.'

Rosemary was certainly not what her parents had expected an Irish grandmother to be. She was the same age as them, but her spirit seemed so much younger. More in common with Lily.

This was her new family now, Lily thought, as she ladled the soup into her mouth. Blended from all the corners of her heart. She ate another spoonful of soup but suddenly started to feel a little off. It didn't taste like normal. Too fishy and the cream thick in her mouth. She put her spoon down, her appetite gone, and stared down at the bowl of rich chowder, which suddenly made her feel incredibly nauseous. Getting up from the table, she ran upstairs to the bathroom, making it just in time before she threw up.

After spraying her face with water, she sat on the side of the bath, feeling a little bemused. The sickness had come upon her so suddenly. She closed her eyes, summoning the last time she was with Connor. She placed her finger on her lips as she remembered his touch upon them. She opened her eyes. Oh, she still felt so sick. She put her hands on her belly. It was there: a tiny vibration. Not an actual movement or sensation, but a resonance, deep inside her centre. Tears trailed down her cheeks, joy merged with sorrow.

Connor had left her one last gift.

Chapter Twenty-Eight

Niamh had learnt how to live again in the ashram in the desert. Here, for the first time since she'd lost her baby boy, she was able to learn to forgive herself. It had been hard, and at times seemingly hopeless, but then when she'd been at her lowest, a small simple sign would lift her up again: an eagle in the sky, a desert rat burrowing in the earth, or a wildflower blooming in the desert. Nature had helped her heal. She looked at the harsh landscape of the desert surrounding her and wondered at how tough the cacti were. Able to survive against all the brutality of the sun, drawing what they could out of the parched dirt. She painted their blooms, fascinated by the rich intensity of their colours: the spikes of orange, gold and pink as they emerged from the barrel cactus. It would seem her destiny had been to leave her homeland forever and live in a place of big, star-filled night skies and endless horizons.

All these years, Bob had been her teacher. She had followed him with the devotion and the humility he shared with others. At first, all she'd wanted was to serve. Working in the ashram kitchen, cooking and cleaning. But after a while, she'd joined meditations and sharing circles. She'd begun to tell the truth about her past. What had surprised her the most was that she'd met no judgement from her fellow devotees.

The years passed in a gentle rhythm of devotion and gradual enlightenment. Bob's hair grew whiter, his beard longer, and his blue eyes richer with compassion every time they talked. Niamh new home with Aisling, Noreen's youngest, who had been minding him while she was away. When Lily had announced her pregnancy, Rosemary had realised there was more for her in America than in Ireland. But most affirmative of all was when they had found Niamh. After they'd hired the private investigator, it had been only a matter of days before Niamh had been traced to the ashram in Arizona. The perimeters of Lily's family had expanded further. If the event of Connor's death had been a golden leaf in fall, Lily was spinning in the air with it. Sometimes plunging into sorrow, and other times lifted in the light of small joys. And sometimes the bittersweet partnership of the two: like the day she'd given birth to her son, Cormac, named after Connor's grandfather.

After Cormac had been born, Lily's dad had tried to persuade her to return to lobster fishing with him, but her heart had gone out of the business. She went out with her father and Ryan just once more. As soon as they lost sight of land and the waves started picking up, Lily had been hit by a panic attack. She'd been stuck behind the wheel, trying to breathe, unable to help the men hauling in the traps and banding the lobster. It hadn't even been a small storm, just a bit choppy. Her nerve had gone, now she was a mother herself. The idea of leaving Cormac orphaned was too much for her, and she told her daddy she was giving up lobstering.

'But honey, I want to pass on my licence to you, and the new *Lily May*.'

'Give it to Ryan,' Lily said. 'He deserves it. Works every day with you, risks his life for you.'

'But what about little Cormac?' her father protested. 'I want to pass on the business to my grandson.'

'Well, let's just wait and see, Daddy,' Lily told her father. 'Cormac might have other plans.'

Her father had looked surprised. Lobstering was what Smyth men did – but lately, Lily had been realising that it was possible for people to change. What she was doing now with Niamh, with Rosemary's help, was a new adventure. They'd built it up all on their own: *Rockland Seaweed Bath Co.* At first, they'd started out small. Selling little muslin bags of seaweed to friends and neighbours. Rosemary had shared her knowledge of aromatherapy with Lily and Niamh, and the women had experimented with different blends of oils, developing a line of bathing products which were hydrating and nourishing, and all natural. Suited for different generations. It turned out that Niamh was good at design, and they created a brand which evoked the sea. Their logo was a pale pink unicorn horn shell. The company had really taken off, with several hotels in Maine ordering their products, as well as lots of online sales.

The women rowed the last haul of seaweed for the day back to the *Connie*. The lowering sun picked up strands of red in Niamh's grey hair as she smiled at her daughter-in-law. Lily had received so much strength and solace from the love and companionship of the two generations of her husband's women over the past few months. Both she and Rosemary had suggested to Niamh she might take a trip down to Cape Cod and visit Jesse's boatyard. Lily had looked him up online. But Niamh couldn't even bear to look at his website.

'How can I?' she had said to Lily. 'After all this time.' She'd shaken her head. 'It would be different if Connor were still alive.'

Which of them was grieving Connor most deeply? All of them, but in different ways.

Niamh and Lily lifted their haul of seaweed onto the deck of the *Connie* and climbed on board after tethering the row boat to the back. They stripped off their wetsuits, pulling on cotton sweaters and denim shorts.

Lily steered the boat back towards land, and watched Niamh sitting up in the bow, her arms hugging her knees, and her long grey hair blowing in the breeze.

When they moored at their own little landing, Rosemary would have the racks ready for them to lay the bladderwrack out on to dry in the Maine sunshine. The forecast was good for the next day. Back at the house, there might be the smell of Lily's mom's baking – she often came over to help Rosemary with baby Cormac, although Rosemary was a wonder with him. There would the tap-tap of Rosemary's keyboard in her room, and later, the baby would be sheltered by the big willow at the water's edge, while Lily and Niamh took little dips in the cold sea. That night, there would be stargazing, wrapped up in light blankets, listening to the crickets and inhaling the scent of all the roses Lily had planted in the garden. Maine summers were the best.

The small boat *Connie* kept on chugging towards shore, as the sun sank behind them, reflections of gold, orange and violet scattered upon the water like a magnificent abstract painting. Lily would keep on going, as long she had land in sight.

A Letter from Noelle

I want to say a huge thank you for choosing to read *The Boatman's Wife*. If you did enjoy it, and want to keep up to date with all my latest releases, just sign up at the following link. Your email address will never be shared and you can unsubscribe at any time.

www.bookouture.com/noelle-harrison

What if the person we love the most in the world is not who we thought they were? Are some secrets unforgiveable?

The Boatman's Wife aims to take you on a journey between two women connected and yet unknown to each other. To Lily in Maine and her life upon the Atlantic Ocean. How it snatches away what she holds most dear. To Niamh, lost in the dark woods of Ireland as she clings on to what she's always believed in.

At the heart of *The Boatman's Wife* is the search for what is true, no matter how hard the consequences. From the wild western ocean to the stark Irish boglands, the landscape mirrors our quest, drawing solace from nature.

The Boatman's Wife is a study of sadness through deep loss and of small seeds of hope. How this pain can expand our hearts to receive more joy ultimately. To understand love is not finite.

I hope you loved *The Boatman's Wife*, and if you did, I would be very grateful if you could write a review. I'd love to hear what you think, and it makes such a difference helping new readers to discover one of my books for the first time.

I love hearing from my readers – you can get in touch on my Facebook page, through Twitter, Goodreads, Instagram or my website.

Love and light,
Noelle

@NoelleHarrison

NoelleCBHarrison

@noelle.harrison5

www.noelleharrison.com

Acknowledgements

Thank you to my inspirational editor, Lydia Vassar-Smith, for gifting the story of Lily. So much gratitude to my fabulous agents, Marianne Gunn O'Connor and Vicki Satlow. I am so lucky to be part of the Bookouture family, and much thanks to them all for their hard work.

Thank you to best pal Becky Sweeney for making my research trip to Maine so much fun, as well as all the encouragement and support. Huge thanks to my friend Alyssa Osiecki for helping me create authentic Maine characters. Thanks to dear Hailey O'Hara for coming to Ireland with me, and to my brother Fintan, his wife Eimear, their daughter Thea, and Eimear's family for letting us stay in their house. Gratitude to dearest Kate Bootle, Monica McInerney and Tracey-Ann Skjæråsen for their love and support.

Big thanks to all my lockdown pals, especially Samantha Kleman-Hood, Laura Lam, Lizzie McGhee, Sandra Ireland, Caroline Byrne, Jo Southall, Bernie McGrath, Charley Drover, Callie Stylianou, Kim Plant, Suzy Wilson and Kat Easson. To friends in Norway: Ila, Nina, Sidsel, Elisa, Ann, Marianne and Joan, thank you! Love to family: Jane, Paul, Mary, Joyce, Donna and Barry. Hugs and gratitude to ALL my wonderful friends and family – so many, your names would fill a book!

A special mention for my stepdaughter Helena and my son Corey, to whom this novel is dedicated. I am so proud of you both.

Finally, thank YOU for picking up *The Boatman's Wife*, and entering the worlds of Lily and Niamh. I hope they bring you on a journey worth taking.

Chapter Twenty-Nine

Rockland, Maine, 8th July 2019

Lily was behind the wheel of the boat as they sliced through the cold clear waters of the Atlantic. The day was cloudy, with scattered showers. Warm, although once they got in the sea, the cold water was bracing on their hands, even in their wetsuits.

'Stop here!' Niamh called to her.

Lily turned off the engine and threw the anchor overboard, before joining the older woman in the stern of their small boat, named *Connie*. Lily pulled up the top of her wetsuit and zipped it over her swimsuit. Niamh was already in hers, and climbing into the small row boat they'd been towing across the smooth sea.

They rowed back towards shore a small way, where they could see a mass of brown bladderwrack, the polyps glossy, honey-toned, and nutrient-dense.

'Good job,' Lily said to Niamh at her choice of location.

The seaweed was so thick here, the opportunity for regrowth was optimum. They both clambered out of the boat, the water only reaching their waists at this point, and waded into the dense sea vegetables, cutting swathes of bladderwrack with their knives and loading it onto the rowing boat. The two women chopped away at the seaweed in companionable silence. It was hard work, but no chore, because they both loved what were they doing, and believed in the vision of their little company.

It was Rosemary who'd first given Lily the idea. She had never returned to her cottage in Mullaghmore. Willie was happy in his was surprised to see in her tiny hand mirror one day that her own hair was turning grey, and for a moment she felt a small, fleeting dart of sadness at the loss of her red locks, which Jesse had admired so much.

But soon she let her vanity go and moved on to gratitude. This had been her biggest challenge in all the years of the ashram. Every time she had talked with her guru, Bob, he had guided her towards feelings of gratitude. It had been a long journey to observe any blessings in her life. But slowly, she'd been able to feel them. A great love had once been hers. She had brought life into the world.

In the ashram, Niamh had found a tiny pool of peace to swim in. She had believed she would never leave. But this was not her destiny, and Bob had always warned her it would be so.

One March morning, as she sat in the grove of orange blossom trees in the ashram compound, painting a hummingbird as it fed on a red bottlebrush flower, Niamh sensed a shift in the air. A presence from old. Without even looking up, she knew she was here. Watching her. With her dripping paintbrush and easel still in hand, she turned around.

Her mam stood before her, behind her a girl with inky black hair she'd never seen before – and in her arms, a little baby boy. The child looked like Connor on the day she'd last seen him.

'I'm sorry, Niamh,' her mam said to her.

She looked into her mother's eyes, then into the eyes of the girl carrying the baby who looked like Connor, and she knew.

Niamh dropped her easel and brush, the deep red pigment of the bottlebrush flower spattering the dusty earth. She fell on her knees onto the hard ground. She had always known. This was her price to pay for the past.